JUST LIVING

Rachel Tejeda Morris

Just Living

Copyright © 2023 by Rachel Tejeda Morris

Paperback ISBN: 978-1-63812-695-9
Ebook ISBN: 978-1-63812-696-6

All rights reserved. No part in this book may be produced and transmitted in any form or by any means, electronic, or mechanical, including photocopying, recording, or by any information storage and retrieval system, without permission in writing from the copyright owner.

The views expressed in this work are solely those of the author and do not necessarily reflect the views of the publisher. It hereby disclaims any responsibility for them.

Published by Pen Culture Solutions   04/18/2023

Pen Culture Solutions
1-888-727-7204 (USA)
1-800-950-458 (Australia)
support@penculturesolutions.com

JUST LIVING

Rachel Tejeda Morris

CHAPTER ONE

BUMBLEBEES

Being dressed up with a yellow t-shirt and black shorts only attract the bees. I guess they think I am a part of their family. So they follow me around. I just don't want them to sting me. I know some people are petrified of bees because they are allergic to bee stings. They could die if stung by a bee. I was on a bus one time and a woman was having a panic attack!" She was screaming" There's a bee on the bus" ``get it out!" She yelled ``I'm allergic to bee stings' . Everyone on the bus thought this woman was crazy, but to her this was life or death. I took my daughter with me to see "Honey, I shrunk the kids," and when they showed the giant bumblebees she didn't get scared. Years later she was scared of bees. I had no idea that seeing the big bumble bees would affect her or maybe she was Just plain scared of the bees because I doubt that she remembered the movie Honey I Shrunk the kids. She was just an infant in the stoller.And when she saw the movie she didn't get scared that i can recall. Well, I got stung by a bee in Church, of all places. There was a bee inside the Church. It was a beautiful day so the doors and windows were open. I had never been stung by a bee before. There was a bee flying around the church. I raised my hands to praise the Lord. The bee was starting to sting me. As I raised my hands. I felt a strange feeling in my hand, like a needle going through my hand. I opened my eyes, and I saw a bee flying away. I thought to myself ``hum" that bee was starting to sting me. Now if this hurt while he was starting to sting me. I hate to find out how it feels when he finishes the job." I told somebody at the Church.They said I should put some meat tenderizer on my bee sting so they went to the kitchen and got some tenderizer. They made a paste out of it and put it on my bee sting. It seemed to help the pain go away and took the swelling away in no time. First time I was stung by a bee as a grown woman. Years later, when I lived in an apartment that was subsidized, I almost lost my sandal. It came off my foot. I slipped it back on my foot, but I felt a sting like a needle. Going through my foot, it hurt terribly. I took my foot out of my sandal and a bee flew out of my sandal. I got stung by a bee on the bottom of my foot. Well come the next summer, I got stung on my right foot again. I don't know if it was the same bee or not. It is said that when a bee stings they lose their stinger and the bee dies. But I don't know about that. I swear it was the same bee on the same spot as last summer. I know I better not wear a yellow t-shirt and black shorts. I don't want any more bees following me. Where would we be without the Bumble bee's well we would not have any honey and forget about using money. Because money can't buy everything you need. It's Just that we are in need to be fed a loaf of bread Instead you just keep walking ahead. Don't Get in over your head, be glad you've got a bed to lay your head on. Stop trying to get ahead of yourself, that you can't keep up, Just remember what is right, hang on tight for what you believe in, try not to drink gin with a grin. You better work out at the gym. Ask for friend Tim, ask him again and again and watch out for what he is in. You better give him a grin, let him know who's within so he can begin a true relationship with the most high. That you may benefit, and not die. Remember To treat others with love and respect, what the heck are you waiting for? Who's knocking at the door? If you let him in. He will dine with you and you with him. This is the best decision that you have ever made. Be glad, don't be mad at the thought of what you think you could have had. Now remember it's not all that bad. Change is on the way, you have been blessed today, take it or leave it, who's to say that you did it your way on this special day. You went out of your way to say. Please stay another day, don't go away, for I need you in every kind of way. That you can think of, Know that I want to see your hopes and dreams come to pass, all you have to do is ask, when you think that you can't make it another day, I will help you and show you the way. For each and every single day is very special in its own unique way, so what people say. That you made it anyway. Hang on to what is good. Remember what you've learned, keep it, hold it, don't let it depart, you know that we are worlds apart, Just remember what you have learned, take it to heart, don't fall apart, you are a piece of art, you keep on showing off your colors, so that others won't suffer. Just remember what you've learned, take it to heart and do not let it depart because you are a piece of art. He is the potter, you are the clay, he will bless you anyway. Don't be shy, because you know this guy. Just remember what you have learned, don't put your fingers in the fire, you may get burnt, as long as you learn a lesson, and not do it again. Just remember what you have learned, keep it to heart and let God be first, so he can quench your thirst. The time for you is coming to an end, In which you need to make very important amends, to come to the realization that you need provision for all your division that causes you confusion in this. Let's take a look at your situation, I come to the conclusion, that you are in delusional, and it causes you confusion this is not my doing that you are in for a bruisin, keep on cruisin, this is my conclusion you will need to pay restitution this is your only solution, to all of your confusion, to be set free from all your delusion. Do I make myself clear you can be a dear, and not have any fear, when you come near to your heart's desires, because you have asked for a very long task, Let us just ask, is it a blast? That you have to keep asking until the task is over and done. Now you can run for fun and not fear, be a dear stay near to the chosen one. He will help you to get things done. In the end you won't have to bend not until the very end. And I say Amen!" You did it again!" I won't have to defend because there is no beginning, nor is there an end. In the end we will win, I tell you again, and again. Isaiah 55: 8-9 For my thoughts are not your thoughts, neither are your ways my ways, saith the Lord. For as the heavens are higher than the earth, so are my ways higher than your ways, and my thoughts than your thoughts. For as the rain comes down, and the snow from heaven, and does not return but waters the earth, and makes it bring forth and bud, that it may give seed to the sower; and bread to the eater: so shall my word be that goes forth out of my mouth: it should not return unto me void, but it shall accomplish that which I please, and it shall prosper in the things where I sent it.

CHAPTER TWO

MILK, IT DOES A BODY GOOD

Now let's forget about the bees for a while and remember a horrible thing you went through as a kid. You call it traumatic." And you have been traumatized for life. Well, my youngest daughter says hers was when she was little. If we happened to run out of milk. I had powdered stuff from a box that you could make into milk. Apparently, I didn't mix it well enough to get the lumps out so my kids had a hard time drinking it. So when I wasn't looking or had to go to the restroom, they would throw most of their milk down the drain. Can you blame them? My daughter says she has been traumatized for life because of the powdered milk. Poor kid. I had no idea I did that to her. My milk was fine. I know when I was pregnant with her it took me three hours to drink a glass of milk. It was very difficult to drink milk. I should have known that it was a sign that this kid was not going to like milk too much. When she grew up, into an adult while in her 30's she became allergic to dairy products and also her son. She would break out if she had ice cream or milk, or any dariy products. So then she became lactose intolerant and so did her son. They took after each other. What can I say or do? Milk is something I didn't drink growing up." Because I didn't eat cereal for breakfast." That I recall, once in a while I would grab a piece of cake or an orange and peel it and eat it on the way to school. I always walked to school. Most of the time I walked alone.' I had never taken a school bus to school or got a ride. I guess I did a lot of walking as a kid. It was a long walk for me especially in the dead cold winter. That's life. Never knew that milk was good for you all thow I did see some commercials and there was always milk in the refrigerator but I didn't see anybody drink it. I do know mom and dad put milk in their coffee. But mom always made kool aid for us kids and mom and dad drank soda. I remember going to the store with empty soda pop bottles and then we got money back to purchase more pop." We ate a lot of pinto beans growing up and spanish rice and lots of flour tortillas. Never knew that the beans were good for you. They are higher in protein than meat. Beans the magical fruit that makes you toot!" The more you eat the more you toot" good for the tummy so beans,beans at every meal." At least we did have some good nutrition in our daily diet." Never was introduced to different kinds of vegetables. That was okay. Sometimes we had corn or green beans but we didn't experience others until I was a grown woman, like squash or asparguas or spinach or kale. We mostly had potatoes. Lots of tortillas. Flour or corn. When my grandma was younger she made tortillas for the store that she lived next to. They paid her to make tortillas for their store. She made them perfectly round and cooked just right. She was a good tortilla maker. When mom started to learn to make tortillas. She would make them all kinds of shapes and sizes. You could swear that she made the map of the united states!" She got so mad that she threw the doe up in the air and sometimes up to the ceiling. Later in years she did better. You didn't have to worry about having some doe fall off the ceiling on top of your head.`` Think again for what you have, be glad even if you don't have much, be thankful and do keep in touch. For Just a touch you must learn from all your mistakes. That there is room to compensate. Please do not be late, do you want to have a debate? Let's compensate, so we don't have to have a debate. Don't let it go so that it escalates, remember to not let things escalate, demonstrate what you have seen illustrated. So that we can demonstrate, please try not to let it frustrate you, I will show you what to do, you don't need to ask Sue, or hold your breath until you know what to do. I'm not quite over you, what shall we do? There is a solution to this illusion that has come upon you. Take it or leave it, it's up to you, What else are you to do? Take it one day at a time, what else do you have in mind ? Now remember to be sweet, and kind it will be worth more than just a dime. You will be glad that you listened to this free advice that you have been given. In the end your time has been spent very well. Shush' please don't tell, the other's think this is a fairytale, I bet you are a nice gale, you can certainly tell even if you didn't open up your mail, now that's swell. Who am I gonna tell ? you can ring the bell your such a gal. I sure am glad that I know you well. And you're quite the gal and you're swell, can you tell ?" oh!" What the hell!" Am I making myself clear as a bell? 2nd Corinthians 10 :4 For the weapons of our warfare are not carnal,but mighty through God to the pulling down of the strongholds

CHAPTER THREE

ALL ABOUT BAKING

Now I was married to a baker who loved sugar. But of course, who doesn't love sugar? We went through bags of sugar like nothing and ate sweets like there was never going to be another cookie in the whole world again. We better get every last crumb. We did a lot of walking because we didn't have a car. So we stayed thin. Problem was diabetes ran in my family. I never thought about it until I got older. I became pre-diabetic in my 60's. Then I had to cool it with the sweets. So anyhow, we did lots of baking. When our girls were toddlers, we let them help bake. They helped all right. They ate the cookie dough. Got to admit, the cookie dough tasted good. And the frosting from the cake was fabulous. We ate it from the bowl and from the mixing pieces and utensils. Then I learned how to make cinnamon rolls from scratch. They were so good. But sometimes I didn't make them right. I put too much flour so they were heavy. When I wasn't around, my family threw them at the wall. One time I didn't bake them long enough. I don't even want to know what my family did with them when I wasn't around. But there was a friend of my daughter's that loved them. She ate them whenever I made them. I guess they were always good for her. I'm glad someone enjoyed them. Yum. There was a cookie jar filled with cookies on the way to the restroom. So since I had bladder problems I had to run to the restroom every few minutes. Of course I had to take a bite of the cookie half way through the day the cookie jar would be empty. My husband would ask who ate all the cookies." I said I just had a taste every little while." He called me mom. He said mom !" you ate the whole jar." I said oops!"

That only meant we had to do more baking." I was glad we did a lot of walking.``Or I might have been obeast. There were times I was hooked on sugar so bad that I ate a whole loaf of bread just because it had honey in it.' And freshly baked right out of the oven. Oh! boy I was naughty when it came to my favorite baked fresh right out of the oven, nice and warm oatmeal cookies. They were the best ever." Banana bread was another favorite freshly baked right out of the oven." I made banana muffins for the girls a lot in the winter so when the kids came home from school They had freshly baked muffins with hot coco waiting for them. That is if i didn't eat them all." We did have a lot of fun making homemade pizza." It was great!"

What would we do without bakers, this would be a dull world. There wouldn't be any fun and good snacks, don't forget about the sugar that we all like, come on let's take a hike, or do you want to bike? Yes the world is much sweeter than we admit, it's great you've got to admit. Some people are blessed with the gift of being great bakers, and some others are such haters. Some people are good at cooking, others decide to keep looking. They never lift a finger to help, what are we to do but yelp!" Don't tell. Be a gal, I tell you not to yell, or I will ring the bell. You know what that means, you must be on your best behavior, so you don't lose out on the many blessings that you can shout about!" Without a doubt, let me tell you what it is all about, don't shout, in a roundabout way I'm happy to say you've had it your own way. Knowing what's ahead, sit down and have a piece of bread. Don't let it go over your head. Instead be glad for what's ahead, it's far better than playing dead. Now come to bed, and lay down your sleepy head, don't hold your breath until you turn red. Stop trying to get ahead of what should have been done, Just accept what has been done under the sun. You try to run, but instead you Just want to have fun. Let's take a run under the sun should be fun. Don't overdo it or you will lose it, you old son of a gun. Let me tell you how to began, open your heart so that we can began, to see what's ahead, let the light shine in, so that we can began the next chapter, I'll tell you the day after and if it's riches that you seek, take a peek at the geek, that you surely want to meet. Be discreet, stand on your feet, be neat, it's been a pleasure to have met the chosen one. In him all things will be done, whether it be here on earth or the next rebirth. All in great wisdom, I challenge you to follow the true one then you will go to his kingdom come, You want him to say in the end well done good and faithful one, welcome to the kingdom. God made sugar: verses man made sugar: Genesis:1-29 And God said I have given you every herb that yields seed which is on the face of all the earth, and every tree whose fruit yields seed; to you shall be for food.

CHAPTER FOUR

COMMON SENSE

Okay let's admit that at times people don't use common sense. On the other hand, I will Say that at times I didn't use common sense, especially when I was a kid,growing up. My parents always send me to the store to get the Sunday newspaper. I don't know why they didn't have it delivered. So, I was the delivery person. Sometimes I cried because I didn't want to go. No matter how hot it was or how cold it was, I had to go. Well one winter the walking was difficult, because everything was icey. I tried my hardest to get up the icy sidewalk. I kept falling down. I threw the newspaper up the sidewalk then tried to get up the icy hill. But I kept falling down. This was getting old. Apparently so was the newspaper." By the time I got myself home the newspaper was all wet and torn up. My dad looked at the paper and looked at me. He said get in here. I thought my dad was gonna spank me because I took so long to get home and when I did the paper was in shambles.' I could not get up the sidewalk that was pure ice. So I cried. I kept trying." I didn't have enough sense to walk on the side of the road. Good thing I didn't. I would have gotten hit by a car. I guess I didn't use common sense. In the long run I made it home safely. That's all that mattered. Okay so what do you do If you don't use your common sense?" you get yourself into an unpredictable situation not only yourself but the people you have around you or with you. Like the time my friend takes me to Target store She says to me remember where I am parked I will be here waiting for you I said okay. Well in the store I am wandering around to find the product that i went to get. Okay so It took a while to find my ride. It had gotten dark outside while I was wandering aimlessly looking for my product.

I kind of forgot what her car looked like because she got a new car and this was my first time riding in it." I went outside in the dark. I didn't see a car where she said she would be waiting." I thought to myself where in the heck did she go!" I decided to walk around to find her car with her sitting in it. But each car That I thought was her car was not hers. The parking lot was quite busy." Why was everybody coming to the store at the same time close to closing. Did I miss out on something?" I was here late because I couldn't find my ride.' and apparently she couldn't find me. Then a thought came to my mind: maybe she made a quick errand while she was waiting for me. I just about got hit a few times by a few cars. I thought what's taking her so long to get back here?" Then I thought maybe I should walk home. But it was too dark to know which way was home?" I got tired of walking around looking for my friend and her car. I saw a chair close to the curb. I decided to sit and wait for my friend to get back from her errand. I waited and waited. You would think it was Christmas time by all the people coming and going, Then I thought to myself ``oh no!" What if I get coronavirus from one of these people who are coming and going.``Not everyone was wearing masks. Truth is most people were not wearing masks. So, I sat and watched the cars going and coming And the people coming and going." Lots of time went by and I thought ``oh no!" I hope nothing happened to my friend.' The sad thing was I left my phone at home otherwise I could have called her and asked where she was. This was the one time I wished I had my phone." Then finally my friend came out of the store door and said there you are" I didn't know what happened to you!" She said I thought something happened to you in the store and I wondered if the ambulance came and took you to the hospital but she couldn't recall seeing an ambulance." I said, ``Where were you?" She said I was Just up ahead to where I told you where I was gonna be waitting for you." I had to move up more because I was on the drop off spot and in the way. I didn't think to look ahead of the spot she said she was gonna be." Just so happened," I went out the wrong door. I don't think my friend will offer to take me to the store for quite awhile. Such a federal case over catching a sale on toilet paper."Good thing I didn't get into a fight with someone in the store over the toilet paper, like they showed on the news two ladies were fist fighting over the toilet paper during the pandemic." It could have been a much longer ordeal than it was." I get into unpredictable situations!" I need to add drama too!" Well that's my story about the toilet paper sale. I told another friend about what happened. She said, ``What an ordeal!" she was right, it was a big ordeal." I don't want to go through that ever again, I am certain my friend doesn't want to either." What an evening!" What an ordeal!" something so simple can turn into chaos!" Who would ever think that you can blink, and there is strife" Should I tell your wife?" About what took place. Ask God he will give you the grace, not so you can fall on your face. Now come along let's get out of this place, don't let anyone see your face. Because it would be a disgrace all over the place. So Just let me leave with at least one sleeve, I don't want to be rude, take a good look at this dude he thinks he is something, when he's nothing, until you humble yourself, you will be nothing to somebody else including yourself try to keep it between you and me. Together we can make it work, stop being a Jerk!" Be on the alert. We might not know the day or time that Jesus is coming to take us home, remember to be a light in this cold and dark world, which is not right. It's plain and clear to see that you are more than just a memory. In the days ahead try not to shutter, that there is no other. When you come to this conclusion, don't think this is a delusion, don't be in confusion at this conclusion. Think rationally, think continuously, think maturely then you will feel security. Listen to this remedy this will make you feel heavenly, remember this remedy

    Doesn't that sound heavenly. Proverbs 16:20 He that handles a matter wisely shall find good: and whoever trusts in the Lord happy is he.

CHAPTER FIVE

FITTING IN

My daughters and I began going to an all black church. We didn't have a car nor did I drive. We got a ride with whomever was willing and able. Now all the older women wore big hats to church. So of course I had to get myself a big hat to wear to church. I went to a hat store and I saw hats there that I saw some of the women wearing at church. I thought to myself this must be where the women from church go to get their hats from. Now I had a big hat just like the other women in church. My two daughters laughed! They thought I was hilarious! I fitted in alright! I had a few hats but not big and fancy like the women wore to church. I had to get a big fancy one like the other women. The girls began to learn the books in the bible. In their Sunday school class they all sang a catchy tune song naming all the books in the bible in the order they are in the bible. I was glad they met some nice Christian friends. I wished I had learned the books of the bible like the girls are. When I went to my first bible study I didn't have a bible. Then a pastor's wife gave me one. It was so big, thick, and heavy. When they told us to turn to a book in the bible I was lost. In fact I was embarrassed." I have never had a bible before. Then someone suggested putting tabs on each of the books so I could find the book to be able to read along with. This was one time I really wanted to fit in. I wanted to know all that I could learn about the Lord and his word. Besides, it was fun going to church more than just once a week. On Sunday there were two services. On Tuesday there was bible study, on Wednesday there was service and on Friday there was Coffee house. Which was a teaching and worship just like on a Sunday service. I met more Christian friends and this blessed my life. These Christian people felt more like my family than my own real blood family. This was amazing. But it was real. Maybe that's how it will be when we get to be with Jesus!" For now the girls can learn what they can from going to Sunday school and about God's word and hang out with some Christian friends. This will be good for their spirituality to grow in the Lord. This was good for them, this was good for all of us. My husband decided that we would try a new church so we did.We stayed for a few years then He wanted to try another church. We'd go for a few years, then he wanted to go try another church for a few years then it was time to go to another church. I don't know why we kept church hopping. I think my husband was trying to fit in a certain church. But if he was trying to find the perfect church He would never find it.' Because there is no perfect church." Then again he was trying to fit in. The good that came from going to other churches is we got to know different pastors and different people." But this came to a stop when my husband went to go be with the Lord. It's almost as if he knew he was going to go home. Because just before he passed he didn't eat or drink any liquids. We went to a bonfire. He didn't talk to anyone he wouldn't eat. He wasn't himself. I wondered what was wrong with him. He wanted to go to the bonfire. I was looking forward to going to my nephew's birthday party. Which happened to be the same day. They were going to have live ponies for the kids to ride. My husband told me we were invited to a bonfire tonight and we're going. That night was different. That was the last time I saw him alive. He died in his sleep. And when he did wake up he was in the arms of love. How blessed he is. No more pain no more sorrow no more shame no more worries no more anger no sickness no more sadness no more having any needs, because he is with the great king and that is the best !"great thing. One day I will see him again. For now I know he is very happy. I know he longed to be with our father in heaven as we all do. He just beat me there. I know I have a few things to finish here on earth and one of those things is putting a smile on your face. Another is telling people about Jesus. And another is to finish what I have started and to reach some goals. But I am not guaranteed tomorrow so I will do my best today and if I fail at least I tried. Now he can rest in peace because he is home now. He doesn't ever have to worry about fitting in because he's home. Where he belongs and someday I will see him again and all the people that have left this earth. We shall be reunited one day. That will be a glorious day that we long for to go home. This is exciting to look forward to no matter what you do, things will get done, although it may not be all fun. Let's take a run of how things get done. This is not a bluff, this is a serious matter, don't climb that ladder. What does it matter from what I gathered this is reality to the degree that I must flatter no matter the batter that makes you fatter, from what I gathered from here on after. There are no two days that are the same. Now I'm not playing any games, for each day is especially made for you, It's up to you in what you do. Make use of each day, try not to waste it any which way, it could give you tooth decay, that could happen anytime, anyway. I think I better hit the hay, let's do it my way, we can do this any day. Let's think about it on our way, then you won't be thinking I'm gay. Now that's the way, I'll give you an A because you deserve it anyway, I say it's A okay. By the way, can you pick me up a milky way candy bar?" Not tomorrow but today, if tomorrow too, that would be really nice of you. I can always make room for another. If you don't want to, that's quite alright!" don't bother, I'll still think that you're out of sight, and that's quite alright!" hang on tight and hold your appetite, you may need it later, depends on the weather, If you choose to go when it's cold, remember your not too old to get a cold, so hang on tight, then everything will be alright now that's out of sight swallow your pride and hide, this is really not a gift, this is just a word of advice, please be polite and nice. If you choose to go in the rain, what do you have to gain? Nothing but a headache and pain, what do you have to gain? Please refrain. I'm not ashamed. dreams shattered, from what I gathered, there is no shame in this game, that you plan to use, refrain from being drained and used. Then you won't have to worry about being abused or used, am I making you confused?" In time you will be infused, you will remember and make yourself usefull don't forget and be peaceful. Wish I could fly up high like the seagulls, and eagles, the time has not been given to us when we can gather in his trust, that we will meet him in the air, and in his time he will bring us to meet him and rejoice when we see him, I cannot bear the waiting is so far and hard. Hard to be apart from all our loved ones, soon the time will approach fast, are we ready for this blast that will last and last. Forget about your past, it has disappeared in the air, you don't even have to care. Because it has all been forgiving, That's if you are willing, to stand tall and strong you have not done wrong for long. Because you've given me the very best. And now you are my quest, be at your best. The time is coming, and it is approaching fast, are you willing to be last? At the thought of you in the past, so come on let us pass through the heavenly gates, where there are no debates. When you come to grips as to what you should do. Remember God loves you through and through. Things are not the same without you. So let it be for you that my home is not here on this earth. We have been rebirthed, Our real home is in the heavenly places that the human eye can not see, for you have been set free. To live a life without any strife, and to live it happily, and abundantly, don't you agree?" Indeed.I 've planted a seed for you and for me, this is what it should be. The way the Lord has planned, he will put it in your hand. Because you have a lifespan, and it's all in his hand this is a demand in which I stand, to be willing, and tender to accept all that has been rejected. In the end we will be detected, that we believe in the holy one. In him all things are done. Because we have won to be united as one in the kingdom. We will have freedom to be happy, and to be fulfilled. This is no joke, this is for real, that we have a special deal to be revealed In and at a special time. This is what God has designed. This is God's special perfect plan that he will put in your hand so you don't have to demand anything that you can withstand. If you understand, take my hand. I'll help you understand because I've got a plan, I'm not trying to be in demand. Know that the Lord is good all the time, and all the time God is good. It's a bit of a pleasure to be understood, at no measure that we can be fully made into his Image, this is truly a privilege to be in the presence of the holy one. You're not the only one who doesn't need to get everything done to have him clean you up. Because he will take you as you are. Remember don't go too far, ahead of him you will soon begin the Journey of your life. You won't have to think about it twice. You better be nice, shake them dice twice. Just when you think you've got this all down, embrace yourself and take a look around, Listen to hear that great sound to be found all around, the day is approaching fast, when the past is the past, and you want to make everything last, that is real good to remember, you are the chosen one, and that you have a Job to do on this earth. You have been blessed because you found newbirth. And you will reign in heaven above with the father and his great love, you will be truly loved in heaven above. You will fly like a dove, In heaven above, where there is more love. You will never feel rejected because this world is hectic, God's the only one that can predict, what's to become if you have chosen the right one to follow after, do it today and not a day after, so that you can hang on to your laughter then you can laugh about it the day after. Then you will live happily ever after. Now this is what I've gathered from the word of God, This is the truth, I tell you no lie, the Lord has a special place instore for you so don't give up and let it get over your head, that all things work out for the good in time you'll be glad you didn't waste your time this is great to keep in mind, remember to shine all the time. Even if you don't feel like it, it's better than you taking a hit. I'm just telling you a bit of what's to come, don't let it become undone, all that you've done truly you are the one to do it so it won't become undone. I'm not afraid in the least bit. Because where we are going, we will be glad, and we won't be holding anything that is spoiling because it is perfect up there in the air now can you spare to be of some sort of help. So that I won't have to yelp!" In the end time won't matter anymore if you just walk out the door. You will see a brighter tomorrow you won't want to pass it up I know you can feel it in your gut. That going forward, and not looking back you know this is not an act you better watch your back until you make it home, where there is peace, love, that you can endure, the time is coming it's coming near and fast, be on the alert and be ready for the time is going to be stunning when we won't have to know what time it is, when you won't have to worry or be in a hurry. Because there will be no more time. We will Just sit and dine and we will shine and sing praises to the king forever more. In him we do and will adore. So don't be shy, Just be yourself and forget about all the troubles. The Lord will take very good care of you so that you will have a better view. You'll see everything new. You will see it through and through, he's not done with you. Now what should we do? I tell you to take a break, And please don't be late. I can hardly wait!" It's time to celebrate that we are headed home some time soon but not soon enough, because we still have stuff that's going to be tuff. This is what needs to be done here on earth. Remembering those who are lost, and those that are blind and those that refuse to be kind. Take a break, don't stay late. God wants all to come to him, won't you let him in so he can begin the work that he began to start, that when the day approaches near you will be ready and have no fear, you will be near and dear. Do I make myself clear?" When you wish upon a star, then you feel so far, no matter who you are. I tell you by far, there is no rhyme and reason for you to believe when you do you will receive the greatest gift of all. And he will help you not to fall, all of you shall be a doll to it all. Because you've taken the time to do things right. He will make your days bright with delight. Remember what I say I won't have it any other way. That the truth will set you free, you will be free indeed, this Is not coming from me, but from the one who is In me.The holy one. You are not the only one. He will get things done. So try not to run the wrong way, If you need a place to succeed. He will be on his way to give you what you need. Maybe not all your wants, and desires. That's okay because you really don't need it anyway. He will take your case,and bring you to that special place that is waiting for you. In time he will see you through. He promises never to forsake you or leave your sight, this is precious in his sight he will be with you day and night now this is truly out of sight that you might not fall into a pit, and take a hit from the unknown. In time you have grown and you can flourish in delight that you have become right that you might endure to the end. Because you have a best friend and that will never end. This is worth the fight, you are his delight and he is yours, remember he's the one that can open the doors, and if you choose to follow him you will be blessed forever more. That you have walked through that door. Try not to snore, so you will be adored. For he has chosen you to be with him In the very end. All things are possible for those that believe, in order to receive, you won't need a degree. You can be set free, Free like the birds in the air you won't have to live in despair. Yes I do care what happens to you I will see you through no matter what you do I will be with you through and through. It's up to you. He has given us a free will, to make the right decision, what do you believe in?" What is the reason for you not giving God your all, there's no time to stall no matter how big, or how tall you need to answer his call you all. 1st Peter 2:19 -20 For this is thankworthy, if a man of conscience toward God endure grief, suffering wrongfully. For what glory is it if, when you are buffeted for your faults, you shall take it patiently. But if and when you do well, and suffer for it, you take it patiently, this is acceptable with God.

CHAPTER SIX

GETTING DRESSED

I know this sounds funny coming from a 64 year old lady. But there are days when I feel like, "what's wrong with me?" I am having a hard time getting myself together for the day. When my mind is going 60 miles an hour and in twenty different directions. I jump in the shower and take a quick shower don't want to keep my ride waitting. I've got places to go and people to see. First of all I need to learn how to dress myself today. I am frustrated because I keep putting my bra inside out! I can't seem to remember so I put the hooks on the opposite side of what they are supposed to be. So now I can't hook my bra together. Well who ever invented these stupid bras didn't make good sense! In the other chapter I was talking about common sense. And now i am talking about stupid sense. How do you like that? Next I try to put this blouse on that I only wore a couple of times last year . It was a strange blouse that had a turtleneck with no sleeves. You wore it like you would a poncho. I had one woman give me a compliment on this strange blouse. Yes you could say it is pretty and different. Or should I say pretty different? Well I finally got myself dressed as fast as I could go. I didn't want to be late. So I grabbed my earrings and was going to put them in my pocket. Then on the way to my appointment I could put them on. But I kept trying to shove them in my pocket. But I kept missing my pocket. Then I began laughing. I thought to myself don't tell me I put my pants on backwards. Then that means my pockets are in the back. Instead of the front. I began to laugh. There was a janitor in the hall and he saw me laughing by myself. I told him I think I put my pants on backwards because I can't find my pockets. The man smiled. When I got to my ride I was laughing and told them that I put my pants on backwards. That I was trying to find my pockets. The driver looked at my pants in the back and she said you don't have pockets in the back. I said I don't? Then where did they go? By this time I am almost peeing in my pants because I am laughing so hard. Then I looked at my pants and said OH! I guess these are not the pants I thought I put on. Because I had two pairs of blue jeans that were brand new that I never wore before I won them from playing bingo. Because when we win in bingo we get to pick a prize that we would like. It could be household Items, treats, clothes, dishes, jewelry. We have a wide range of selection To choose from. And it is fun to play. So there I was looking for pockets that weren't even to be found in the back or front or sideways, or upside down, or inside out, or rightside up, they were nowhere to be found. I had a good laugh! I amuse myself! I entertain myself. I don't have to go far for a laugh! So this is one of those days. I'm glad this doesn't happen everyday. I would be in trouble! Deep Trouble! Be careful for those kinds of days! A few weeks later I did put those pants with pockets on backwards where my pockets were in the back two days in a row, glad nobody saw me. Another time I put on a pretty blue dress for church. It was only worn a few times. So this nice family from church picked my girls and I up for church. They had a big family with seven kids. They had a big van. They were such a sweet family. As I stepped up into the van I felt like my dress was choking me. So I thought to myself. Why is this dress choking me? Did I gain 50 pounds overnight or what? As soon as I got to church I quickly went to the restroom to look in the mirror. There was a long big mirror there so I could see what was wrong with my dress. I began looking and It turned out to be that my dress was on backwards.I couldn't remember how the dress goes because I only wore this dress a few times." I guess I made it a different style than it was before" I began laughing." I couldn't stop laughing." I tried telling the man that drove us to church. But every time I tried to tell him I burst out laughing." the man said what?" He began to laugh because I was laughing. He didn't even know what I was laughing about.' I finally calmed down to tell him why I was laughing.' Then he laughed with me about the situation of choking myself with my dress and how I was changing the style of the dress. Once I was down in the dining room and a waitress called me over to her. She whispered to me that I had my shirt on wrong. Now I don't remember if it was on backwards inside out or upside down right side up or what?" But I had my shirt on wrong. I was glad she told me so I wouldn't be wearing it that way all day. There was a time when it was time for me to get ready for bed. I noticed that I had my shirt on wrong. I said awe!" I had my shirt on wrong all day." I laughed and said to myself ``I hope nobody noticed." Another time my husband and I took our daughter to the U of M hospital to see the Dr. I went to the ladies room. When I pulled my pants down I noticed that my pants were on backwards. I began to laugh and a young girl came in. I was laughing. I felt stupid that I am laughing by myself. So I told the young girl. You see what happens when you get old." She had no idea what I was talking about." I told my husband and daughter why I was laughing. I couldn't stop laughing. So my husband and daughter started to walk ahead of me as if they didn't know me." I swear they were trying to ditch me." Well this time I was going to the store with My I L S worker, this means Independent Living Services. They help with everything you want help in. And they take you out in the community, like shopping, and other errands. Well I put my sweater on but I thought I could zipper it up in the car. It's kind of hard for me to zipper things because my left hand and fingers are not as strong as they used to be because they used to be paralyzed, from my head injury. Anyhow I zipped my zipper, then I reached for my cane, but I could not find it so I said to Alex ``where's my cane?" What happened to my cane? We began looking in the car for it. Then we both saw it in my sweater. I had zippered it along with my sweater. We both laughed!" This was funny."There are plenty of situations that I got myself into, now this is a new trick on me about trying to put my socks on, well I put bag balm on my feet because apparently I have diabetes feet, One time they got dried up so bad that I got big holes on the bottom of my feet, so I had to start putting some lotion or therapy cream on them to keep them from getting dried out so bad. Funny thing is my feet don't have an odor to them. I think that is strange." Everybody else has stinky feet or an odor to their feet. Why am I so different from everybody else?' Not that I want stinky feet, but maybe a scent. I just tried a new way to put on my socks, okay. After I put my one sock on I tried putting my other sock on but I was having a difficult time trying to get the sock on. Then I thought that maybe my sock was stuck to the other one. So I tried to pull the socks apart. But they would not come apart, so I thought maybe the other half of the sock is not going on because it's inside of my slipper and I am stepping on it so it won't budge!" I thought, ``What the heck!" Why am I having so much trouble putting my sock on?" Come to find out that I was trying to put my sock on from the heel of my sock, and not at the top of the toe part. When I finally figured out why I was having so much trouble getting my sock on. I sure had a good laugh!" and a half" I think my cat did also, Or he thinks I'm crazy." Anyhow, this was a new way I tried putting my sock on." don't you try it!" it will never work. Not unless your foot is deformed." This is the case that you need to embrace, all that you have learned, as you were growing up, that there's more to life than meets the eye, that you can look up at the sky, and feel like the clouds are moving and yet they are staying still. That it is you who can't be still, be careful or you may become I'll. Now stand still, so that I can give you the bill. Don't let it make you I'll. This is the real deal, I'm not lying, I can be underlining that you are dying. From this day forward I will be a good stewward. I will keep looking forward, at the thought of living heavenly, is the greatest gift of all, I will be standing tall, and I will be having a ball, at your presences I won't have to

Worry that I'll fall at the ball. Where there are important people, they shake your hand and they say see you. In reality they don't see what you see. Now can we agree? Just between you and I, we can look up at the sky, and not have to worry about something going in your eye. Let me tell you why, so you won't get a stye in your eye. Because life is sweeter on the other side. Let me tell you what it is all about, don't shout!" Let's go in and around because this will take some time. Don't let me waste your time. Is it even worth a dime? Let your light shine, if you don't mind. I am not to decline, It would be a waste of time. Come over here and wine and dine. Don't waste any time, tell me what's on your mind. Don't decline, of what's on your mind. Be a light and let it shine. Because I have you on my mind. Let the good times chime, now that I have you on my mind. Don't pretend everything is fine when you have a lot on your mind. And you're pressured for time, keep me in mind like you do when you're on time, waiting to shine all the time. Remember everything takes time, keep this in mind. Time goes so fast, try to have the last laugh then your mind will be fine. It's about time you won't have to stand in line. Having a seat doesn't make me repeat what's on your mind?" That you don't want to spend time, I assure you I'm worth more than a dime that is worth my time.

Time and time again, you will see the wind come and go, you will still be here and yes you shall see that I do this for you and me. There is an eternity, in which we will make beautiful harmony, so Just let it be, you know the reality, In which there is history, I give him all the glory This is the end of this story. Let us move on to the next chapter. Come see what I'm after, Live in peace from this day and after remembering all that you have learned don't forget the laughter that came after, soon the rapture will come then everything will be undone. The father's will will be done. Don't even try to hide or run. When everything is done the way it's supposed to be. We will live eternally. We will be so much happier than you've ever been. Because there will be no sin within, And to be quite honest, you shall be my guest. On request you will be made up fresh, there shall be no more sadness, sickness, or pain, nor shall there be games, or shame. You will be reunited with loved ones that left before you. Don't be sad or blue. The time will be made right that you will shine bright. You will hear beautiful voices, and music that you've never heard before. Now come on, walk through that door as you did before. You're the one that he adores, don't be shy, don't let nothing get in your eye, go through the door so you can give what you need to give. Then you can truly live. In peace and harmony, together we agree that you will be set free to do what you have been called what to do. Now put on the right shoe, so you can function like you are supposed to, that you do what you gotta do and move forward. There is nothing that can beat your ambitions down, if you guard your stand, and you're holding the right hand. He will gleam all over this land. And you can dream all that you can. While he holds your hand. This is our land that he gave to us. We have to obey him and trust that he will do what needs to be done. His will will be done in heaven and on earth. Be glad that he gave us a new birth. No we won't die from a lack of thirst, because he has remained faithful. I will rejoice, and be thankful, I will also have an attitude of gratitude, always in my heart I never want it to depart. Keep it deep in your heart. No matter how hard it is, you can be sure that he will not give you anything that you can't endure for he has made sure that you will never be alone. In this he has truly shown that you are not on your own, that the bible is the word of God. We ought to live by faith and not sight, take another bite of his word then you can be endured, he will spread his great light, he will always be in sight, he will always fight your fights, he is your delight be polite he will also shine a bright light so you can see, All that is needed for ahead, In God's word you should have read what's ahead. Don't look the other way instead. Be ready for what's ahead, it's far better than bread and even better than the butter that you can spread. Remember what's ahead. Now turn out the lights and go to bed. Try to not bump your head, instead move forward as best you can, ignoring the strong winds that keep you afloat. Listen to the billy goat that wants to be a lamb because he knows who is the keeper of the sheep. Now this is neat, try to stay on your feet. Take discrete as a tool, then you will not be made a fool you better not drool. Stay cool, you know what to do. Deuteronomy 22: 5-12 The woman shall not wear that which pertaineth unto a man,nor shall a man put on a woman's garment: for all that do so are an abomination unto the Lord thy God.

CHAPTER SEVEN

GOING ON VACATION

The girls and I went camping for a few days with the church. It was time to get away from the cities. And breathe in fresh air and to see the view of the country. We could see the stars so big and bright." We could see the moon so big and clear. We could see the clouds so close to us. It felt like we could reach up and crab a piece of cloud. It looked like cotton, but of course it wasn't cotton. Nor was it that close to reach up and crab a piece." We did bow and arrows, that was fun." We rode on horses which was amazing." Well I tried but for some reason I kept letting go of the regin and apparently that's what controls the horse. Plus I was leaning to the side so it looked like I was going to fall off." I must have looked funny." No wonder people were laughing at me, The man had to keep coming back to get me and my horse. My daughters laughed at me.``After a few times I think this man was getting annoyed with me. I spent a lot of time walking from our cabin to the main headquarters. Because my girls were there playing with the other girls. At the cabins It was kind of chilly when the temperature dropped down at night and the wee hours. I was in a hurry to get a shower and shampoo my hair. I grabbed the wrong bottle and poured sun tan lotion all over my hair and I said oh!" This is a different texture than mine, so I thought I took somebody else's shampoo. It did smell good" I thought to myself I hope whoever's shampoo I am using I hope they don't get mad. Come to find out it was sun tan lotion!" ewe!" I thought that if this works like hair dye Then this will be cheaper to use than hair dye. The trouble is you don't know what color your hair will turn into or if you have any hair left when and if your hair falls out!" This is crazy to use as hair dye. I think I will use it for what it was made for and nothing else that way I won't get people mad or sad or try to sue me. I 'd stay on the safe side.``This is not the time or place to try to invent new products. This is time to relax and have fun. Me relax?" I don't know how to relax!" With me being a single parent running back and forth and to and from, being on the run it's not all fun. keeping an eye on my girls there was no such word as relax in my vocabulary. I might as well train in to do a walk a thong as much of walking I did all day long. This was hard work trying to keep up with two little girls. In fact I really need a vacation after going on vacation." I needed a real vacation but of course this was not reality for me. It was good to get out of the city for a few days. While we were here The girls had a lot of fun. But it was a lot of work for me. As long as the girls were happy I was happy. I was worn out every single day and felt like I was training for the olympics."The kids wanted to go swimming. So we spent a lot of time down by the lake. Minnesota doesn't have beaches. We only have lakes and rivers" I tell it like it is." After all that's what we are known for, 1000,00 lakes,That is our slogan and the loom duck as well. We only spent a few days away but it felt like a week. It was much needed. And it was greatly greeted. I didn't have to tell anyone to beat it, Instead we had a wonderful time, to get away from the cities, was really a blessing in disguise, we could hardly recognize how important it is to get away and reminisce on what's good and important, sometimes we forget about ourselves, because your so busy making sure that you have got the cure for everything you can endure. When you stop to take a break, don't you hallucinate, what I appreciate, you don't want to go in a debate, your kind of late to negotiate you should appreciate, come on let's celebrate, all that you want to dedicate, In order for us to regulate all things appreciated, we can delicate it if you don't deliberate it. Then you can participate in it, so that we can liberate it. As long as you have time to refresh, let me tell you this has been a blessing. Yes you never want to negotiate, you can participate, let's not get into a debate. Please don't be late for this important date, In which we want to celebrate this special day, when you can have it your own way, all day what can I say you did it your own way, and that's okay for the day, I will remember you always keep on moving forward, do not stop, and do not go back, and miss out in what you could of had. This is not so bad, so come on and be glad, look to the heavenly one he will help you to get things done. It may take a while, so give us a big smile, and go the extra mile. It will be worth your while, get on the phone and dial, not for a little but for a while, you will smile on your own, because you know who sits on the throne, you better not groan and complain, for this is dangerous, to reminisce, and try to gain, on the wrong thing if you know what I mean, I am not a teen, please don't make a seen and make me scream. I have been redeemed, do you know what I mean?" I Am not a machine. Please don't lower my self esteem, I need to gleam like a beam. I do not intend to scream, can you be a light in the darkness, and lend a hand when there is a demand, take my hand, as we can stand stronger, for one another. We can go a lot farther if we choose to do what's right, and shed the light in the right direction, can I get your attention?" Remember the resurrection of our savior, please be on your best behavior later you will be rewarded for all of your deeds you have done when you get to kingdom come, God's will, will be done. In which we will become one. It has been done, the battle has been won. 1 Timothy 6: 17-19 Charge them that are rich in this world, that they be not high minded, nor trust in uncertain riches, but in the living God, who gives us richly all things to enjoy; That they do good, that they be rich in good works, ready to distribute, willing to communicate; Laying up for themselves a good foundation against the time to come, that they may lay hold of eternal life.

CHAPTER EIGHT
BEING A PARENT

    I never thought I would be in this situation of being a mother and father. Nowadays it is common. My two daughters were close in age so it was like having twins. Well I didn't even know that my oldest daughter left the house and was in front of a bakery sitting on the curb of a busy street playing in the rain. In front of a bakery a few blocks away from our house, for a few hours. I was so busy doing laundry I didn't even notice she was gone. It's a good thing that she had a book of mine that had my name. So the bakery called me, and told me that my daughter had been playing on the street curb in the rain for a few hours. I just freaked out when they called me! It was a miracle she crossed the streets safely to get to the bakery. Those people probably thought that I was a bad mother for not taking care of my baby like I should have. I felt like a single mother. The sad thing is I wasn't single. I had a husband that worked two jobs to pay for our cost of living. So he was never home. I had no help, I was blind in my right eye, and I had physical and mental problems. I was calling 911 all the time because I needed help with one of my girls. And it happened to be the oldest girl all the time. I bet those policemen and firemen and paramedics had a good time laughing about me and my situations that I somehow got into. When I would call 911 they would say is this the woman on juliet street? I said yes it is. Once I called them because my daughter was locked in the closet and I couldn't even open the door, there was no door knob. Another time my daughter got her leg stuck in the rocking chair and her leg was stuck she put her arms up for me to pick her up. But I couldn't. If I tried I would have broken her leg. But my baby didn't understand that

I couldn't pick her up into my arms. So here comes all the sirens of the ?"police, fire truck, and ambalance. They put dish soap on the leg to make her leg slide out of where it was stuck. My baby and I were very relieved. I bet the whole neighborhood was talking about me and my girls. I bet they had a bunch of laughs about us and my many adventures with my girls. At least I could cheer somebody's day up. Consider the tasks that you do each day, not keeping track because it's not an act. As a matter of fact, you can crack my back. If you stand in the middle, I'll tell you a riddle. That will make you giggle, If you stay in the middle and not toss to and fro remember you got to go, with the flow you gotta let go. Please don't make fun of my riddle, It's just little, soon I will get better, sooner or later. Then you can spend more time wine and dine. Without so much as a chime. Make up your mind, don't commit crime, keep in your mind what you want to do, so that you won't be made a fool, don't drool over the fact that you've been caught in the act. When all the day is done. You know that we have won that which doesn't belong to us. Remember in God we trust. Because he has done it all for us. The battle belongs to the Lord, remember he's the one you adore. Please do not ignore. I am sure that you can make things right whether it be little or whether it be big, remember you have been given what you need to succeed, Do God's word and you will agree, that you have all that you need. In order to succeed, then you can truly be what God wants you to be. When my youngest daughter was in grade school, if she got mad at me, she would do things to me that I didn't know, like hide a piece of my coffee pot so I couldn't use it. Then one time she poured all my body spray out and put mouthwash in it." I never knew it, I just kept using my body spray everyday. It smelt fresh to me. Boy was it fresh. My daughter never told me until many years later. Kids will be kids. Titus 2:4-5 That they may teach the young women to be sober,to love their husbands, to love their children, to be discreet, chaste, keepers at home,good,obedient to their own husbands, that the word of God be not blasphemed. Women are naturally more nurturing than men because they were designed to be the primary caretakers of their children. Discipline and instruction are integral parts of being a good parent.

CHAPTER NINE

WHAT YOU SEE IN THE DARK

Do you ever see things in the dark that are really not there?" Maybe it's your Imagination some things look spooky in the dark, practically everything looks scary right!" Well I am sure you all have stories of what you thought you saw. Well my problem is not only in the dark it's in the daylight as well," When my son was little He got up during the night to use the restroom. He screamed and he sounded like a girl screaming." He said there's a big rat!" I jumped out of bed." and ran to the kitchen. My husband turned on the light. We both said ``where?" It was a drinking cup that had fallen off the dish rack onto the floor. It sure was a big rat!"The boy scared me half to death."Now I was looking out the window one morning. It was a nice sunny day. I began looking around our yard. I saw something weird. I saw a green object that looked like it had eyes on it." I thought to myself what the heck is that strange thing doing in our yard." I am thinking to myself ``what is it and where did it come from?"It was big and green and had two eyes. I'm thinking maybe it's an oversized turtle." I kept looking at it, waitting for it to move. Where did it come from?"I'm thinking maybe he's sleeping with his eyes open." After all, I have a husband that sleeps with his eyes open." You don't know if he is sleeping." This was dangerous if he were driving and he fell asleep."So I waited for this creature to move." I waited and looked, waited and looked for it to move or do anything. To no avail It did not budge" It finally moved. The brush of wind made it move. It was not an oversized turtle, It was not a green creature, it was a big piece of plastic with two eyes which were not eyes." I then thought, `` I sure do make a federal case out of nothing. Then I had to laugh at myself." I sure do have a wild Imagination! All though I did experience an uneasy scary situation I had to not think about what had happened to me. I had to remain calm and not dwell on it. It was the only way that I could keep myself from getting spooked out!" Or scarring everybody else out. Right!" Let me tell you what I am talking about." Well one night I was getting ready for bed, and I was putting my pajamas on. I happened to look over to the other room while I was getting dressed." I saw something freaky!" I got so scared!" I saw an image that almost looked like it was from star wars." It was a guy with a black helmet, face and head." and he was wearing a black cape!" I put my pajamas up to cover my breast because I wasn't dressed yet. I made a sigh of noise Like I saw something freaky.!" And yes it was freaky." I was scared to be down in my apartment." By myself I was scared that I would see that thing again. I had no choice. I had to because that's where I lived. I have a friend who specializes, In cleansing homes from anything spiritually, mentally or physically but she charged a 100.00$ to come out to your house to do it. I didn't have the funds to do that otherwise I would have. At the time she was going to give away one free cleansing of the house. I wished that I could have won it because after what I saw I needed that. Plus I would have felt more safe if I had it done. Well my daughter had a friend who had a gift for picking up unwanted things in a person's home. And thank goodness she did not charge us for coming over to do this. She went around the house as thoroughly as she was trying to feel for something in the atmosphere. Then she said everything is fine, there is no icky spirit in the house,whatever I saw is gone now there's nothing abnormal in the house. She did put our minds at ease. People have different gifts for different areas in life. You may or may not be surprised." So then I prayed over the house and put anointing oil on the door frames and windows of the house. After that I felt so much better I felt the peace of God. Philippians 4:7 And the peace of God, which passes all understanding, shall keep your hearts and minds through Christ Jesus. The peace only God can give.This is Awesome!" all three of us women had gifts, but we used our gifts in a little different ways but we all wanted the same results. We have a great God to bless us like he does. Don't make a fuss, just because you know what I mean, don't try to pretend that you are a machine, to avoid what you need to do, stop acting like you're a fool. You remember when you want and you hear what you want to hear, you've gone for so long, doing what you please, let me put your mind at ease. You don't have to worry about me. Because I am free, free as can be, come on let's have a cup of tea, relax now you're with me, I'm not your aunt bea, remember me you can plainly see that it is not all about just you but it is also about me be free indeed. Then you can be me. Don't go up that bark and go to the wrong tree. Be simple, be real, then you can be set free, indeed you will be able to agree that you can proceed what I mean about to proceed in what you need. Don't be afraid of what you see, you know what I mean? Continue on your Journey but don't be in such a hurry, take it one day at a time, God has a set time for your destiny, I reassure you this can truly be all that you see is only a remedy in reality to your conclusion. This is a matter of constitution, in the evaluation of your confusion, Get away from the delusion of this pollution. Come take a break from all this confusion, when you pay restitution, to your delusion this will pay off, for you will shake the dust off, now who's the boss? I'm not trying to tell you off. I just want you to see reality for what it really is. This is not a bliss, but it can be a wish, in the true bliss. Do you mind if I give you a kiss? Then you can make a wish after you have your favorite dish. So don't miss out without a doubt what it's all about, then you can give a shout!" Don't pout, you have a reason to shout. Now this is what it is about.`` Don't be blinded by the cloud, no doubt you need to shout and not pout you know what I mean, my name is Dean please don't scream, if you are good I'll get you some ice cream that shall make you beam with a smile for a while anyway. Let's do this another day. Do you know what I'm trying to say? You can have it your way if you stay, will that be okay?" I'm on my way. So please pray I make it there safe, I'm not trying to be gay Hey hey!' I'm on my way, okay stay that way so you can have peace of mind. Please don't forget to be kind and keep this in mind. Don't waste my time, let's flip a dime then we can know what to do next. You broke up with your ex, you gave it your best. Take a while to guess what comes next. Remember give it your best then you can rest knowing you've done your best. Don't second guess it, but have a positive attitude then things will come through with flying colors, you will be overwhelmed at God's blessings because he is the King and Lord of everything, let me show you what I mean don't worry about that old machine, you know what I'm talking about you don't have to shout. I can hear quite well, can you tell, you're quite a gal, What's that smell? Please don't make me deaf by all you're yelling, who are you going to tell about that smell?" Because we don't want to yell, he will give you your heart's desire. I'm not the umpire or referee, don't spring this on me. Because I want to be free, If you choose the path that is right. You know God will bless you in all you do. It's really up to you, or do you want to hang out with Sue? As long as you stay on track and don't pretend to be a class act. As a matter of fact, I'll be right back this is straight from the heart, so don't drift apart Remember your manners, be sweet and kind, don't speak your mind until you think before you blink and draw in ink, what should be done. This gotta be so much fun, until it's done let's rest in the sun, you're not the only one that wants to have fun in the sun. You better get things done. Don't run, take your time, what did you have on your mind?" Don't worry that it could make you hurry, then you can't think straight, don't be late because we want to celebrate, the date in which we began this ordeal you know it's no big deal and that I'm for real. Psalm 139:12 But even in darkness I cannot hide from you. To you the night shines as bright as day; darkness and light are both alike to you.

CHAPTER TEN

GET THAT CAT

Our cat went up the tree in front of our house." My husband decided to go after the cat. He must have forgotten that he had on his slippers. Well don't wear slippers if you plan on climbing a tree. My husband tried as best as he could to climb up the tree to get the cat! He looked so funny. Now we know why slippers are called slippers because you easily slip all the time." We were all laughing. He looked like he was ice skating on the tree!" This was hilarious! I was surprised I didn't call 911. Aren't those firemen famous for rescuing cats!" While we all were laughing because it looked like a cartoon we were watching. My husband was getting mad that we all were laughing at him. He was getting frustrated. But he kept on trying. Instead of going and putting on normal shoes. He'd rather entertain us with his bark slipping on the tree. He was barking alright!" As my husband kept trying to get up the tree he was talking to the cat. He was telling the cat that he's coming to get him and to not worry. Well we all are laughing yet at the same time we were worried that my husband was gonna get hurt." But he would not give up. He got a hold of a big strong branch then he pulled himself up the tree and got the cat." A few days later my husband decided to chase after another cat. Because the cat was bothering the bunny rabbit. I let the bunny roam around the house. I had a barnyard of pets. It even smelt like a barnyard. EU!" Pew!" So my husband began chasing the cat around the house. Everyone told him to stop. To leave the cat alone. But of course he didn't listen." He kept running around the house like a mad man." he jumped on the furniture like the cat did. We were worried that my husband would hurt the cat if he caught up to him. We kept telling my husband to stop!" But as usual, he didn't listen. I guess he liked to entertain us." Acting like a wild man. Again he looked ridiculous!" He looked like a cartoon.``He did make us all laugh again. And we all thought that I was the comedian in the family!" People kept walking into my screen door. Because it didn't look like there was a screen there. My husband got angry about people walking into the screen door. He said, ``What's wrong with everyone!" why can't they see the screen?" I can see it just fine." As soon as he finished saying these words he walked right into the screen door, like everyone else did. We were trying not to laugh!" but we could not keep it inside any longer." Then my husband says ``oh!" great !" Now I walk into the screen door like everyone else." Then he started to act crazy again. He went on his knees and was being dramatic and loud." He was talking to God but entertaining us again." He said okay Lord I stuck my foot into my mouth then he tried putting his foot in his mouth. And he was making all of us laugh hysterically" He said yeah I was talking about everyone running into the screen door then I go do it myself. Like I said, we all thought that I was the comedian in the family." Guess what I did?" I tried to feed the cat orange juice this morning, Well I usually make sure that I have my orange juice and milk for my morning breakfast, every morning when I have my bowl of cereal I give a little bit milk to my cat, well this is our daily routine then I brush his hair but some days I am running slow motion, things are a little different oh the routine gets done but not in the order we usually do them in. I think my cat gets a little annoyed about it. You see, cats don't like changes or a different kind of day. They like that things stay the same old way anyhow let me finish my story. I have blue glass bowls so it's hard to see the color of what was poured in. Right!" Well I poured my cats milk in the bowl then I noticed it was a different color so I smelt it but of course my sense of smell does not work the greatest but neither does my taste buds don't function too well you would think that I have coronna virus all the time.`` But this is the norm for me. To continue my story about pouring milk for my cat. I thought and said to my cat, ``Is this milk bad?" because he wasn't drinking it. So I tasted it but I couldn't taste it well then I opened the lid of the cup that had the milk too and found that this was not milk i was giving to my cat, it was orange juice." Poor cat!" It's a good thing he didn't drink it and it's a good thing I didn't pour it in my cereal. So I rushed down to the dining room and got a cup of milk for my cat and I. " Good thing my cat doesn't talk. I wonder what he would say!" I bet he would say we're just living!" and of course we would have a good time laughing about it!" Just when you think you've done it right, You turn around and you have another fight with the inter man, for the spirit is weak but the flesh is weaker, Now you're going to have to be sweeter, but you can't keep her because they have been given to us without a fuss. Just because we are caregivers for a while. Please don't be in denial. For a while you've got to be in style when you walk down that aisle with a big smile. This will be worth your while. 2Corinthians12:9 But he said to me, my grace is sufficient for you, for my power is made in weakness." So that the power of Christ may rest upon me.

CHAPTER ELEVEN

BIKE RIDING

If you haven't been on a bike for years It will come back to you. Maybe you won't be as confident as you were when you were younger. Maybe you will have to relearn not to be fearful but safe and maybe it will take you too long to have enough guts to cross the street when you have the right away. But you are not sure if you should cross so you let the light change lots of times to be sure you can cross now. When it comes to crossing a bridge you are terrified that the bridge is going to collapse once you are halfway across the bridge. So the people you are riding bikes with are losing their patience with you because it's slowing everybody down. And what about the man holes that you happen to fly into when you wipe out!" Take a good look at all the bruises, scrapes, and scratches all over your legs from when you wiped out on your bike." While we were biking on a bike trail that had been damaged from a bad storm. It looked like we had an earthquake, hit us with the trails all torn up upside down. Huge cracks in the pavement and pieces of the road lying everywhere. And Then you were drowning in two inches of water because you flew off your bike because you didn't see the crack in the road. And landed in a swamp. Then you stunk so bad when you got home. And the babysitter says to you ``what happened to you?" And you say I went for a swim." But you reak so badly! you have to take a shower so you don't make somebody puke!" Including yourself!" And what about the people that you are biking with? They treat you like you're in the army. My husband acted like he was the drill sergeant." He would yell at us to keep up the pace!" and make you go uphill all the time." Like we are training for the olympics." In the long run training to go uphill really benefits you for long trips. Anywhere any time.'' Everywhere you go by car you can by bike" "We biked all day. We took lots of snacks and water. We stopped at all the parks so the girls could play at the park while we took a snack break. We carried two bike trailers, one with supplies and food and one with the girls in it.''If we had a trial or things didn't go as planned. The girls had a good time. Once we got stranded in some small town .The girls and I waited for the guys to fix the problem." While in some store, it was nice and air conditioned in the store and there were some puppets that the girls were playing with and they were having fun." I was having fun watching them. Even though we were going through some trials the girls were getting blessed with a good time." If they were happy I was happy." Even if we biked down a hill on a super hot day and it feels like flames of fire hitting your face." Even If it stormed on you you considered it as a shower." And it felt so good. One thing for sure when we made it to and from a trip when we got home we felt like a champ. When winter time came we got the bikers blues. I wanted to bike in the snow and ice but it was only a thought, maybe even a crazy thought. We couldn't wait until winter was over so we could go biking again. This is the beginning and not the end, will you be my friend in the end? You shouldn't get bent out of shape. I'll give you some tape. If you need it, don't be late, open the gate, and please don't be late for a very important date. Come on, let's go out and celebrate. Open the gate wide so you can lean on your side for just a short ride. This will subside, don't take this personal, be a gem and go to rehearsal, when you think you got it down pad. You will think this is the best thing you have ever had. Then you will be glad that you have this down pad. You'll be glad and think this is the best thing that you have ever had. Aren't you glad? Others will think that you are mad, but don't you be sad. Don't give satisfaction to those that want you to be the opposite of what you want to be. Because you look to the father and it's no bother for the others to see your strength that comes from the holy one, you won't have to threaten them with a gun, because you are the chosen one that God desires to bless, now take a guess and give it your best. Then you can rest after you give it your best be my guest. 1 Corinthians 9:24 Do you not know all the runners run, but only one receives the prize? So run that you may obtain it.

CHAPTER TWELVE

LOSING YOUR RIDE

When you don't drive you get rides from different people so it's always a different car and a different color. There are times when I forget what kind of car I came in. So at times I go to the wrong car. Especially if there are more than one car that are parked next to each other that are the same color. But what I don't understand is how can I be so confused as to how I get so confused as to trying to get in somebody's car who has a car load full of people." I open the door and the lady says to me ``sorry we're packed full.`` I say oops!" wrong car" the car is full of people and I laugh!" Or how about my friend taking me grocery shopping in a van right" and I come out the store and go to a truck with two big dogs barking at me and ready to bite my head off!" Now you think I would know better." Nope, not me." How about the time my husband took me to the thrifty bread store. He says to me now I am gonna park up close to the door so when you come out of the store you will be able to see the car. Well I still went to the wrong car. I went to a totally different car than ours. There was a woman in the car. She did not see me trying to get in her car. She was busy looking for something in her car. Then my husband beeps the horn and waves to me he wasn't in the spot that he said he would be. So It wasn't all my fought. But yes I should have not tried to get in a car with someone I didn't know." And the sad thing is I didn't even know the person whose car I was trying to get into. No harm done because she didn't see me trying to get into her car. Good thing I don't drive I would be getting arestted for trying to steal somebody's car." In fact I am Just trying to get home. I even went to the wrong house. I was going to visit my grandma and mom because my mom was at grandmas taking care of grandma. I went there everyday for a walk and to see mom and grandma. I was walking so fast that I passed my grandma's house and I went to the neighbors house. I knew this wasn't the right house, it didn't look familiar.''It's a good thing I didn't try to go in their house, they might have thought i was an intruder. Oh boy! I'd be in deep trouble. No thank you, not today. Loseing your ride, standing up and trying to swallow your pride, trying to touch the sky with your eye. Being focused on the things that will last for eternity you have to have some kind of dignity if you know what I mean. Don't scream, I am only a human being, you know what I mean don't be mean, or I will make you scream at the thought of a living being, you know what I mean?" Don't make a scene just to be seen, to reveal that you have been redeemed. If you know what I mean, look to the skies and realize that it is not all about you just because you didn't stay in school. To learn what you need to know so you can go out on your own, and yes it's a bit scary, don't be hasty, and call Larry." The time will come when everything is undone. You will want to run. only God can fix it. The sooner you take this to heart people can not tear you apart. So don't be left un intended, but be on guard that the one is coming, He will not let you drift apart he will be dear to your heart he will always be faithful so do be careful, for what you let inside you whether it be physical, spiritually, emotionally, mentaly, remember he's got the remedy, and he can make melody and it truly will sound heavenly. Not only to your ears, but to everything that appears, to be here for a while. Please don't be in denial, Because it's just for a little while that we have to wait, let's try to negotiate, try not to be late. For the most important time in history, When Jesus will come back in his glory. Now it's important to remember this story. For it's the most important story that you ever want to hear, Remember he is here and dear. So don't fear when the time comes near so be a dear do not fear. The time is coming oh!" so stay near my dear. Hang on tuff, because things will get ruff but he is tougher than any thing that is being, because he is not a human being. He is the king of all and he stands mighty tall, be careful not to fall; you want to be on your best behavior before you meet the savior. For as the sun and moon comes up then goes down the sky will fall down, when it does you want to be with the one that can fix anything that is un done. Because he has won." Yes

God doesn't change,Hebrews: 13:8. Jesus Christ, is the same yesterday, and today and forever. He remains true to his word. And for this and many other things I am thankful and grateful. Now if I get confused and lose my ride, I don't need to worry because Jesus is right by my side. But I must abide to his word, and keep his commandments, and to be a light. That everything isn't bright, that's alright with me, as long as I keep his deed. That I will serve him day and night. That i will keep shining bright. To minster his love to others,and to bless others in ways that can express showing humilaty, and love as if they are my special guest, at my best then I can lay my head to rest, I also benefit, peace in my heart soul spirit, mind.body. As I remember to be kind, yes I have to keep it in mind all the time. Lest I shine without giving time, so I keep this in mind, in the end it; is worth my time; Don't prolong in doing what's right, you better hurry before it's out of sight, Just remember you'll be alright

This is really cool, and it is all new. To a few,how about you, do you know what to do? Be ready to fight for what is right, You will be glad that you're not mad. Instead of playing dead, continue your Journey, don't make your eyes burley, you only have one life to live so give yourself the benefit of the doubt, now shout!" because that's what it is all about. I am telling you for your own good, please don't misunderstand the difference between good and bad and everything you have had. It can't be all that bad. Is this a fad?"Give it all that you have. You'll be glad and not mad. So count your blessings one by one and don't leave things undone. Do it for pleasure and not for fun then you can sit in the sun, but don't run, until things are done. Proverbs 3: 5-6 Trust in the Lord with all of your heart, and do not lean on your own understanding. In all of your ways acknowledge him, and he will make your paths straight.

CHAPTER THIRTEEN

DONATING PLASMA

My husband and I were at the dollar tree store. When a man who looked like he was homeless came in. The man started talking to us. He was talking loudly in the store as if he wanted everybody to hear what he was saying. Although there were not many people in the store. The man was telling us that he just came from giving plasma. That he makes good money donating blood at the plasma place. So my husband and I thought we would try it. Well we didn't know it took all day your first time," So we spent most of our day trying to give plasma. They said for a couple we could make good money a month. We went along with the peperations, come to find out my husband couldn't give plasma because he was on a certain type of medicine. Turned out that I could not give plasma because my veins were too tiny. That they could not even get a good vein. Now how crazy is that!" It had to have happened to us." Never did try again. I guess we were not meant to give plasma. That's a shame because I've heard that giving plasma helps to get rid of headaches.``especially migraines. I guess I am supposed to keep my headaches, But I really want to give them away." But who wants them?" Now if they did get a good vain my vain would have fainted." What I really mean is they collapse then they would have to keep sticking needles in me so I am glad they didn't try again and again. I don't feel like being a pincushion" today or any other day!" No thank you." My second husband gave plasma all the time, that's how we got extra money when we needed it. He did have a job but he didn't make enough, at times we needed extra cash So this was another alternative for us. He had no problems at all. He had good veins and he did not take any medications" I felt bad that he had to give plasma for extra income. But to him it was no big deal. There was a female neighbor who came around to ask for money. For some reason she would try to hide her Identity. She wore a really big hat but it was not fancy or pretty, it was huge," she also wore big old sunglasses." She couldn't hide her identity from me. I never borrowed money to her because I didn't know if she wanted it for something foolish like cigarettes or booze. So I offered her some food but she said no thanks." I wasn't going to borrow money to someone that really didn't need it." Besides, my husband was giving plasma for us. Not to give it to somebody else. Call me mean or heartless or whatever?" But if I feel the Lord wanting me to help a person I will. At the Cub Foods there was a young man holding a sign as we were coming out of the store. I walked past him then I went back to him to read the sign that said I lost my job can you help me. Something to that effect. He could have been lying. Just to get money I don't know so I gave him what money I had in my hand which was only a dollar. I usually don't have any cash on me. The young man was so grateful." He probably thought I gave him a twenty dollar bill or bigger." Boy he's gonna be disappointed when he unfolds his dollar bill. The woman that I was with said ``why did you give him money?" When he's young he can go look for a job instead of begging for money. Which she was right but I told her it was a dollar that's all I had. She kind of chuckled a bit then said ``well a dollar is a dollar." We could say Jesus gave his blood not for money. But to pay our debt that he didn't owe, but he was a ransom to pay for our sins. That we may live life to the fullest, and live it abundantly, he has paid the price so we can live free from the bondage of sin. For this I shall be ever gratefull. Just when you think you have it bad take a look around. It will make you feel sad, You will be glad that you are mad for the things you may have said. This young man was healthy and in good shape. The woman that I was with was right. This young man should have been out looking for a job, Instead of begging for handouts he should have been going about doing what's right he should have been putting up a fight!" That's right to either get his Job back, or get a better one than he had so he shouldn't be taken advantage of other people's kindness. He should have been more willing to be of use to others, but he didn't bother to lift a finger to do what was really right to do. Now what's he going to do? Go around and say boo hoo. He should be thankful that he is able, instead of pretending that he is disable. Now i know if there was a table filled with food he would be able to sit at the table, he would be truly able, In fact he would be stable and help himself with no problem, because he is able but not willing to do his part in this society from his heart, that he could really do his part, but he needs a change of heart to do his part. Now he truly is a piece of art, he better keep it together and not fall apart. Maybe in time he will make up his mind and put the past behind, and try to reach for the stars, and to be able to dream again, this all has to come from within. Then again he can't pretend again, and again. As long as he doesn't give up on himself who's he going to tell that maybe he's on his way to hell. Please don't let this be, you can pray for this lost soul you know you have to be bold. Because you may be the only one that has seen this man come undone. There is Just one gesture, tell him about our Father in heaven, and tell him about the word, for it is living active and powerful, this is not to be kept a secret for yourself, this is meant to be shared with everyone else, In hopes that he won't run the other way, but to our heavenly father and that's okay that you spent your time that way in doing God's will, don't be afraid just stand still. Be a light to where it is dark, you can be a spark in the dark. Not for just a while, please do not be in denial I'm telling you this and not for just a mile. Go ahead and smile for a while because you have been given that chance to embrace the goodness of our heavenly father, and to know him and his ways for the rest of your days. Here on earth, you have a chance of rebirth. This is not our permanent home, so you can roam around all you want. There's no harm done until judgment day comes, you'll be glad that you did the father's will. And he already flipped the bill on that hill called calvary. He wasn't in a hurry, yet he bore all our sins. Even though he was perfect without blemish, he made a pack to finish the father's will. You should be glad that he paid your bill. He even gave us a tip, which is the holy spirit that is within, that we might communicate with him, and to have spiritual gifts to use. That we can edify one another with brotherly love, and to be kinder, now mind your manners, for this is God's will that we love one another, as he loves us. It's easy to trust in him, If only we let him in, and not try to do things ourselves. There really is no one else that we can depend on. Mankind will fail, But the Lord stays true no matter what you do. He so loves you in hopes there is no other, that you will trust in him even when things get tough, remember you have the right stuff. To go on to the higher calling. Don't be afraid of falling. The great I am is calling. Please do not ignore his call. He will be there for you when you fall. Time and time again, he is the only one that can wipe your tears, and also your fears. When he forgives you of your sins, he remembers your sins no more. He doesn't keep score. He's the one that you should adore. Let's move on to hear what I've got to say. Pay attention anyway. Now, not the day after hope you are getting some laughter here and there and everywhere you can. Because this is the beginning and not the end. Hebrews 10:22 Let us draw near with a true heart in full assurance of faith, with our hearts sprinkled clean from an evil conscience and our bodies washed with pure water.

CHAPTER FOURTEEN

ROAD RAGE

Road rage has gotten ridiculous! It's gotten out of control. Even if you don't have a car people still treat you like you have a car and maybe you're riding your bike to the bank and you go to the drive through to get some cash out and the people behind you beep their horn at you. What's their problem? Just because you don't have four wheels and you only have two you're a person too. And what about if you don't have any wheels at all? People still have road rage. When I was walking I wanted to mail something by the post office. They have mail boxes outside the old fashion blue mail boxes. Well, I was mailing my stuff and a man came behind me and peeped his horn! Then he hit me with the fender of his car, and on the back of my legs I became furious!" When this person hit me with his car." I got angry, and turned around to look at the driver. I yelled at him and said what's wrong with you! I was here first! If I wasn't so angry about this guy hitting me with the fender of his car I would have tried to memorize his license plates,and called the police as soon as I got home. But I was too upset. Now I have never thought that just to mail some envelopes, that I would have a crazy guy doing road rage when I didn't even have wheels. Another crazy driver was going to hit my girls and I. We were walking home from the store. We were in an alley and some crazy driver tried to run us down. He backed my girls and I against a brick wall. I think the guy was just trying to scare us. This guy was a jerk. Get this my husband and I got runned off the freeway by a big semi truck. Now what was his problem? I'm telling you all that road rage has gotten way out of control. Whether you have two wheels, four wheels or no wheels at all!" It's getting so people are afraid to leave their home if they don't have to. Even my husband had road rage a few times. He got mad about something and he put on the gas. He was going too fast !" for where we were, we were not on the freeway. But he acted like we were. I started screaming, let me out! stop. But he did not pay any attention to what I was screaming about. I even wanted to jump out of the car. I screamed ``let me out!" stop" stop" Let me out!" I thought he was trying to kill us!" I frantically yelled and screamed ``let me out!" i thought he was going to commit suicide and take me with him."I was so terrified!"I was hysterical!" I wanted to jump out of the car so badly!" But I knew that would be a wrong move." Either I die in the car in a crash" or jump out of the car and get run over a few times by cars coming towards me or die instantly When i hit the pavement!" Which was the best choice?"After a while my husband finally slowed down. He only gave me a half heart attack!" I really thought we were going to die!" There was another incident where we were on a busy street. And a truck was going to hit us" to avoid getting hit my husband had to swing the car to the right then my husband lost control of the car because he was driving fast. This was not road rage, this was ``watch out for your life" rage. We were shaken up a bit because it was a miracle that we didn't hit one or more cars by swerving to the right and left on the street out of control. I wasn't as shaken up or as scared as I was when he was driving like a wild! maniac ' going 90 miles an hour down a street that you were supposed to be driving slow." Too bad my husband didn't get to shooken up and was scared sick like he made me during his road rage episodes!" I had a freaky episode while I was in the car with my son. We were on the freeway going fast and it was storming hard and we couldn't even see in front or back of us. Because the rain was coming down so hard and fast I was trying to see the freeway and I couldn't see anything but the rain. For some reason I just freaked. I began screaming because the rain coming down on the car was making me dizzy somehow" My son kept on driving and didn't say a word. I thought he might tell me to be quiet because he's trying to drive. But he didn't say a thing. I must have screamed for a good 15 to 20 minutes. Well we finally got off the freeway. Safe and sound." I was relieved." I don't know why. I began screaming. Maybe I had back flashes from bad experiences from the past I do not know. The other times I had bad experiences was when I was a teenager. My brother crashed my dad's car and I hit my head really hard on the dashboard. I blacked out for only a moment. I never told anyone what really happened to me." i Just said I hit my head. But the truth was I hit my forehead really hard on the dashboard.``I didn't know what happened to me when this happened, that's why I didn't tell anybody. I did get a bump and bruise.`` Not a thing happened to my brother or my girlfriend."I guess they were lucky! Now I really did not need a bump on the head." If it did my brain good then that's okay but if it made me more daffy then I definitely didn't need it. Other than that we were all fine. I was glad everybody was fine. But my dad's car was not fine." It was totaled.Then there are people that are on the road driving and maybe they are not mad or upset they Just don't care." Okay I was in the parking lot of the dollar store when a woman backed up to me she hit me and I fell on the pavement hard flat on my back. Some people saw what happened to me." They were astonished!" At what they Just witnessed." The woman that hit me was Just sitting in her car looking in her mirror she was just looking she didn't even bother to get out of her car and ask me if I was okay she Just kept looking in her mirror to see if I was alive as soon as she saw me get up she took off in her car fast." When My son heard a thump!" He knew something happened to me. He came running, he helped me up." Then he asked me what happened?" I told him that the lady hit me with her car. He said, ``Let's call the police." I said no we are running behind schedule already. I had planned a family reunion. It happened to be father's day. I picked the wrong day to have a family reunion. Anyhow I went into the store and the people that witnessed the car hitting me came up to me and asked me if I was okay. I said yes I am fine.The family reunion was no reunion it was a flop!" Only one brother showed up and one uncle. It was father's day and everyone was spending time with their father's. So, I Just threw away money for nothing and I managed to get runned over by a car. I paid for the pavilion And it was a big flop!" There were some other people there having a get together. They turned out fine. They were cooking on the grill and playing volleyball. So much for family reunions"The first one I had was a blessing. It was a great turn out everyone had an enjoyable time but no one knew who put this event together they didn't know it was me. Until my aunt and uncle asked,

"Who put this event together?" Then I told them it was me. They were so kind to send me a thank you card and a gift card to dine at Applebee's. That was very sweet of them." I don't think I will be having anymore family reunions in the near future. Road rage, what does it really mean?" Are you mad because of the way people drive or does this make you want them out of the way. Because you can't stay, you have to be on your way. People are coming and going so fast you've got to make the moment last. Then you will have a blast, because you made fun of the other driver, and you couldn't stay beside her. Then you lose patience and self control. Let's face it, you're getting old. But you are in denial for a while. Then you give a big smile, and you want to dial on your phone, so you won't have to be alone. So you zone on your own, but if you would have known then you could have known what to do. When the situation had approached you, you would have known what to do. You would have known what to pursue. The pressure is not on you, you will know what best to do. Don't be a fool, and lose your cool, you better learn and stay in school. Because this is the right thing to do. So please don't be a fool. In whatever you do. Don't sue, then the blame won't be on you. Now what are you gonna do?' It's really up to you. Be very careful of those crazy drivers, don't you become one of them, I tell you over again, that this is a real trial, so don't be in denial, If you do, let it be for only a while. Then you can smile for a while, give the biggest grin that you can give, so that it will last, like a long lasting kiss. Please don't miss who you are and how far you have come. You still have a ways to go. Let's get this show on the road, let's get it done nine days in a row. Tell your brother Joe, to not be too slow. If you miss out on all the best. You can be my guest, you can rest at your best. You will not be left behind, Just take a look and see what you can find. Please remember to be kind, when you zip some wine, let your light shine keep this in mind. Now let's wine and dine. Go ahead and take your time. Everything will be Just fine. Now give it your best then you can rest. Try giving your best, I can only guess give it a rest, It's not enough it's less, be my guest give it your best. Yet I can't remember. I can only second guess. Why are you being a pest? I can only second guess you wore your best, yet nevertheless I can only guess what is best, for you have to give it a rest. So you won't second guess. You only want the best now please give it a rest let me guess, you want to give it a rest when you're not nearly done. But if you feel it's necessary, to carry the burden, If you do you will surely be hurting so lay your burdens down at the feet of the cross you'll be lifted on high, this is the truth, I tell you no lie, I'm not a spy that came from the sky don't be shy I tell you why, take that stye out of your eye. I tell you the truth, no matter why. So you can see clearer, and brighter than before, then you can walk out the door, and do what you are called to do. Now this is what you need to do, do it for the sake of love and devotion, and to remain faithful and true no matter what you do. When you do it with a pure heart, no one can rip it apart, because it comes from your heart. Only one person can see you from afar, no matter where you are. When you have done all that is required, you will take a deep breath, sit back and think to yourself ``I'll do it all over again, Matthew 11: 28-30 Jesus said, come to me, all you who are weary and carry heavy burdens, and I will give you rest. Take my yoke upon you. Let me teach you, because I am humble and gentle at heart, and you will find rest for your souls. For my yoke is easy to bare, and the burden I give you is light."

CHAPTER FIFTEEN

WEARING THE RIGHT SHOES

Okay my husband and I went bowling. We were having a good time. I was waiting for my ball to come up. I was trying to get my ball and somehow my hand got smashed between the balls. We laughed about it then I threw my ball but the ball wouldn't let go of my fingers, or my fingers wouldn't let go of the ball. My fingers were stuck inside the ball. When I pitched the ball down the lane I started to go with the ball. I almost went with the ball down the lane. But instead I kept myself from falling. In the process of keeping myself from going down the lane with my ball I looked like I was having a ball not to fall at all on my face. Isn't that a disgrace? I must have looked so funny, trying my best to keep from falling I could have gotten a strike. If I went down the lane and striked. We laughed about it. We did have fun laughing about the silly things I did. Now it was time to go home. We left the bowling place and were on our way home. Then my husband said to me ``look down at your feet so I looked down at my feet and saw that I still had my bowling shoes on and I looked at my husband's feet he had his bowling shoes on too". We both busted out laughing. We had to go back and get our shoes. We quickly rushed back to get our shoes and return the bowling shoes. Nobody ever noticed What we were doing. We had a good laugh. Next my husband and I went to a class at church. It was in the dead of winter we got done with our class and were in the car. My husband says to me, look at my feet, he just noticed he had gone to church wearing his slippers. So I look down at his feet. He was wearing his slippers. Alright." The whole time he had been wearing his slippers." We both laughed and said nobody even noticed." Now how could he not notice that he didn't know he had his slipper's instead of his shoes because it was a dead cold winter. He should have felt the bitter cold on the back of his heels. Not only that. It was a miracle that he didn't keep slipping and sliding after all isn't that why they are called slipper's?" In the first place. He should have been slipping and slideing all the way from the car to just get to the building let alone to make it inside the building without falling a thousand times and in the whole ordeal" I'm amazed that he made it to the car without slipping and sliding most of the time. To be able to drive us to church, if he had he would have come out looking like a live snowman himself." And his clothes would have been soaked and wet." And practically crawling on his hands and knees so he wouldn't fall any more!" He would be looking ruff!" but he is tuff" Hope next time he will wear the right shoes.``As for me I have to put the right shoes on myself as well. One day in the summer I was in a hurry to get out the door. I got on the elevator and went up to the laundry room. I happened to look down at the floor and noticed I had two different sandals on. Then I saw the maintenance man when I got off the elevator. I said look I got two different sandals on he made a funny face as to say that I am strange. Once I put tennis shoes on my daughter. Then I looked at her shoes. I said it looks like I put the shoes on the wrong feet. So I switched them around. That should be all right now. I looked again and I'll be, they still look like they are on the wrong foot." What the heck!" I was getting confused!" My poor baby was getting tired of having to switch the shoes around. Now if It were up to her she would rather be barefoot. That's how my husband wanted to train them to like being barefoot like the flintstones." He says it will toughen their feet. Well I finally figured out that there were two different sizes of the same tennis shoes. I thought there was something wrong with me." Now when I was younger I did a foolish thing. I took off my socks and shoes and decided to walk home barefoot from school in the ending stages of winter where there was snow and ice and alot of slushy melted snow." Oh no!" Now that was a foolish thing I did." I have no idea why I did that, nobody dared me!" nobody threated me if I didn't do it they would beat me up" nobody made a bet with me.`` I Just did it!" I don't know why I did such a crazy thing like that! I am surprised that my girls didn't do a crazy thing like that with their Flintstones feet!" I guess they aren't as crazy as me." I didn't even have flintstone feet.''I never told them what I did, they might have tried it themselves. We will never know. Which way do I go? Do I go to and fro? I really don't know which way to go. Because I have not been told that I'm not too old to be bold, no matter how old I am, I will tell you again and again who I am because from where I stand I demand an explanation, hand and hand. Where there is freedom to others. Some are in bondage, with their knowledge and they try to be set free but it's a real key to the trick, don't stick out your neck, Oh what the heck!" you're damned if you do, you're damned if you don't. Don't be a people pleaser, be a God pleaser then you won't be a teaser you will be a God pleaser. People will watch every move you make. They will try and take whatever they please you won't feel at ease, until you get things right now that's out of sight, Am I right? I like things bright, In the middle of the night. And that's alright by me you can surely see what's in it for you and for me. You can truly be committed, can't you see the mystery of history. This is not a mission of tolerance, this is about your commitment to one another. And to the king. This is what I mean, you must have a heart that is clean and spotless. Let me guess at my best that this means clean from all sins. Then we can start the process, now give it your best each day that you tackle will be a plus for you. Then you will grow and flow the way you should go. To be a light in the darkness, a flame to the game you once knew. Just remember all things are new. When you give your life to Christ. Everything is new, yes you will be unsure what you can and cannot do. For old things have passed away. All things are new, you are on the right track this is not an act by far. Now you will shine like a star no matter where you are. All things will flow according to his will. Please be still and know he is God!" He has said he will never leave you or forsake you. He is true to his word. And if you abide, he will be by your side forever and a day. I must be on my way. To make it a special day. Romans 8:28 And we know all things work together for good to them that love God, to them that are called according to the will of God.

CHAPTER SIXTEEN

ANY WHICH WAY

Now it is okay to change your mind about things but it is strange to have a favorite color one day then the next day you change your favorite color. Or to say one day you like chocolate then the next day say you hate it!" Now that is strange, well I know somebody like that." Maybe they ate too much chocolate one day so they got sick of it and decided they don't like it anymore. But this is not the case." When my oldest daughter was a toddler I constantly put a sweater on her because I got cold so I put a sweater on me, and my daughter then got hot then I would take it off, then i took my baby's sweater off. This went on all day." So a few years later my daughter began changing her clothes every little while. The room was such a mess with clothes all over the floor you couldn't find the floor in the room. Because my daughter has changed 20 times a day!" Was it my fault !"She changed 20 times a day?" Maybe I was going through some hot flashes!" That didn't mean my daughter was having hot flashes.!"After all I went through menopause in my early 30's So I made my daughter go through menopause as a toddler. Now I had drilled into her mind that she needed to change every few minutes. How was I going to convince her otherwise?" Poor kid, I was confusing her small world.``Now I have to untrain what I taught her and re-train her." Sounds like I'm talking about my pet. " Once we went out to dinner and we took off her jacket she had my bra on over her shirt.!" We all laughed, this was crazy!" But we were kind of embarrassed!" How in the world did we get her jacket on her without seeing my bra on her?" Must have been a trick she learned but from who?" My husband put a bodysuit called a onesie on my daughter. He thought it was a shirt!"

it had snaps on it, how could he not know that it was a onesie!" the poor girl no wonder she dressed strangely and so did her father dress her strangely. She was not a baby anymore to wear a onesie and that's not how you wear a onesie." So that's where she learned to dress." When my daughter grew up to be a woman she still had a strange way of dressing when it was warm out she dressed like it was cold and when it was cold out she dressed like it was warm she never did get it quite right only now she is with Jesus so, now she is dressed perfectly. And will always be. Staying focused is tricky for me. At times!" my mind can go any which way." You can be sporadic in your way of thinking, and your mind can be racing a thousand miles an hour. If you happen to get anxious, or panicky, or worried, or stressed or have anxiety. Your world will swirl and even cause headaches, buttaches, and every kind of ache in between. you can end up walking around in circles. Once I was having a meeting I decided to go do something else, and the people I was having a meeting with asked me where I was going. They said, ``Come back over here, we are having a meeting." I don't know what made me wonder off. Another time when I lived in the ministry home. We had guests over. It was a Christian doctor and his wife after dinner I went down to my room and did my own thing, instead of fellowshiping with the guest and everyone else that lived here. The only thing that I can think of is that when I was a kid, if mom and dad had company over they told us kids to go play somewhere because they didn't want us to hear their converstion. So my mind went back to when I was taught that. I don't know why I didn't think I could stay for fellowship, besides I did want to do my own thing as well. Now that I think about it seems kind of rude that I did that without saying goodbye and nice to meet you. At the time I didn't think it was rude. To our guests, goes to show, you never stop learning. Because maybe the way you were taught something as a child does not mean that this is the right way. You can learn a new way that could be better, and more polite than you ever knew of. There's always room for improvement. Right!" Isn't it impossible that there is an obsticle in the way to make you delay, for you to say this isn't the way to get things done while you are on the run. Until you get things clear my dear, without any fear that you can get things done right. As a matter of fact you can make them bright then this will help your sight in a manner of speaking, this has true meaning, as I am speaking, this for your thinking. That all things are possible to those who believe, you can truly receive all the best that is meant for you. If you know what to do, you know what's in store for you. Take it one day at a time, make yourself shine. Don't be blind to what you left behind. In time you will blow my mind, trying to keep peace of mind. If you don't dine Just one more time. In time you will shine, all the possiblities are mine. Because you don't want to take it back now this is a fact, this is no act. That is that, come on back where you belong, then you can be strong. Please don't do anything wrong, keep yourself strong, and don't do wrong or you will prolong, don't know for how long, But it is you who belongs to the king of kings. All year around and not just spring now this is the thing if you know what I mean. Take it easy, I'm not a machine. Let's work together as a team. Then we can beam from cheek to cheek, don't be a geek, or a freak. Stay petite, because you don't want to be bigger. You want to stay small. But that's not all. So be a doll and carry on in your business, don't be a busy body or a menace. Why are you trying to get in the world's book of guinness? It's time to reminisce, so take a guess at what's best for you to dwell on, let it be good, so it can get better than you could of Imagined. Your imagination can take you places that you could have not thought of yourself. At times you don't want to tell anyone else. You would rather keep it to yourself, and not tell anyone else. Then you can go where you want to go. You Just got to know, for your own peace of mind, you can unwind don't spend a dime, and waste my time because I've got alot on my mind. Now dreams are kind of the same as far as keeping them to yourself, and not anyone else or you can share them if you wish so that maybe you could try to interpret them. So you can begin to make sense of what the dream meant. Can I give you a hint, you will never figure it all out. Because this is what it is about, don't shout because it is meant for us to wonder, and be curious. Only our Father in heaven knows what they mean, we need to stay clean in our thinking and our Imagination. It would be nice to take a long vacation. What location shall we go?'Try to make it easy as you know, you Just have to be on the go. Stop going to and fro, Just so you know the location is not the matter from what I gather It's how long you'll be gone, Just as long as you come back in one piece. I'm not trying to live in luxury, remember the fact that this is not an act. But subtract all your misery so you can live in victory. Now this is history, and this is my story that God gets all the Glory. For this is his territory, in which you can keep it near and dear to your heart. In which you will never let it depart. For this is true to human nature, that we belong to the one and only creator of the universe and the whole world. That one day he is coming back. Be ready, and be on guard for the time is at hand when we can go home to the place that we are longing to be. Just you and me, so let it be soon Lord. For times are hard but this is nothing that you would regard. Don't push too hard for there is a reason for every season, And a time for every purpose. Just know that the one who made you all up I can feel it in my gut, that the time is nearing. Don't go on fearing, but be glad for what you have had. It's not so bad, don't get mad but be glad for what is ahead. Now you can rest your head on your bed and be rest assured. That God's got your back, Just be glad you're on his team so let yourself beam from seam to seam you know what I mean.Every way you go, I Just want to know, you can go with the flow, now I'm on a row, if you must know which way you should go. Make sure it's an even flow so that you know who's to show!" Then you can let go to say no, If you must know. Be yourself and don't tell anyone else. This is in the best interest for you. Then you will know what to do. Just go until you have peace in your heart and mind, and spirit and soul. You've got the right idea, keep this in mind, you need time to unwind, so that you can have peace of mind. You will feel alot better and not under the weather. Now come on get it together, now from what I gather it really doesn't matter how long things go wrong. Because you are stronger than you know, so let things go. That's not important in this life, I think that's pretty nice. Give me a smile that will last for a while. Go that extra mile you'll be glad that you did. This will give you the energy that you have hid, you will feel uplifted Instead. Don't let it go over your head. Remember to break bread Instead, go ahead and anoint yourself with God's presence, It's not an essence to have your presence at the moment but if you'd rather take a tip be glad in the Lord for all things are stored, in the heavenly places without any traces or fumes from the tomb, you must resume so you won't lose your place. Ask God he will give you the grace, In this place, In your face. You can see Jesus all around, Please be quiet, don't make a sound." Come on!" I'll show you around, you must stand on solid ground, to be profound you've got to be around and stand your ground. Look up!" things will get better. If you lay your burdens down at Jesus' feet. Do I need to repeat this over again? I don't think so, Let us begin all that is within. I'm not going to tell you again my friend. I'll love you till the end. I say Amen!" I'll say it over and over again, This is not the end, now I can bend on bended knee, I must agree that you can be free, free indeed if you know what I mean, and if you do, you're more mature than I thought, you want to keep growing, this is serious and not boring. Don't fall asleep and start snoring. This could get quite boring, not to mention annoying." On your Journey you won't have to worry, you will not be alone. I garentee my helper the holy spirit will guide your every step. And yet the future is unknown to those who groan and moan that they wished that they had chosen the one and only son that could get things done. While you're on the run. Running here and there and everywhere. Let your focus be on the right one. God's only son and his word, Then you will see what you need to see in order to be free indeed. Philippians 4: 6-7 Do not be anxious about anything, but in everything by prayer and supplication with thanksgiving let your requests be made known to God. and the peace of God, which passes all understanding, will guard your hearts and minds in Christ Jesus.

CHAPTER SEVENTEEN

OVERCOMING OBSTACLES

There may be things that stop you from achieving your goals but don't give up on what you want to achieve, don't give up your dreams. Yes there may be obstacles that are preventing you from moving forward. That doesn't mean to give up or quit." Just because you're shorter than most people just because you don't use common sense, at times just because you are different than the average person or just because you don't dress yourself right, like people want you to dress. If I say the way you speak spanish is to just add an o to any word and that makes it spanish wish it were that simple," But it is not." Say you are at some place in the public and a caucasian man or woman is speaking spanish and you happen to be hispanic and you don't know what in the heck he or she is saying. Makes you feel like you are worthless!' Because this is your heritage." But your parents didn't teach you. All though your grandparents talked to you in spanish but didn't ask you to speak back to them in spanish." Or how about you go visit someone in the nursing home and an hispanic man sees that you are hispanic and comes up to you expecting for you to understand what he is saying and expects you to engage in his conversation.`` And you feel and look like an idiot!" The man is looking at you like you are an idiot!" But you are not.``Mom always says that nobody taught her she just picked it up." Or how about you are at an hispanic church and the pastor is taking roll calls. All the people are answering him in Spanish so you answer in Spanish and everyone giggles because they think you are a comedian." because they know that you only speak english.``Maybe you took spanish class and your grandparents and other relatives speak spanish to each other you may know some words but you don't have anyone to speak spanish to then you Just speak what you know best. But if you don't speak the proper grammar then you are stuck between a hard place and a rock. Then your Just out of luck, don't pass the buck, it's just your luck. Don't get so excited, don't buy it, deny it. Take a deep breath, remember to take it slow then you will know the process is slow,get on the go. look what you've done. In what you have won, getting things done. I'm on the run, don't rush ahead and jump in bed, and want to sleep all day. There is nothing on display, of what I want to say any old way. I want you to stay, But in your own way today, not yesterday, or tomorrow, If you need to drown your sorrow, remember there's always tomorrow to get things right this shall be a delight. If tomorrow comes for you. It will be brand new, for each and every day is made by our heavenly father. Do not bother to make it up. You can get it unstuck, remember to take a big breath, don't forget to let it go, So, you won't cause death because you held your breath, so you could rest. Just to let you know, this is not a show, What are your intentions to grow? If you don't know then you've got to go. Because this is not a show where you can lose control. Let's take a stroll, so you can know that all things given to us are a gift from our heavenly father. Now how can you bother to holler about what you don't have. Be glad what you do have, for we have only one True God and he's not odd. We are made in his own image, consider it a privilege that he chose you, And he loves you no matter what you do. He will never fail you nor will he turn his back on you. He stays true to his word indeed. There is no other that can fulfill you. Make amends with him, he'll renew you from the top of your head to the bottom of your toes, and even touch your nose. Be true to him, he will never leave your side, but you must abide in his word and in him. This is where it all begins. I say Amen!" And in the end, you will be glad that you trusted in him, he will forgive you again and again, remember the great I am. He is waiting for you to come to him, each and every minute he desires to be with you. Whether you feel ready or not, he has never forgot, what you were before you existed. He will not be resisted in any shape or form, for he is adorned in nothing but beauty, it is our duty to become more like him. Then we can begin to grow maturaly to want to reach your goals. And to wait patiently for when the time is right, you will know in which way to go. Don't say no, for in the end he will win because he is within and he will make it right!" and your future is bright because of him. So be glad he is near so don't fear the one that can get things done. For he has won the battle. 1 John 4:4 Little children you are of God, and have overcome them. For greater is he that is in you than he that is in the world.``

CHAPTER EIGHTEEN

WHEN PARENTS EMBARRASS THE KIDS

One of my daughters didn't want to go to a public place with my husband and I. According to her we always did something to embarrass her." She was right about that as I examined the times we did something stupid in public" Instead of the kids embaressing us we embarrassed our daughter. Okay so there was a sale on the bread well my husband began to yell at me that I could only have a certain type of bread I said no the coupon says mix and match." So here we are in the store arguing about what kind of bread we can buy with the coupon. Well my daughter had to walk away as if she didn't know us." Then my husband yelled for my daughter which is more embarrassing than ever.`` I think she wanted to run away after that!" Then another time my husband and I were arguing about a certain curtain rod. We argued for a bit then my husband threw the curtain rod up in the air!" it was a heavy iron rod so it made a loud noise when it landed and boy if we didn't have the attention of people before we sure did now." Next thing I can recall is when we were in the store with our daughter, the one we had to promise we wouldn't embarrass!" We were on our best behavior so far so good." So, okay the store has a long line for people to check out their items. We were standing and waiting our turn. Our daughter says please do not embarrass me!" Everything was going good What happens next is very peculiar my husband is Just waiting for our turn to pay and go. He was holding a case of soda pop Well out of the blue all the cans began to fall out of the case cans were rolling down the aisles and all over the place. We could not believe this happened out of the blue. But my daughter could believe it!" She knew that it was too good to be true that we didn't make a scene." That was the last straw for our daughter to go to the store with us ever again!" "Next we went to register our daughter to get photos at her school. Our daughter pleads with us to please not embarrass her. We say we won't. Everything is going well, we are almost done. Then I accidentally tip over the basket of all their paperwork. My daughter was so humiliated and embarrassed. What can I say but oops!" Now the parents are embarrassing the children. What is a child to do? Just walk away like they don't know you; this can't be true. What are we to do? But try to be on our best behavior, no matter what, something always happens when we least expect it. This is not our fault, no doubt without a shout so my daughter will pout and that's not our fault, no doubt it's not our fault that this came about, makes you want to shout, tell me what's it all about? It can't be real that we embarrass our child and steal her moment that is supposed to be all about her now that she can't endure what had appeared, that was not supposed to happen again, that we shamed our daughter. She says to us she'd rather take a bus or walk home if she can, she doesn't want to be with us because somehow we mess up her day she wished she could have it another way. We can't say we're sorry because she's so in a hurry to get away from us, don't make a fuss with us, and she doesn't trust us to be in public with her no matter what she feels in her gut. That we will do something to embarrass her again and again. Later we all talked about it. Then we have a good laugh, except my daughter she remains mad at us. That's okay, I know in time she will forgive us anyway, Just as long as she's not with us in case we make a fuss, and if we do, that's on us.There's really no one to blame isn't that a shame, this is not a game, let us reframe what will we gain? How can we gain trust from our daughter? Why should we bother? Because she is ashamed of us, because somehow something goes wrong that doesn't mean we should keep a frown, and let it get us down. We are not clowns that have been found, we are merely just ordinary people but we are unique and specially made. From the great king, the great I am together we stand hand and hand. This we can demand. Forever and ever again, I say Amen." Over and over again, where do we begin? Start within your heart, do not depart until you ask for a clean start, you won't fall apart then you have begun a good start. This will not tear you apart, because you choose to do the right thing, then healing can begin so that you can get rid of all the stuff that you thought would make you tough. Now that's enough. Then you can live the life that Jesus died to give us. He brought me up also out of a horrible pit, out of the miry clay, and set my feet upon a rock, and established my goings. And he has put a new song in my mouth, even praise unto our God: many shall fear enter In, then you can begin to know what to do, you can pursue what's on your heart. You will never let it depart this is a start, now that's smart, don't let it tear you apart. There is a better future ahead, keep this in your head so you can stay out of bed drawing in depression, this is my suggestion, keep your head up, and think for the best. Stay positive in yourself and think only good things will come. Believe in yourself and don't give up. Things will get better. This you will see, believe in yourself, also believe in me, you'll see that better days are ahead for you and for me. I'm sure you can agree. Better days are ahead for you and for me. Indeed.'Proverbs 22:6 Train up a child in the way he should go: and when he is old he will not depart from it.

CHAPTER NINETEEN

FINDING MY WAY

Having to deal with one half of an eye, and having depsure vision which I cannot tell how close or how far things really are. My right eye is totally blind. I wear a fake eye. My left eye is blind on the side they call it left field vision loss. Also known as peripheral vision loss. This is from my head injury, if you want to know what kind of head injury you will have to get my first book Running into the arms of Love, then you'll have to get the second part called Resting in the palm of Love. Then you'll have to get all my books because you are curious about what kind of person I could be. Sure glad I don't drive I would be a danger to society. I've met a few people that drive with one eye. But I think they have been driving their whole life. So they are comfortable, myself forget it." it's not an option I would be lost forever and a day. Besides that I am colored blind and I see the wrong size of things. Once while I was at my moms house my mom put two frozen pies in the toaster oven which she Just happened to get recently. I went to check how they were doing. My brother was there. I told my brother to look to see how the pie is getting big. My brother looked inside and then he said It's not getting bigger. As far as colors go I miss match the colors of socks. Now I am doing better because I don't even do the laundry. And I don't burn the food because I dont cook." As far as getting lost well that's a lost cause. I am still working on that one. Well my balance is kind of rocky so I need to use a walker but when I go out in public I use my cane. My daughter says that I am not using my cane, that I am just carrying it." So she laughs at me. She says mom you're not even using your cane, your Just carrying it. Now if we are in a resturaunt And I need to go to the restroom I usually will get lost or go to the wrong table so my grandkids have to look out for me to make sure i am not wondering around trying to find my table. Such a shame that I am having to have assistance for every little thing." For walking outside I have to be extra careful because if I don't see a crack in the sidewalk I will go flying. Let me tell you I fly higher and farther than I ever thought I could.``Now if we happen to start laughing and I am tired Oh boy!" I can't seem to stop. I better not wet my pants. So I am not looking forward to being in my nineties. Such is life getting old. It's human nature to living. I am goofy now. How would I be as an older woman!" Watch out world because I'm coming. I'm not coming to fast, Please don't pass gas when I'm near you I don't need extra fumes especially if they don't smell fresh take a second guess, please don't make a mess, now I'm impressed at how good you did on that test, when you didn't study much but that you only guessed your best, now you can rest, what's next?"Do you want to play tennis with your ex?' If you do , give it your best, then you can rest knowing you gave it all you could, when nobody else would nobody quite understood, where you stood because you miss understood, of what's under that hood that you keep on hiding under, don't be afraid of the thunder, It's a no wonder that you cannot win again and again, use a ballpoint pen. Then you will clearly see that the best is hidden indeed, but you let yourself go, remember which way to go so that you won't track back, and have to do it over again then you will see where you began. Then you can win again, and again. I say Amen!" Finding my way in a very special way, what can I say, help is on the way this very day. When I began to sway the wrong way. He catches me before I fall too far away from him. Then I can begin to see what he wants for me, because I can't be what I want to be, If only I can see what I should be, but to me I'm not in a hurry, to see what I should see and to feel what's really in me. And that I can please my father so that I will be no bother and that he can shower me with his blessings, because I want to be a blessing to him. In that I can begin to shine the light to those who are lost. That he did pay a great price. This is no tip of the ice, don't be surprised this is not a disguise. We can never begin to thank him enough. That's why it is up to us, not to make a fuss. And all we can do is trust. We are called to love one another, as he has loved us. It is up to us to do what is right, even if you have to fight for your rights.

Because in the end you will receive a prize right before your eyes, that will lift you off the ground, and it could never be found here on earth. Remember there is a new birth, let this be the first, when you stop to think of it, It is not from the pit, that you have been hit, with reality. That this is the way to eternity, so please let it be for you that you know what to do, I promise you will never be blue, you won't have to bother tying your shoe. Because everything is new. When you think of it, this does belong to you in everything you do. It will be refreshing that you may be God's special guest, so be my guest, be at your best, then I won't have to second guess, now be at rest. For you have the best. And the best at that, for there is no other that can give you what you need because you have been freed, you will be kept up to speed. To live a life to the fullest, and abundantly, you can agree that there is no other, like the Father. So don't bother to try to find what there is not to find you need to get out of this bind, keep it fresh in your mind. There's still a time, when everything falls in place, he will bless you with his grace. Just remember your place. He has made you special, and he wants you to be with him, but it's all in time that this will happen, Then when you realize, don't be surprised you have been told the truth, don't act like you did not hear, that the time is coming near, when the great king will come to our rescue, It is if you are in him, and him in you. All things will be made new. 2 Corinthians 5:17 Therefore if any man be in Christ, he is a new creature: old things have passed away; Behold, all things become new.

CHAPTER TWENTY

LOSING KEYS

How many people can say that they locked their keys in the car?" or that they lost their keys and they can't find them." scary feeling right!" not knowing where your keys are, you get a little frantic!" and panicky!" Not a good feeling. You're wondering where they are and if somebody has them. Well I had a very busy day. I went for a walk and got a very much needed haircut. I got inside my apartment building. I could not find my keys to get into my apartment. I said my keys. I can't find the keys my girlfriend says are they in your pocket ?" I checked my pocket nope not in my pocket. My friend asked me again did you check your pocket ? I said yes but I will check again. So I did. Then my friend said, ``Did you check inside your purse?" I said yes I checked twice. I was getting so nervous. My friend said to calm down they can't be too far away I began walking around in circles in a panic mood" This is what I do when I am having an anxiety attack or panic attack!" My friend is freaking out watching me be a crazy lady. She said let's back track of where you have been. I said well I managed to get in the building. My friend said yeah that's right well where did they go?" This is a mystery lets keep looking when you panic or have an anxiety attack you can't think rashally so you need to take some deep breaths and try to calm yourself down so I take a few deep breaths, you don't want to hyperventilate" Then you will be trippin and have me trippin!" Girlfriend, don't do this to us not now , not ever"I looked down at my left hand and long and behold" I found my keys!" I was holding them in my left hand all along." I said to my friend ``hey look!" I've got my keys in my hand," We just busted out laughing" I asked my friend why didn't you see me holding them in my hand she said why didn't you see them in your hand I said because I am not left handed my friend said what difference does it make if you are left handed or right handed?" I said to her ``Never mind, this has been a loooong" day." But my reasoning is because my right eye is blind and my left eye is blind on the side I guess they call it left field vision loss. I probably got that name wrong. I am not sure what they call the left side of your eye blind. God knows what I'm talking about. And maybe some of you all know what it's called Left field something!" Well my reasoning is because I don't see out of my left eye all the way. If that makes any sense to you all. But it makes sense to me. I guess that's all that matters. Now if I'm repeating myself about something this is another habit that I developed while growing old. Enough of growing old, I've developed strange habits getting older. Must be old age syndrome." There's this app on my phone, it's Tom the talking cat, Okay, he repeats everything you say right!" Well it's so cute" I get a kick out of it. It makes me laugh!" So I have to have it talk to me sometimes. I have to say hi to my cat then my cat comes up to the phone to see what's saying hi to him. And saying his name.This is just too cute!" Speaking of cute, I had a friend over to play skip bo card game with me. Right, well my cat nibbled at her toe she said to my cat did you just bite my toe? My cat nodded his head up and down saying yes, we busted out laughing this was too cute!" Now back to getting older, sorry for going off track I think this is also a growing older habit." We both busted out laughing. This cat is for real. I swear this cat is human. Yes as we get older you better look over your shoulder, because you don't know who's watching you. I know you can second guess, go ahead and give it your best. You're not in any trouble, hurry up on the double for your trouble stop mumbling, and crumbling of what should have been. You don't know what's in store for you. You better know what to do. When that day comes, you will be ready and be on guard. You've never tried so hard to fit in, because you don't want to be left behind, share what's on your mind. Please be kind if you don't mind, get yourself out of this bind, but you don't have to be so rude and unkind. Share what's on your mind. But be kind if you don't mind. Don't be blind to see what you want then you shut the blinds because you don't want to be unkind, and this blows your mind that you have to stand in line. Let your light shine if you don't mind. I promise you I will be kind, for this is always on my mind. So if you can't find your keys, remember to have peace because in the end you will win favor with the father, because this is a desire for you, you'll know what to do next, give it your best then you can rest, knowing you did your best so that you can rest. Knowing that you gave it your best. Don't second guess that you gave it your best, you need to rest and be at your best for the next guest. This is a request that you do your best. Then we both can rest. That's the best."1 Corinthians :16-13. Be on guard, stand firm in the faith, be courageous, be strong.

CHAPTER TWENTY-ONE

THE WRONG FAST FOOD PLACE

Did you ever get mixed up or confused as to what fast food restaurant you are at?" Well on good old Robert street it is easy. They have restaurants one after another next to each other even though some restaurants closed their doors for good because of the pandemic they managed to have plenty of fast food places on that street. Well one day there was a sale on the whoppers at Burger King you could get ten whoppers for 10 dollars. I wanted to catch that sale well. I figured I could freeze a few in the freezer, that was a good deal!" So I get to go and catch this deal right!" I get to the counter to be waited on. The young man says can I help you? I said yes, can you give me 10 whoppers ? The young man says to me mam we don't have whoppers here. I thought maybe this young man didn't hear me right so the young man said, "Can I help you? I said yeah can you give me 10 whoppers please the young man says mam we don't have whoppers here So I am thinking what is wrong with this young man can he understand what I am saying I ask him kindly can you please give me 10 whoppers he said to me again mam we don't have whoppers here I am thinking oh! They ran out. I guess I must have missed the special. And I had my heart set on having a whopper. Or should I say my stomach is set on having a whopper?" Well I walk outside and I look up at the sign and it says Mcdonalds I busted out laughing" I couldn't believe that I thought I was at Burger King no wonder the young man kept telling me that they did not have any whoppers I bet he and his co-workers are gonna have some laughs about me.`` Why didn't this young man tell me that I was not at Burger

King? I know why because he wanted me to order something from them and not Burger King. Well the next time there is a sale I hope to get the deal and make it to the right fast food place."It's a good thing I don't go out to eat much. I usually don't go to fast food places. My place is at home. That was a good laugh of the day. I usually amuse others." And tend to make their day. Going to the wrong fast food place, you better not lose your place, make sure your shoelace is in place, so you won't be in disgrace, that you fell on your face, in this busy place. Where people are in a hurry. Don't you worry, because if you happen to be at a different place than you thought you were in, then you can start all over again. You can start from the beginning, what is the beginning and the end. Remember you can't win this battle alone because you have shown that you need the father and there is no other that you can depend on, For it is God's great son, that the battle has been won. When it is all done. You will be glad that you choose the right one, In whom all things are done. Then you can have some fun in the sun while you out run the one who has been after you from day one. Yet you have come so far, no matter where you are your heavenly father will guide you through. Even if you don't know what to do. He will see you through the next phase.So don't be in a daze, get up and face the unknown. In what the father has shone, what is not possible with man, he has shown you again and again that he is the great I Am. Isaiah 55:2 Why do you spend your money for that which is not bread, and your labor for which does not satisfy? Listen diligently to me, and eat what is good, and delight yourselves in rich food.

CHAPTER TWENTY-TWO

THE WRONG BANK

My friend took me to the bank. Now we are back at famous Robert street again, they have banks next to each other, Just like they do restaurants. Now whoever developed this street was smart because if you need money to go get something to eat wa-la you can be right by your bank. Or anybody's bank for that matter. So my friend took me to the bank. Well the bank was closed. I said to my friend, Maybe they got robbed. But the truth was the bank was being bought out and they changed their name. We ran out of time. So on a different day we went through the drive through so we gave the woman my bank slip and ID and bank card. My friend rolled the window down so she could hear the woman. The woman kept pointing to the right but we couldn't understand what the woman was trying to tell us. My friend said what!" and the woman kept pointing ahead of us and we kept saying what!" The woman was talking and pointing her finger as she was speaking. We could not figure out what the woman was saying and we wondered why she was pointing. We both decided to look in the direction that the woman was pointing to. Well she happened to point at my bank, the bank we were supposed to be at." Then we said ``oh!" were at the wrong bank, we felt so ridiculous!" We just busted out laughing. The woman had the biggest grin that you've ever seen. She said to us it happens all the time."Every time we go to the bank we are reminded of our visit to the wrong bank.You begin to wonder where you wander to see or be, take a look at that tree and see it with a different perspective, this is the way life is. You either learn and do your best to make a life that is the best you can. Then when you become an old man, you can see what you did with your hands. Then you won't be in any demand. Make the best of it and do what you can while you are able to stand. Come and take my hand, for you will be secure and be able to withstand, all that is thrown at you without any plans You can laugh if you want. But it's only for awhile, that you will be in denial go the extra mile in style, with a great big smile don't be in denial if you do let it be for Just a while so you can go that extra mile, Now come on give me a great big smile, that will last a while.

Proverbs 16:8 Better to have little, with Godliness, than to be rich and dishonest.

CHAPTER: TWENTY-THREE

RESTAURANT MANNERS

Now my two daughters and my husband and I go out to the restaurant called the ground round, for a meal it doesn't exist anymore. It closed down years ago way before the pandemic came around. They had stools that you sit on and they were tall so it took a lot of time and effort for me to get on these stools. The girls and my husband were laughing at me they saw that I was having a hard time getting on the stool. Finally my husband helped me to get on the stool. It only took half an hour to get on!" I am exaggerating " But it sure felt like it." We ordered our food then we were eating our food and all of a sudden my husband started choking!" my girls began to panic" They said pat him on the back I said what!" they said pat him on the back, I said to the girls who's pat? I did not know that my husband was choking while sitting to the left of me. I couldn't see because I am blind in the left field, whatever they call it." I can only see half of what is really there. Once we went to a Chinese restaurant that we lived close to that we liked a lot. It was a family owned business, well my daughter Tammy acted like she owned the restaurant. She took her shoes off and made herself at home. She even went to the back where the employees are working. My youngest daughter took her shoes off as well, she had to copy her big sister, and since they had flintstone feet they Just had to be neat, and of course they made themselves comfortable. My younger daughter was not as forward as my older daughter. She didn't walk around the place as if she owned the place. My husband and I were totally shocked that the girls were acting like they were. We were embarrassed by their behavior!" Well, another time I took the girls to that restaurant we walked there because we only lived a few blocks from there. They began having better manners going out to dinner at a restaurant. So that was progress. Now when we got done with dining it was time to go home there happened to be a blizzard.! Well my youngest daughter didn't take it too well. She was so upset she never wanted to go out of the house again. ``We had to bribe her to go outside of the house.''Snow is here one day then it's gone for a while. We can't be in denial, don't forget to smile awhile. You're not on trial, not even for a while. This is my style. Can you stay awhile? I promise you a good time, you won't have to spend a dime, you're on my time would you like a glass of wine. Then we can have a good time and dine. You've been on my mind in a nick of time, we will be just fine, sit down and enjoy your wine, don't waste any time as we dine. Let your light shine. Will you be mine ?If you don't mind. Everything is totally fine. Mind your manners when you are in the care of others, then you won't bother others with your burdens, and act like a fool. Instead be polite before you take a bite, know that this is out of sight, that's alright by me Just as long as we agree to keep it cool, so you won't be made a fool, and drool all over you because you want to give an good oppression, in my direction, not to mention, all the cares that you've had, some will make you glad, some will make you sad that you've mind your manners no matter what, you are Godly and presentable no matter what, keep this attitude in your gut no matter what. If you do, you will go far indeed. Now go on and proceed, with your character, and charm, don't be alarmed that the father will carry you far if you intend to do his will. You will succeed in deed, you will not prematurely endure what is ahead remember the father is the head keep this in your head. Then you can break bread. And move ahead, Instead. Don't be afraid of what lies ahead, try to reach for the stars instead, you can blink once or twice, remember to be nice at a price that has been paid, don't be afraid. Just be glad you will be amazed at what can happen when you put your full trust in the one that loves you no matter what. And if that is not enough. Be glad that you are still here no matter the year you put yourself in gear. And do not fear. For the one who is near will be coming back soon. So put down the broom, and stop acting like Martha, and be more like Mary, to learn of things that are far more important than the things of this world. For the things that matter are so preccious, by far.

you will see in time, your world will shine. It's all in a nick of time. This doesn't have to rhyme to be fine, you Just need to sit and dine. Take your time no worries, don't be in such a hurry for when you take your time things go more professionally. I'm sure you can agree. That all things will be heavenly, I'm sure you can agree. That the best is still to come, this will make you want to get things done. Isn't this fun? Now I've got to run, so I can get things done. 1 Corinthians 15:33 Be not deceived: evil communications corrupt good manners.

CHAPTER TWENTY-FOUR

MAKING EXCUSES

When you feel like a change in your life is coming upon you don't fight it, go with the flow, don't be so afraid of change that you let fear take control of your life But rather you take control of your feelings and actions. Remember who's in charge" now you can let your emotions take control of your mind but it doesn't stop there. This will make you act like a crazy person and do stupid stuff like make wronge decisions and get yourself in trouble with friends and family or in trouble with the law. Think more highly of yourself and have a mind set that you can do what you need to do even if you don't know how to do It if you are meant to do it every thing will fall into place and you will surprise yourself and others You all will be truly amazed at what you can do. You see I had no Idea what I was going to write about In this chapter and here I am rambling on and on. I probably am not even making any sense but that's okay at least I am making a chapter and it's better to have words than empty space. If this is your case, you better embrace all that you can so you can be the best at what you can. Then you can sit back and not have disgrace because you've tried your best. Now if you would rather I shut up because I am boring you. Go write your own book then you can say whatever you want. I'm Just saying stop making excuses. Whatever you have been called to do or are calling yourself to do what you want to do. Stop making excuses for moving in a totally different direction that you never even thought of doing. Some people don't know what they're going to be when they grow up. Until they grow up. I can't spell right. I don't have good grammar, I don't speak proper english. And yet I'm doing what I've been called to do. Now it's up to you to not be bound up in fear, because fear is the devil's faith. Fear tolerated is faith contaminated. I may not speak good grammar at times. But hey there's not one person on earth that is perfect. That's why we need Jesus, because he can fix us and turn us into what he wants us to be. but I keep on keeping on. Because it's better to be able to say at least I tried." So stop making excuses, don't let fear rule over you, you be in control. That's what I have to say about making excuses. You can take it or leave it or shove it!" Where the sun doesn't shine!" it's up to you.``Well you can make all the excuses you want for not pursuing your dreams. Maybe you don't have any dreams or goals that you want to achieve. It's possible that your Just here taking up space and you don't want to make a difference in this world. That's possible also If you are afraid to dream big that's okay maybe dream little at first. It's okay and maybe you don't know what you want in life. I am sure you are not alone. Then there are people that think they know what they want but they keep Jumping from Job to Job and keep moving from place to place. And never seem to settle or be content or satisfied. Almost sounds like a rich person. They have anything and everything and they are never satisfied." I wouldn't know because I am not rich and I really don't know anyone who is rich. I know guys want to befriend me because they think I am rich. So, I decided to not talk to any men online. This way I play it safe." Besides, I`ve been married three times already. I say that's a strike out!" No more for me I guess I never found my mate for life. My third husband died. So I will stay a widow until Jesus comes and takes me home. I don't know the fathers will, but I know I want to do all that he wants me to do, and I will need his assistance to go the distance that he wants me to go. Maybe everything won't go in a flow. I can tell you this, our timing is not like his, and our ways are not his ways. He has everything better for us. Than we can ever imagine, for his ways are higher than our ways, and his timing is different than our timing. All we can do is trust in him that he only has the best for us. In him we can truly trust, for this is a great must. This is the truth that I share with you, even if your eyes aren't blue. This is the truth that I share with you, there is nothing more important than this truth he will be with you no matter what you do, this will all come true if you desire all that is waiting for you. Don't be shy, don't be blue, let all of heaven's reign on you. And he will make all things new, It's up to you what you do with the truth, please let the heaven's reign on you all things will be made new. I assure you. Matthew 12:36 I tell you on the day of Judgment people will give account for every careless word they speak.

CHAPTER TWENTY-FIVE

LET'S TALK ABOUT TALKING

I thought about maybe having a talk show of my own one day, just because I want to be the first Mexican American woman to have one. Plus I just wanted to experience the fact of having a talk show. In time I decided not to because your privacy is taken away and you really don't have any freedom. Or live in peace. This is not for me. Because you're always running from the Paparazzi's and lies and rumors are always being said about you then you feel like you're in the zoo caged up in your mansion. What a horrible life to live. Sure glad it was only a thought and that i hadn't bought or sought this gesture it would have been a short term pleasure. My daughter looked it up online and she says there is a latina woman that had a talk show. And then there's George Lopez If you want to consider him as a she, I don't think George would like that. But you can ask him." And when I don't speak proper English and my grammar is way off base. Plus I say the wrong word and I say things backwards. I pronounce the words wrong" Or I say the wrong word and I have no Idea. At least when the wrong word comes out we can laugh about it. What about the people that say a swear word every other word is not pleasant to hear. Or uses God's name in vain. I just close my one half of an eye and pray silently, I ask the Lord to forgive them because they don't know any better. This is not a laughing matter, at least not to me. But to some this is funny, everybody has a different sense of humor. Now when I get in a giggly mood. Oh boy!" I can't contain myself, then I get everybody laughing, then I'm not alone, with the giggling.Got to admit it is contagous!" Same when someone yawns, then person after person take turns in yawning. Have you ever noticed it ?" Next time pay attention okay; When I start laughing I can't seem to be able to stop. Will I reach my goal or not? Nobody knows but the Father. Now what about the people that talk too fast? You have to keep saying pardon me, or what did you say? Or sorry I didn't quite understand what you said. Can you please repeat what you said." and you can tell they are getting frustrated with you. Or what about you are trying to get things settled over the phone about your bills and they decide to do a fire drill in your building, to test if the fire alarms are in good working condition. And you tell the person on the phone you're sorry for the noise because your building is having a fire drill. Then you feel embarrassed and the guy on the other end of the phone keeps talking and won't shut up. Now you would think that the guy would have enough sense to be quiet while the alarm is making loud noises." And you have to keep saying what?" or can you please repeat that!" And the stupid alarm keeps going on when you think they are finally done." And there happens to be a lady to come and teach a class on ringing bells. I guess they are called tone chimes. I Just bet they had to cancel the class because of the fire drill. Anyhow, why would we need to take a class in ringing bells? Why would we need to be ringing bells?" Even the bell ringers for the salvation army don't have to take a class on how to ring a bell properly. And they do it once a year at Christmas time." I know it's Just for fun, but it was a bad day to have the person come for bell ringing because of the stupid fire drills, but they do sound pretty when you can play a song in unity. But they are annoying to have right next to your ear. If you didn't have a headache before you started ringing the chimes, you surely will get one when you are done with ringing the tone chimes." Maybe next time the person comes there won't be any fire drills. Okay so I ordered an arnie plamer which is an ice tea with lemonade, Then James asked me if I told them to put gin in it. He was trying to be funny." I said to him no I don't need help to grin." Then I gave him the biggest smile.`` This was supposed to be funny, but he did not laugh. Oh well He didn't make me laugh about the gin in my drink so now he didn't owe me a laugh back right!" Such is life!" When you have a lot of strife you can think twice as to what could be nice. I don't need ice to cool me down. I will Just put on an upside down frown, and keep my feet on the ground please don't make a sound so that I can think of what's the next step, don't let it get over your head. Just do a little at a time then you can unwind and have peace of mind. If you don't mind. In due time you will shine, for all time.``Speaking about talking, In the dining room Linda and I were talking about childbirth. Then James came down to the dining room so he could order his lunch. He sat with us and was listening to our conversation. After hearing of our experinceing our child births James said, I lost my appetite. I'm not hungry any more. We all laughed, I said this is the girls club. And you are the investigator. Tune in for the next topic. James says he does learn some things, from us gals. Okay Alex and I went out in the hallway, and it was freezing in the hall. The 3rd floor is the coldest floor in the building, with the air conditioning on. And that's the floor I live on, well we got out in the hall Alex says oh it's freezing out here, I answer back, yeah it's cold in the freezer, we laughed because i called the hallway the freezer because it feels like a walk in freezer. Then we ran for the elevator before the doors shut. I say hurry up, get in the phone booth. We laughed again, because I said the wrong word again. Alex repeats what I say every time. Then we laugh more." Once upon a time we used to have phone booths, today it is rare to see any phone booths. Then down in the dining room the waitress asked for my room number, I started giving her my telephone number. I started to give her my area code first, then she laughed and said not your telephone number, but your room number. We both laughed. Now people that have strokes sometimes lose their speech. Not me I lost my grammar. To begin with, my grammar was not the best. Not that I had a stroke, but the results of my head injury, the side effects are like having a stroke. If you have read my first and third book you would know that I have a head injury. In the autobiographies.Running into the arms of Love and Resting in the palm of Love. And while you're add it, pick up the book called Morals and Values of Tales for all Children, Teenagers, Adults, and Old Folks. This has 207 short stories for all ages. I promise you and your family will be super duper blessed. Don't forget the book signs of the end times. The new book coming out is called Just Living, this has some laughs in it. Be blessed and enjoy" Now I don't want to talk about sad things, but this is life and I'm Just living. I don't know where my grammar is coming from the east or west, north or south, but boy do I have a mouth. Of words that I didn't even know existed. No swear words, or cuss words. Just words that come out of my mouth I didn't intend to say. I either say the wrong word or I pronounce the word wrong or say it backwards. This is very peculiar, don't you think?" Usually we just laugh about it, whoever I'm talking to. Even my daughter's friends make fun of my words like sugar blood, instead of blood sugar. Instead of saying pillow I say pickle Instead of saying iron I say onion,

Instead of saying vegetarian I say veterinarian. Instead of saying shy I say sky, for the word asthma I say amnesia, there's this store that I just went to and everything in it is 5 dollars and cheaper. I just loved it the whole time I was there I kept saying ``oh wow!'' oh my gosh!'' I know the people in the store were marveled at how I was acting my first time in there. The store is called 5 below, and I called it 8 below. Probably because of the Disney movie about the eight dogs called 8 below. As far as the dogs that are white with black spots, The Dalmatian dogs I call them the one hundred and one Dalmatian dogs, because of the Disney movie. Not a dalmatian dog. If I want to say encourage I say encounter, for the word corn on the cob I say it backwards, cob on the corn. I have a very strange way of talking and reading. Now that's a whole new chapter. Instead I say a new chapter the computer has to correct my grammar. Instead of saying principal I say pitiful. Can you imagine going to your child's school for an important meeting, and saying to the principal ``Oh so you're the pitiful.'' Instead of saying principal, they will never ask you to come in for an important meeting, a short meeting, a conference meeting, or any other kind of meeting.'' I can tell you that you won't have to make any excuses of trying to bail out of going to meetings any more. These are just samples of how I say or read the wrong word. Yes, my daughter and her friends have a good time talking about the silly things I say and do. They bring that up all the time among themselves, and laugh as If it just happened. Glad I can make people laugh even when I'm not present. There's never a dull moment with me.I call Amazon Amazein but Alex,my ILS. worker knows what I mean. She orders stuff for me on that site all the time. There's never a dull moment with me, unless I'm sleeping or not around. You better keep your feet on the ground. Be quite don't make a sound, when I'm not around put your feet on solid ground.You will be astonished at what you have found. When you put your feet on solid ground I will be glad that you have been found because I want you to stick around.

Psalms 71:24 My tongue also shall talk also of thy righteousness all the day long: for they are confounded, for they are brought unto shame, that seek my hurt.

CHAPTER TWENTY-SIX

BECOMING MORE LIKE MOM

I called my daughter one day to ask her something but it Just went to voicemail so I tried again but it went to voicemail again. The third time she answered. I started to talk to her but she seemed to be too quiet. Was I boring her?" I started telling her then I said ``are you there?" She got back on the phone but she was laughing so hard that she couldn't tell me." She took a while to tell me she finally told me that she put me on mute." Now this is one of my habits. laughing so much that I can't tell the person why I am laughing." any how we both had a good laugh!" I know we both wet our pants from laughing so hard and our tummies were sore from laughing." As far as wetting our pants this messed up our bladders from having babies. A lot of women deal with this." When my daughter was with her friends, she happened to speak and act like me. They all laughed and said she sounded like me. Glad I am amusing to some people and make them laugh. Even if I'm not there in person. The thing is I also make myself laugh too!." The strange thing is I never spoke another language, only english." Usually people who speak weird are people that talk another language. You see, what I mean about my grammar is way off base. I had to be corrected by my Labtop. I was trying to talk about speaking another language. I said I never talked another language. The correct grammar is spoke or spoken,another language. When I tried to type the word labtop, Instead I typed laptop. Even the computer speaks better than myself, and it doesn't even speak. So you see I need a lot of help!" Lord have mercy!" Okay you get what I am trying to say. For a sentence I would say, even my daughter says this is true. And the correct way to say it is even my daughter said this is the truth. I only know this is because the computer corrects my grammar and spelling and everything else in between. I tell my daughter she has alzheimers and I have sometimers. You get my drift?" not dreft but drift" okay. You got it!" good." dreft is a baby detergent, did you know that? If you didn't, you do now. Yes I'm a barrow of laughs Oops!' I meant to say a barrel of laughs!' you see what I mean" When my daughter was hanging out with her friends they all were laughing and having a great time. Just doing girl stuff my daughter laughed Just like me." Everyone all said at the same time you sounded Just like your mom!" Then they all laughed even harder and louder my daughter said great I get to inherit my mom's looks. I get to have her laugh, her complexion, her cowlicks, on the back of her head. This only gets the girls talking about the things I say or do that give them a great memory. That every time they bring it up they laugh and laugh just like it had just happened. Oh!''By the way, have you ever heard of a momzie?" Well not a zombie, but a momzie, a momzie is a mother that is sleep deprived. A mother that is in very much need of sleep and rest, because sometimes moms are running on empty, Moms can't afford to get sick, they are needed too much. But sometimes everything catches up on moms. And they need a break, but sometimes they don't have help to get a break." So they end up getting really sick. Then it's up to the most mature child to take care of mom. This is hard if the family only has one parent involved in their lives. And no family or relatives call you or drop by to see you more than just when there is a funeral or wedding or maybe even a holiday once a year. Well every year around the same time I got the flu, And my youngest daughter took care of me the best she could. But some things remained out of control like the two girls trashing the house. One day the girls had cereal all over the living room. We had a small trampoline, so the girls dragged it to the living room and they were jumping on it with a box of cereal in one hand. Eating while jumping on it." They should have been in the circus with that trick!" What a terrible disaster!" And how about trying to take care of a special needs child. You try to stay awake but the Doctor gave you something to help you sleep better. But your daughter has bipolar and is manic, and wants to stay up all night. She wants you to stay up all night with her. Because she needs an ear to listen to her. You know that this is very important for her so she won't get suicidal, And if you are not paying full attention!" They get upset that you don't care. When in reality you can't run on empty. You try your hardest to stay awake, Then you look like a drunk person trying to focus on what's really important right now. You have to be a crisis counselor now to your daughter that desperately needs help. So you make a huge pot of homemade soup and tell the kids that's your meals until you get better enough to be able to cook or eat yourself. Such as life right!" Matthew 12:49. And he streched forth his hand toward his disciples, and said, behold my mother and my brethren!

CHAPTER TWENTY-SEVEN

EYE GLASSES

One day as I was getting ready for the day I noticed that I was seeing everything blurry As the day went on I began to get concerned of why everything was looking blurry i began to panic because I only had one eye and a half because My right eye is blind and my left eye only have some vision I thought to myself If my left eye goes blind then I will be totally blind I got so scared Just thinking about it." I began to worry that something was wrong when I got my mail. I tried to read it but I couldn't read it. Everything looked too blurry. I began to panic when my niece was over and I asked her to read the mail to me. I was getting teary eyed. I was very disturbed that I could not read. My grandson was having a concert that night so we were planning to go see him and his classmates they were going to be singing So we didn't live to far from the school so we walked there it was winter out the sidewalks where icy and snowy my daughter was holding my hand and she was rushing me she was pulling me along so fast that my cane was flying in the air. My daughter was laughing at me. I am yelling, ``Slow down, I'm going to fall." but she thought this was hilarious!" I probably looked funny with my cane flying in the air. It was not doing me any good. The concert had already started. I walked up to the bleachers where we had saved seats for us. I got up to the bleachers and my other daughter who was already there watching the kids sing, looked at me and said, ``Nice mom, I said what !" my daughter said to me, ``you're wearing my glasses, I said what?" She says you're wearing my glasses. I busted out laughing. I could not stop laughing. I said good I am not going blind after all. I was relieved that I wasn't losing my eyesight totaly. Everybody was annoyed with me because I couldn't stop laughing. But they didn't know what I had been through today thinking that I was going completely blind." I laughed through most of the concert. Sometimes my daughter tries to be helpful but then she does damage instead. Like the time we went to see somebody do ballerina, the place was very dark, almost like being at a movie theater. My daughter took my hand and was walking me down the stairs. I fell down, and hurt myself, I really hurt, but I didn't want to make another scene, so I said I was okay. Even though I hurt, Now my daughter runs me into a wall. Then we laugh about it." At times when I fell down my daughter would scream and scream loud." I always seem to laugh!" when I fell. This was getting dangerous!" but even when I went to the eye Doctor the last time he gave me a prescription for new glasses, I couldn't see out of them too well." I wondered if he made a mistake because I was having a hard time seeing. So I kept the new glasses that I had gotten and dealt with the fact that I couldn't see well with them. I thought maybe I just have to get used to the new glasses. I never thought that maybe the Doctor made a mistake. Or maybe the people that make your glasses made a mistake. I went to a store and saw a friend there. They laughed and said that the right side of the lens of my glasses was all fogged up.!" I said, ``That's okay that eye can't see anyway." We both laughed." So I told my daughter to Just let me walk without her trying to help me. I did do a lot of crying for my daughter when she was little because she would always take off on me. I didn't know where she was. Now I don't have to cry any more because she's in heaven with Jesus." But I miss her so much. But I know someday we'll be together again." Let's move on to the next chapter before I get all wishy washy." Don't get wishy or washy, don't have the audacity to be what you want to be, even if it's just wanting to be you. And nobody else but you. What do you do? Don't act like a fool, because everything is new, don't be blue, I'll show you what to do. So be cool, and don't drool, so you won't be made a fool, I bet you knew what to do. But instead you pretended that you were dead instead watch out for your head, so you won't shed in the bed that's ahead of you. You can't see further, you can only see a twinkle of what's now, Now take a bow before our Lord and king, because he can surely bring the best out of you, this is what he wants to do. For me and for you, so don't shy away, and pretend everything is okay. When there is no reason to dress for the season, now you can take it or leave it. You Just got to believe it!" This is real as real can get. How much do you want to bet?" That there is a brighter tomorrow, don't drown your sorrows, In what could have been your tomorrow, Just be glad and rejoice within. For the time is coming soon when we will be out of room, to live in this world. There is something better ahead, It's so hard to wait I can truly dread the wait by far. Don't let it become a scar. No matter how distressed you are, you can deal with it, and go way far. Farther than your dreams can dream, farther than your visions can Imagine, this place is called heaven. This place is extra special, because it is perfect, there is no sadness, no sickness, or no pain, truly this is one thing you want to gain. May you refrain from all unrighteousness, Come on I have some things to discuss. Please don't make a fuss. It's Just us. In this place called heaven, there is no sadness, no sickness, no shame. I'd like to play this game, you will never be in need in order to succeed then you can proceed, yes indeed, all that's important, You got to know this is more than a fortune in time you won't waste any time, If you step out of line. For time is a factor, you'll be able to live happily ever after. This is a true factor, that you will see then you can agree that this is the only way to go. Even if you get old. Because in heaven there is no catch eleven. If you want to go to heaven as long as you stay true to the master, you won't regret it the day after. This is where you want to be. In hopes there are others you hope to see. So let it be the last and the best thing you ever did, for in this decision that you have made. Be the best you ever did. In the end you would have done the best thing yet. I bet you won't regret it. You surely don't want to forget it. This is the way to go Just go with the flow then you will grow spiritualy this will be heavenly I'm sure you can agree. Just wait and see all the possibilities. Matthew 19:26 But Jesus looked at them and said, with man this is impossible, but with God all things are possible.

CHAPTER TWENTY-EIGHT

CAN I TALK TO A LIVE PERSON PLEASE!

Nowadays it's hard to get a human person on the phone. This is very frustrating. Okay I dial a number then I wait an ½ an hour to get a human person on the phone then they put you on hold again to connect you to the right department. So you are waiting another half an hour. You finally get a human person on the phone then they say ``Let me put you on hold for a minute But they hang up on you." Here you are waiting another ½ an hour another human person comes on the phone yay!" progress" So you think, all these different people are telling you something different. Nobody knows anything so now you are more confused than you were when you first started your ordeal of phone calls. So then you try again right! Now you wait another ½ an hour then a recording comes on and says there are unusual high volumes of calls at this time. Try your call later. When it's not so busy. How do you know if it's busy or not when you call and you have to wait an hour just to get a recording. So now you are frustrated. Now you don't want to talk to anybody. Because nobody knows anything then when you cool down from being frustrated, you decide to make your phone call again Okay so you wait an ½ hour again a live person finally comes to the phone then you can't understand what they are saying you have to keep saying excuse me, I don't understand what you are saying. Then they get mad at you because you don't know what they are trying to say because they are from an foreign country. Then you get upset because the person on the other end is being mean and rude to you because you cannot understand them. You finally get the directory when you press the button to the department you want, a recording comes on to answer your questions. But you can only ask the questions that they want you to ask! What the heck? You wait and wait. You finally get a human being or so you think! Maybe it's really a robot! The website is always asking you if you are a robot and maybe they are the ones that are a robot right!" Then a voice comes on and it's really a human person. You don't believe it because you have been fooled too many times So, you can't believe it! You keep saying to the voice on the other end, are you really a live person? They say to you that they will connect you to the right department for your issue because he is not qualified in that area but the person puts you in the wrong department so you wait another ½ an hour just to be told that nobody is answering the phone so, maybe you can try your call later. Then you just want to scream! So you say the heck with that! I am calling it a day. This has been a loooong day! But this is Just Living right!" Even the people that service you with the internet don't want to talk with you; they would rather that you text each other. This is Just plain crazzy!" People don't want to do their Jobs, They want the robot or the internet to do their Job. They want the easy way out!" No doubt, let me tell you what it's all about. Don't shout or get loud,and don't pout, when I tell you what it's all about. No wonder you get asked if you are a robot. Right!" But hey that's living!" You're not really living until you start giving, then you can sit and start chilling. It's only the beganing, not the ending, so stop spending all your attention on the wrong things. Things that don't matter Here on earth, Now if you've been giving new birth here on earth. These things shall pass away. But that's okay, because what matters are the things that are above, for they shall last forever. Forever is a long time, so don't waste any more time and don't waste another dime. Just reach for peace of mind, If it takes you all day to get a hold of a human being you won't be stealing anybody else's time. Keep this in mind, remember to be kind whether you are stressed. Let me guess, there is no rhythm or rhyme, Just take your time you'll be next in line. To be declined, rest your mind, then you can shine without a double mind. It's all in good time. It seems the days are shorter, we can never get enough time, there seems to not be enough hours in a day to get done what we want to accomplish. We are all given the same amount of time in a day , but that's okay anyway you spend your time, once you have spent your time. You can never get it back, so it's your loss if you didn't spend your time, the way you should have to have peace of mind. I'm trying to be kind, If you don't mind. Let me rephrase what I said about us all having the same amount of time. Some people's time here on earth are shorter than others, some become mothers, while others are here for a little while, we can't be in denial, well maybe for a while if that's your style. We all have the same amount of hours in a day. What can I say, spend it the way you may. It Just goes to say, make it as good as you can, what can i say have it your way any day, oh by the way, you need to pray. Because it does matter. When it's gone it won't be long you think ``What did I do wrong?" You still have to be strong, for how long?" As long as it takes so you don't make any other mistakes. Now this can be forever, from what I gather, It's now or never. Don't scatter no matter what you gather, This could be quick. If you'd rather it doesn't matter from what I've gathered, Just take it day by day that way you can focus on the here and now. No matter how low you go, as long as you have peace in your heart and mind, and you accomplish a little more at a time. You haven't wasted your time. You surely got things done, for you have another day ahead of you, so you can focus on what you want to do even if it's not new, so you give it your best and don't second guess. Make sure you have a nest so that you can rest. . If you have another day make it special anyway. Then you will have a brighter tomorrow. Be glad for what you have today, make it special anyway, and if tomorrow comes for you be glad in all you do. The Apostle Paul says in Colossians 4:6 Let your speech always be gracious, seasoned with salt, so that you might know how to answer each person.

CHAPTER TWENTY-NINE

DOING LAUNDRY

The strangest thing ever is that I can't seem to recognize my clothes. I think they belong to somebody else and my clothes are disappearing little by little. Soon I won't have any clothes then I won't have to do laundry anymore. Then I would be like that fella the emperor's new clothes. But he is not wearing any clothes. Only long john's underwear, I don't think that i would look good in long John's i think that's a guy thing. I really don't want to be like him. Okay I ask my grandson is this your shirt because I don't recognize this shirt. Later after examining it awhile I realized the shirt belonged to me. oops! I sure hope I am not giving my clothes away. I really don't think that I am. I can't find some shirts that have been missing for a while. Okay the cat was lying on my bed I thought the cat was my pair of shorts I kept trying to grab my shorts but I couldn't seem to get a grip on my shorts." My shorts are black the cat is black. Now I know I am color blind but to mistake the cat for a pair of shorts is crazy. I amuse myself sometimes. I'd say there's never a dull moment with me unless of course I am busy or sleeping. I can be pretty boring if I am sleeping. I don't know why this cat didn't move so I could tell it was a cat and not my shorts. I swear this cat was playing a joke on me. Well now my clothes are still disappearing little by little. Did the machine eat the clothes? Did somebody steal my clothes? Why are my clothes disappearing?Anyhow, enough about the laundry for now. Nonsense, I still have a bit to say about doing my laundry. Except when I did the laundry To match the socks were a riot!" I would pull the socks to be the same length and one sock was a different color than the other and one sock was longer than the other sock I would pull the socks and wah-la they made a pair of socks. Did you ever hear people say the socks always disappear when you wash clothes? They say the machine eats the socks well. I think they eat more than just socks. Let's move onto the next chapter. I don't want to bore you with my laundry Issues." I just have to mention one more thing about my laundry. Okay four more things, Okay so I don't know how to count!"Speaking of counting!" Well I guess you can call this another chapter." If we were going to talk about counting." then I will leave the laundry alone. I didn't seperate the laundry according to colors because it cost to much money to do it that way so I Just threw all the clothes together well some of the laundry had fuzzy little balls on the clothing, So when we were someplace like public waiting for our turn This was the time where i had time to waste so i picked all the fuzzy balls off of the clothes I was wearing. I had no idea why there were fuzzy little balls on some of our clothing." from not separated according to color. My five year old son's shirt was practically the same size as mine. So my friend that took me to do laundry every week would tease me and hold up my son's shirt and say, ``whose shirt is this, yours or your son's? I would say leave me alone.``But we Just laugh!" And if my friend and my son were bored she would give my son a ride in the laundry cart if there weren't any people in there." Once I lost my clothes in the laundromat. I couldn't remember which washing machine had my clothes in it. My friend and I went around the place asking everybody if they happened to put their clothes in with mine. The place was busy with quite a few people." This was embarrassing and funny as well. We finally found the right machine and the right clothes. Now where I live the people do your laundry for you I heard people complaining that they never got their clothes back and one woman said when she finally found her clothes they were still damp and smelled like mildew!" So she had to get them washed again. I wondered how long she had to wait until she got them back!" I've never had trouble with my clothes other than losing socks. Me and my big mouth," But now my laundry is missing along with my laundry basket." And little by little my clothes are disappearing. What should I do?" Up until today I had no problems. The thing is I have a very special blanket in my basket of clothes that my daughter brought me from Mexico. My clothes are gone along with my basket." sure hope

I get everything returned." Now you don't think the machine ate up all the clothes along with the basket do you?" All I can tell you, these people are in denial, all the while nobody knows where my clothes were. I'm tired and on a vent, trying to find my missing pieces. If this keeps going on, it won't be long that I'll be wearing my birthday suit. I don't think this should happen, then again I'm not laughing. Get this: come laundry day I wondered why my laundry basket was so full. I never have my basket this full, well it turned out I didn't put all the laundry away from last week. So I had towels folded nicely on the bottom of the basket not knowing this. It's a wonder why my laundry basket was full. I also noticed that my linen closet was not as full with towels. I never put two and two together, never even dawned on me that I should check the laundry room to see if i left some towels there. We laughed about it!" Like I said there's not a dull moment with me around. I amuse myself, I don't have to go far for a laugh." Revelation 22:14 Blessed are those who wash their robes, so that they might have the right to the tree of life, and may enter by the gates in the city.

CHAPTER THIRTY

VERTIGO

Now if I had my choice of having headaches or vertigo I would pick the headaches." Even though the headaches can be very severe" and you are so sick and tired of being sick and tired." And you just want the pain to go away. You wish you could just chop off your head then there would be no more pain." But that's stupid thinking because then there would not be anymore of you!"Right." The reason I say I'll take the headaches is because I am scared to death of the dizzy spells." I start to scream because everything is spinning so fast and I can't stop the spinning no matter what I do. Actually I can't do anything. All I can do is be still as I can until it passes, So you have to stay in bed because If you try to get up you are so dizzy you feel as though you are gonna puke!" And you're scared to puke!" And if you happen to be out and about you better not get a dizzy spell you could fall in the street where you are trying to cross then get hit a few times because people are ruthless they don't want to stop to see if you are okay." nope" they don't want their plans interrupted because they are already a few minutes behind schedule and they can't afford any more delays!" Everybody is in a hurry!" Now if you happen to get dizzy in a store or restaurant trying to get to the restroom. You forget which way the restroom is so you turn to the left then you turn to the right then you turn to the left then you turn to the right a few times real fast" you bring on your own personalized verdago!" Then you stagger as though you had one too many drinks so the people seeing you are thinking that it's a little early in the day to be drunk." And you feel like an idiot!" Because they think you are tipsy and you're not!" So you smile a weird kind of smile because if you smile like you're embarrassed then you feel like a fool, then you gave them the impression that you are tipsy!" and if you smile like you want to laugh then you just gave them the impression that you are tipsy when in fact this is normal for you then again you're just living right!" Just remember to Just live right." I say Amen!" When you get dizzy, don't be afraid of your misery, and get the victory. This is not a mystery, this is history, we can make it melody in harmony and it shall be treasury but not in the balcony. Only in the heavenly. There were a few times that I had virago, this was so dangerous for me to even leave my room and home. Once I was crossing the street I got a dizzy spell, then I almost fell in the street. If I had fallen, I could have gotten run over a few times. What a way to get thinner." Right!' Not going to happen that way to lose weight.`` This was scary, not knowing when the dizzy spells happened. Out of the blue they appear. Another time, we were having a baby shower for my oldest daughter. I had virago. So I couldn't be there even when it was upstairs from our home. I made some pinto beans for the shower. Ahead of time the day before the shower, Not knowing that on the day of the shower I would have virago. Then I had the girls, put them in a crockpot to keep warm. Not knowing that it would make the beans hard. Like they were not done. What a flop!" I was embarrassed. I had to stay in bed because the virago was so bad, I felt like I was going to puke!" After my daughter's shower was over. My daughter came downstairs to get me to come and eat something. So she held my hand and walked me upstairs. I don't remember how long this virago lasted. But I'm glad that it didn't get bad like that again. Yes It is scary, but eventually they go away. It's Just a matter of time. And sooner is better than later. What do you do when you get vertigo?" You can scream all you want, nobody can help you. So just take it slow as you go around and around, or until you fall on the ground with no sound. Then you must be deaf, if it is your best, to rest on the ground or on your bed where you still are ahead, take your time, so you won't fall no matter how tall that you can recall, all that is important to you. No matter what you do. Play it safe, don't make a disgrace of yourself. Please don't tell anyone else, you know your downfalls, and your strengths. You know where you began, and where you end. You know your struggles, you know your victories and your trials, make it a plan to get over the hump. You Just gotta Jump. Make sure it's for Joy. Don't leave it for the next boy. So live life but to remember to have Joy. Now that's my boy, so enjoy!" Nehemiah 8:10 Then he said unto them, Go your way, eat the fat, and drink the sweet, and send portions unto them for whom nothing is prepared: for this day is holy unto our Lord: neither be ye sorry; for the joy of the Lord is our strength.

CHAPTER THIRTY-ONE

WHAT'S THE DIFFERENCE BETWEEN OBSESSIONS AND COMPULSIONS

What is OCD? Obsessive Compulsive Disorder: Or could be a brain disorder.

Obsessions: They are thoughts, that have ideas, and Impulses, obsessive thoughts have the potential to interrupt your daily life: Compulsions: are physical or mental responses to obsessions you may experience the need to repeat. For years now I have developed a strange habit of counting things I could be at the Doctor's office and if I am waiting I have time on my hands I will start counting the squares on the ceiling I will count one by one then I will count them by two's In my mind not loud." I will count them over and over. At home I may count a desigh on a piece of furniture over and over then I will count them by two's over and over.``Wherever I am I will find something to count over and over.``It's not just a habit I picked up." over the years and can't seem to shake!" I just found out this is an anxiety disorder. They call this mental disorder OCD." Now obsession and compulsion become a cycle that's difficult to stop. The time you spend on compulsions might began to take up most of your day that you find it hard to get anything else done." This can affect your school work, or personal life leading to even more distress.`` Compulsions can happen physically before starting work. Each day you need to arrange the pens and pencils by height and color then you have to wash your hands three times for 20 seconds each time. And also each time you touch something that someone else may have touched." And that is why you shouldn't paint your nails pretty because with all the washing of hands the polish only lasts for half of the day. And it feels like you took all day to polish them. And it's hard enough for you to be still until your nails dry." Every time you get your nails polished you decide to do something you just can't be still." Now if you happen to have to go to the bathroom while your nails are still wet!" Then you've got toilet paper nails." Then you have to take what you have on your nails off and start all over again.`` And so you have wasted time and beauty products. What can I say but oops!" Then you try it again. Do you start from the beginning or the end?" That depends where you want to end. Can we make amends?" Remember where you are and where you want to go. I suppose you ought to know where you came from and how far you have come, You remember what you have done. At the time you thought it was fun, now that you are done you won't run anymore, because now it's a bore you've already had your fun. Now it's time to reminisce and rest in the sun. At the end of the day, you've had it your way, and so you think there needs to be another way but you will save it for another day. Isaiah 41:10. So do not fear for I am with you, be not dismayed; for I am your God; I will strengthen you, I will help you; I will uphold you with the right hand of my rightousness.

CHAPTER THIRTY-TWO

WHAT'S STREET TALK?

Talking in an accent or a different language We hear all kinds of talk. It's no wonder that anybody speaks proper english." They say that English is the hardest language to learn." Well I tell my daughter that she has Alzheimer's- disease and I have Sometimmer's disease. There's this woman that lives in my building who says she has CRS " I asked her what does that stand for she says CAN'T REMEMBER SHIT!" I just laughed. It was cute!" When I came inside after a walk I banged my walker into the door and I said to the receptionist ``reckless driver!" about myself she got a kick out of that" She laughed!" and said that was funny. So glad I can make people happy when they are sad" and when they are crying I can make them laugh!"Well that's all I have to say for now because I don't want to start talking about my laundry again!" Because now they found my clothes but can't find my special blanket that my daughter brought me from Mexico.``I will not complain because I have nothing to gain right!"Then again I'm Just living." I Finally got my blanket back. I was releaved." I don't use the blanket, I just have it on my bed because it's pretty to look at, and I guess you can say that my cat took over the blanket he lays on it and sleeps on it." I just wanted it back because it was a nice and special gift from my daughter from another country. Now enough of this blanket stuff." I am driving myself crazy!" What about the street talk that I am supposed to be talking about." Well how do you deal with people that use the F word about every other word that comes out of their mouth?" You pray for them or you end up talking like them." How about when they use the word God to swear!" I usually close my eyes and pray for them and I ask God to forgive them because they won't ask God to forgive them because they don't think they have done anything wrong." Nowadays if there is no swear word in a movie it's not a good movie. The day is coming when the commercials will have swear words too!" And before long the news will join them." because that's the normal thing. Then people will have to accept it because you got to go with the flow and according to mankind we're Just Living." That's what man and human nature thinks and seems to know right!" But that doesn't make it right!" Not only do I talk funny, I also read funny. For instance if I see the word wrong, I would see the word strong, like for instance If I see the word tile I would see the word file. Or maybe I don't see the letter f, so I see the word smile, but only for a while. Then if I see the word mile I would see the word ``while." A woman wanted prayer for her migraine and I thought the word was nightmare is what I saw on the prayer list. Then a person named Daniel needed prayer and I thought the name was Janel. Crazy right!" That's me, Now when it comes to reading I get frustrated, because I lose my spot where I was reading then It takes awhile to find where I was at. My daughter says that would drive her nuts." Another thing that is anoying is when I keep reading over the same sentence over and over again." Drives me crazy!" I also miss reading words a lot because I don't see the whole word. So if it doesn't make sense then I have to reread the word, until it makes sense. This is very annoying, and time consuming. Very fustrating. Now if you are doing what you are called to do. This may not be new for you. You know Just what to do. Don't be unsure or blue, ask your friend sue. She'll know what to do, because she's so in love with you. She will agree for the best for you, because she doesn't want you to be blue, she'll know just what to do, she's done it so many times, she keeps repeating herself like chimes, She'll even take you to dinner the next time. Because she likes to dine and wine. That's Just fine," all in good time. Be positive, and shine like a chime.`Matthew 5:16. In the same way let your light shine before others, that they may see your good deeds and glorify your father in heaven.

CHAPTER THIRTY-THREE

DIFFERENT SPICES FOR DIFFERENT OCCASIONS

Well my son went to school to become a cook so he learns about the different spices. Right!" He learns how to mix and blend the spices, to work to his advantage, let's Just say for comfort. So when he wanted to put my girls to sleep or to calm them down, He knew what spices to blend together to make the girls sleepy and that calmed them down" I thought this was a great thing to know because He would make tea from the blends of spices." He would have the girls drink it and in a few minutes the girls were calm and cool." It was like they had been drugged" I couldn't believe it!" But I had to because this was really happening." It was unreal what a few spices could do. It was unbelievable but it was real. My son could make a hotdog taste so delicious" he had that special touch to make things taste really good. Yes this was really cool by the time you know it they were down for the night. I've seen a woman put soda pop in her coffee, when we were at the Mall of America." Maybe that's how she made her flavored coffee." There are creamers that are flavored But to each their own." Now there are days when I am thirsty and I can't quench my thrist" So, I will have a coffee somewhere in the house that I put down somewhere, and I will have a water and a tea somewhere else." I usually drink my coffee cold because I wait for it to cool down Then I wait too long that it gets cold." Then I have to reheat it or drink it cold which is what i end up doing." Now I was going to heat my coffee again So I put it in the good old microwave for a minute now it's too hot so I let it cool again" Well this time I decided that if I let it get cold I will drink it cold." Right!" Well, I was going to take a sip of the coffee to see how hot it really was. But I was afraid to burn my lip and tongue because I saw the steam coming out of my coffee cup." So I tried to get a sip but each time the coffee got close to my lips I'd jerk back afraid that I was going to burn myself. By the time I had enough guts to take a sip of my coffee it would be luke-warm So I began to take a sip and ewe!" icky !" taste it was not the coffee that I had been heating up five times ago It was the soda pop!" How horrible I spit the pop out of my mouth." And I am not a pop drinker and after drinking hot pop I will never drink it again." Know your spices, know your drinks."Just saying." Now when it is hot out I don't mind drinking cold coffee. When it's cold out I don't mind drinking the coffee lukewarm. Now I have heard that Tea has more caffeine than coffee does. I'm not sure if this is true. I think that yes it does. Just by my experience of drinking both. So I don't have any Idea how my son got my girls to go to sleep after drinking the tea. You should have seen, they looked drugged up. Exodus 30: 34 And the Lord said unto Moses, take unto you sweet spices, stacte, and onycha, galbanum; these sweet spices with pure frankincense: of each shall there be a like weight:

CHAPTER THIRTY-FOUR

OUT TO DINE

    I had a friend that she and her husband were struggling financially. They were a young couple, friends from church and they had a bible study at their home which was only two blocks from me. Well one day my friend was driving my son and I home from church. We happened to see an ambulance and they were carrying a person on the stretcher. Our friend says to my son You see, they are taking someone in the ambulance. " My son asked, are they taking him to Jail?" My friend got a kick out of that!" He had a good laugh in a half." The person was probably dead; they had him covered up." Well my friend's wife wanted to go where the homeless people go to get a free meal. I didn't want to go there but my friend didn't want to go alone. So, I went a couple of times with her so she wouldn't have to be alone. I felt guilty going there to eat when I could eat at home. I knew that this was for the really needy people, So, I dined out with my friend a couple times and never went back because that was not my idea of dining out." I am not sure if my friend ever went back or not but I wasn't going to go with her anymore. She could find someone else to dine with. I felt embarrassed to go there. Just because it's free and you don't have to cook doesn't make it right but maybe my friend really didn't have any food at home. I do know before she got married she really didn't have food. She lived on peanut butter sandwiches because she didn't have a Job and she had a lot of college student loans debt and her fiance was trying to help her. But he was struggling himself to make ends meet." They had two babies, a boy and a girl, then my friend died of breast cancer." She beat it for eight years then came back and took her life. But we know she is with the Lord so, no more suffering for her. Now she can dine with the king. Forever and ever and one day I will see her again. Until that day I will be glad that I did get to know her here on earth. That she is my sister because we are all children of God. That one day we will be reunited in heaven with all our loved ones that left this earth before us. Until then we will hang on to our memories and treasure the times that we have had together. For now it seems like a dream but it is just memories that we treasure for our pleasure. For ever and ever." Until we meet again. Amen!" Well so much for dining out How did I get from dining out to death and breast cancer, and whatever else that became of this chapter. Such as life, when you take your time to unwind so that you can dine, remember this is not a shrine. This is for real, Do not steal my Ideal, I'm telling you for real, this is the real deal please don't steal my appeal in order to make a deal. Now I can reveal all that needs to be done, This is a bit quite fun. When you sit in the sun, getting well done, you are having fun being in the sun. But you're only half done, your tan makes you look nice and tanned. Yet you criticize others for the color of their skin but in reality you want to be like them. Let me rephrase my case because there's no other place that you won't be disgraced. Just in case you were wondering which is the path to harmony, You can seek and you can find, keep this in mind that the true color that you are looking for, is straight ahead. Just open the door, just when you think that you are done. It's Just the beginning, isn't it fun? When at the end of day you have made it special in your own way. And that's okay by me, as long as you stay true to the one who's loving you, day in and day out. He will tell you what it's all about. Let's give a shout of praise, let me rephrase, to the Lord of Lords, the king of all kings. He is the beginning and the end. You won't have to bend because he is the Alpha and the Omega, and you can truly depend on him, from the beginning and the end because he is your best friend. He will never leave you on end. 1 Corinthians 10:31 So whether you eat or drink or whatever you do, do it all for the glory of God.

CHAPTER THIRTY-FIVE

THE SPIRIT OF CHRISTMAS

Have you ever noticed that around Christmas time most people have a change of heart? They are more caring, more sensitive, more kind, sometimes more patient and more understanding. Keep this in mind it's only for a period of time. Their hearts are a little more softer. Well, it is because the spirit of Christmas is at hand, and in the air. The Christmas season most everyone is more loving, kind giving and a little more peaceful that only lasts for a season and that's only to reason for the season." Wish this could be all year around but it's only for a season don't know the reason but we have to believe in that the spirit of Christmas is here all year around we need to be open to the possibilities that we can have love, peace, Joy,giving, kindness we can keep all year around If we pay attention and walk through the door that has been opened up to us. And to press forward to the next level that is waiting on high that Jesus the messiah ls the king of all kings he is master and the maker of everything If you believe you shall achieve only through the grace of God that all things will fall into place for the Lord will give us the grace. You will never fail. I will tell you that God has a special place in his heart he will never leave you nor will you depart. That the spirit of Christmas is always near and not far, Will you take it to heart?" Remember why we have this season for the very reason that we celebrate our Lord and savior's birth and remember what's this all about don't forget to give a shout!" and praise that we have a savior that we can depend on no matter the day, time and season or reason. I really don't need a reason to call upon his name. Now be for real and don't play any games. For this is the reason for the season to be glad and rejoice in due season. That is why we celebrate our Lord's birth. We need to get down to earth and spread some love and cheer and to be glad that Jesus is near. I can feel his very presence at times I get goose bumps!" and the hairs on my arms stand up in attention. For I know my Lord is near, now I don't have to fear because my savior is near and dear he is waiting to hear from me and he is blessed when I seek his face. For he will give me his strength and grace to do what I can't do on my own to follow the path which he set before me I will be glad to follow him because I am his chosen one and when all of my deeds are done I know that I am blessed to be his own in due time he will come and get me and take me home for I am not alone. Remember the child of God to be happy, be full of life and spread a little love and life and remember the time is near when the Lord and his angels will appear to all of his chosen ones far and near we will reunite one day soon one day it will be clear. So do not fear, my dear what is near, for the just shall endure all the possibilities are here. In him we can trust, we do not need to distrust. Because you are his dear. He will always be near and dear, do not fear, do you hear?". We have seen his glory, the glory of the one and only son, who came from the father, full of grace and truth." Luke 2:14 Glory to God in the highest, and on earth peace, good will toward men."

CHAPTER THIRTY-SIX

TWO WRONGS DON'T MAKE IT RIGHT

Now if someone has done you wrong It won't be long before the truth is known even if it seems that nothing is being done won't be long before the doing is done. So, Just hang on to your bridges time will tell who's the one doing wrong it will be revealed who's at fought there's no rhyme or reason or a thought that can make up the truth in tale that you're not miss night and gale. So, don't worry about getting even all though there is a time and a season. That you can reason the tale of a night n gale. Just remember the one who fights your battles is mightier than mighty Just remember he is sitting on the throne he will keep you close as his own. Maybe you feel like you have been defeated. In time Your battles will rattle the truth because what is hidden in the dark will be revealed in the light of truth, to tell you that you're not a light in dark and if you cannot listen to reason in time there will be a season to reason the thoughts away in spite of who's telling the tale, that you're not miss knight n-gale in time you will learn to walk away.'' When you do walk away you are not a coward as some people may say. You really are a born star no matter what people think or say you did it right you did it God's way. That's all that really matters, the one you should please is the one who gave you life and peace. He's the one who deserves all our praise!" He's the one that can make something out of nothing. He's the one that can wipe away all your tears and can erase all your fears. And Just when you feel like you can't go on, He will give you the strength to carry on. Remember whose child you are. He is the great I am the prince of peace, he's the one that will never leave you alone. He's the one who gets things done. He is the great I am. He is the beginning and the end. He is the son of God; He will never leave you time and time again. Just remember He is the great I am." He is the king of kings!" He is the reason for us living. He is my prince and knight in shining armor. I am glad to be his child. He's the best Father in the whole wide world. He is the reason that I live and breathe. He is the one that takes my breath away. He is the truth and the light there is no other way. I tell you the truth today,be happy and be on your way." For this is going to be a better day by the way keep a song in your heart and a smile on your face. Therefore there's no better way to give praise to the Lord our God. There's no one else that deserves the very best, so be my guest and give it your best. That he is the one we adore, he's the one who bore our sins so that we could live another day. In the end this will only begin a new and everlasting life and abundantly, this is quite the real possibility. So rejoice and be glad that these are the best days that you will ever have, because this is only for a while, so don't be in denial that the best is yet to come that his kingdom will come. In the end this shall begin, time and time again. If you put your trust in him, then you can surely begin to see things get done. Whether you are on the run, let's make this fun before it comes undone. No matter what you've done, the battle has been won. Because of God's son, In what he has done for us. And what he is still doing for us right now, right this minute, He is legit. For there is no other that can ever compare. Oh don't you dare make a bet, for he is not done not just yet. When the day has come all things will be done, in his time and in his way. Everything will be okay. Because he will have it his way anyway. So surrender yourself to him. Then you can begin to truly live as a gift from God. Because he keeps his word, I hope you have heard that this is the only way to have true peace and not for just your niece. But for all mankind, so just unwind and take a closer look at what the Lord has for you. This will surely do for me and you. To be happy for eternity just you wait and see what the Lord has for you and me. Just let it be.

    Romans 12:17-21 Do not repay anyone evil for evil. Be careful to do what is right in the eyes of everybody. If it is possible, as far as it depends on you, live at peace with everyone.

CHAPTER THIRTY-SEVEN

GETTING BOTOX

Okay after battling with severe headaches of all types and forms, big and small, for years. On and off. I finally get to see a Doctor that knows what they are doing. But it is her last day working here because she was moving to another state Wow!" wouldn't you know it`` We met and she's an awesome Doctor. She says to me that she wishes that she could do something to help me with the headaches. So, she asks me what kind of headaches I have so I tell her sometimes I have them 24/7 never having relief unless I am sleeping. I told her I can't sleep my life away.``Then I have headaches in front of my forehead and it feels like somebody is squeezing my head. Once I had pain so severe that I couldn't even make a move. I had to be very still because the pain was unbearable." Then there's the pain in the back of my head. It feels like i Just banged the back of my head on the wall or hard pavement." Then I told her sometimes the pain is constant from the time I get up in the morning to the time I go back to bed at night." Then there's the migranes,and I wish I could chop my head off. But then I wouldn't be here, silly me" I would not be alive." Then she starts talking about getting botox at the time I didn't think much of it. I guess it didn't phase me." Well then I had to get an approval from my Insurance company that they would pay for this treatment. Well I did get the approval to get this procedure done. But the funny thing is, I don't remember us talking about botox. The only botox I've heard of was the kind that the famous Hollywood actors and actresses and famous musicians get to stay looking young." I didn't mind getting old and looking old. I just wanted to be done with these alfull headaches. Apparently, this is the same botox that supposedly takes away headaches. At this point I was willing to try everything that was offered to me that could possibly give me some kind of relief So, not knowing what I was getting myself into I decided to go with it to see if this could take away these headaches." My appointment was already made for my next visit to see another Doctor. A colleague of this Doctor That I have met. Come to find out that I already had an appointment to get the botox. I thought I had to make an appointment to get the botox. Okay turns out I was late so they refused to keep my appointment. I had to reschedule another appointment for the next visit. I had to wait another month to get in for another appointment. Okay the day came for me to see the Doctor. I was a bit nervous!" I called the Dr. office a week ahead of time and asked if I could schedule an appointment for the same day that I saw the Doctor. They told me that this was my appointment to get the botox. To my surprise!" I had an appointment already set up to get the botox. Well no backing out of this now I have the okay with my Insurance company to get this procedure done I might as well give it a try. I was on time this time. I was nervous" I didn't know what to expect. So this person that was going to give me the shot was not even a Doctor!" What!' Are you kidding me?" Why me?" Why couldn't I have a real Doctor." She is a PAC whatever that stands for." I sure hope she knows what she is doing because my life is in her hands. So, she says to me Just let me know if you get too uncomfortable we can stop and take a break. " I don't know what she means by this" I assume it is going to be painful from what she just told me. Too late to back out of this now!" So, she tells me that I will feel some pain so bare with her. I say okay I am used to pain. I don't know what it's like to have no pain besides I had to diagnose myself that I have fibromyalgia." and in the other chapter I diagnosed myself from having an anxiety disorder. I don't need a Doctor to tell me what's wrong with me. I know exactly what's wrong with me." Well let's get back to my first botox. So, this PAC or cia or bie whatever you want to call her is sticking needles in many parts of my face, neck and back. She's waiting for me to react with a scream or shout or anything!" She's just amazed at how calm and cool I am. She says don't tense up or this will not work, it will prevent me from the benefit of these shots." I am thinking they don't want us to tense up. I feel these needles sticking me so I frown at times, And jerk back at times how many times is this person gonna keep sticking me,: The needles are so thin but very long and when I am being stuck with them over and over everywhere that can be possible It feels like my skin is being scratched really hard." But I let this person do their job. It's gotta be over soon. She's got to run out right!" Okay any day now" My skin is screaming help me!" But I don't want to make a scene after all she said ``If I didn't work with her this won't work, in other words all this pain that I'm going through is for nothing.!" So, I keep that in my mind, all this we are doing will be for nothing." It won't work. So I will be as still as possible and not make any faces or frowns or jerk back or move at all." Because I am not going through this pain for nothing. I thought it was going to be one big shot when I signed up for the procedure.`` I am thinking when is she going to be done. She's just so impressed that I am sitting still and not screaming that it hurts. She says to me, ``Do you know how many people that I've had that don't be still or scream and cry and make it hard for me to give the shots?" But you don't yell and scream or jerk around. She says ``do you know how many people I see for this botox. Then she says hundreds But what I don't understand is why did it take so long. She then says I've got a little left for another spot she says do you have TMJ? I said yes I do," she says then I can use the rest for your Jaw So, at this point I am all shot out!" Then she says do you know how many shots I gave you? I said nope `` Then she asked Sarah my ride, if she counted how many times I stuck her ?"Sarah said no. well she says 33 times."I wanted to fall out of my chair.!" I couldn't believe it. No wonder it took so long. Then she says ``you come back in three months then we do it again there will be snow on the ground when you come back, It will be winter." So, she goes on to say that I might not get any results for a while. I am thinking that in three months Is that how long it will take for the pain to go away or what!" Then they give me a ton of paperwork about what to expect and the side effects. Why didn't they give me that before I had the procedure done, I know!" So they wouldn't scare me away. Well if I didn't have so many aches and pains already I wouldn't mind any side effects." One of the side effects could make your eye look like an lazy eye, I keep looking in the mirror and I could swear that one eyelid is dropping like an lazy eye."And on the information that is on the paper work it says There is no guarantee that this treatment method available for diminishing or curing" headaches or neck back pain. That this product has been FDA approved. I sure hope this does good because going through all that I say it better be worth it .!" But that's living. I can't believe that I am going through such a thing because normally I would pray over this matter and then the pain would go away." They say that rich people like the Actors and Actresses and famous musicians, get botox to get rid of wrinkles, and to keep looking young well my daughter says I have wrinkles on my forehead especially when I frown right between my eyebrows looks like a butt crack" I said what" really" she says yes go look in the mirror so I go look in the mirror and I'll be damned she's right!" I never knew that before maybe I seen it before but didn't pay attention about it.`` Well now that I am aware of it, it would be nice if the botox takes care of it. That would be a bonus for all the pain you go through. On my second visit we were on time but the receptionist told us that my appointment had been canceled. I said what!" They said that a woman named Debbie called and canceled my appointment. They asked me if I knew Debbie. I said no." So we made a trip for nothing." I said to Sarah, ``I don't believe this." But I had to believe it because this is happening.

So we rescheduled another appointment. I went for my second treatment, and this was very painful. Why did this hurt so bad? It feels like this is my first time, I didn't feel this much pain the first time." I think it has a lot to do with your state of mind. I was nervous and anxious!" They asked me if it was okay for me to go in alone, normally I would have said yes. But because I was nervous and anxious, I told them no I wanted Sarah to come in with me. She went to use the restroom so we waited for her to get back. So they started sticking me with shots, let me tell you this was very painful. I couldn't help but to frown and jerk and say ouch" This was way worse than the first time. I could feel it so much more, I am not sure how many times she stuck me but I couldn't wait to get it over with. This did go faster than the first time, maybe she didn't stick me 33 times this time. But she did. I was glad she was done because this was too hard to be still or not frown or jerk back. I already feel some relief. I haven't had headaches 24/7 and don't have them everyday. So I must say there has been improvement." The first time, I got headaches more often before they got better. I am amazed that just after two visits the headaches are not everyday, sometimes 24/7 wow!" I am glad I went through with the treatments. Progress is wonderful. After all that's why I went to them to get some progress in doing this treatment. They don't guarantee that this will work to take away headaches. I'm just glad that it is working for me. Sometimes I get a headache but it doesn't last all day. It's kind of like a headache is coming on then it will stop, which is great for me. It is good to not have them everyday is great. Enough about headaches, and Botox I don't want to bore you. Matthew 9:12 Jesus said, It is not the healthy who need a Doctor, but the sick.

CHAPTER THIRTY-EIGHT
HAVING COMPASSION"

What do you do when you see a homeless animal? Well me I like to take them in and nurse them back to good health. Then I try to find them a good home or adopt them myself. But what if you get too many animals at one time well you will have to work fast at achieving your goals as an animal lover and caregiver. When you have a really big heart but your place is not or someone reports you to the office, that you have lots of animals when you're only supposed to have two. Then you gotta find homes for all your pets when they were not your pet but they became your pet because you got attached to them and now you want to keep them. But everything you have in your home has pet hair. No Matter how clean you are you can't get away from pet hair. It seems to follow you wherever you go. This can be a bit embarrassing." We were having some kind of celebration in the party room and in the sugar bowl we could see some particles in the sugar and it was hair from one of my cats.' We tried to take it out before anyone noticed." So, that's one disadvantage of having too many hairy friends or should I say family members after all they are a part of your family. right." Even human hair is nasty if you happen to find it in your food," That's Just as nasty as the pet's hair especially if it's real long hair. Now when my girls were toddlers I had really long hair like down to my butt." But I never wore it down, I always had it french braided and up." I couldn't stand to wear it down. It was too thick and hot and heavy for me." Every once in a while my husband would find a really long piece of my hair somewhere unwanted."Let's face it, the only place that we really want to see hair is on our head to cover our head. Women don't want it on our legs or underarms, so we have to shave all the time." What a nuisance or should I say a pain in the butt. Now men can look like Gorillas if they want to." And some women prefer not to shave their legs, hopefully they shave their armpits." In other countries women don't shave their legs, I've heard. Anyhow sorry for rambling on and on about hair, well maybe this chapter should be called ``Hair, hair, hair." This was or should I say this started out to be a chapter about compassion and I ended up rattling on and on about hair. Well maybe we are supposed to have compassion on the people that don't want to shave. And they look like a Gorilla." Or maybe we are supposed to pray for them. And maybe I should stop talking so I won't put my foot in my mouth so to speak." Do you dare care what is available, and what is to scare, or do you care?" Please don't stare. This is rude and unfair!" When you get to where you want to be, take a deep look and see what are the possiblities there can be. If you just open up your eyes to see. What's in it for you and for me. You can truly see all the possibllities there are for you and me. Can we agree?" Just you and me. You want to be stable and not disable, for the time is approaching, my dear. When all fear will disappear in a twinkle in an eye. Please don't be shy, and don't let no sty go in your eye like a spy, you can do better than being shy, because you need to look up at the sky. And see what is in the air, I can see you truly don't care, Oh!" but Just you wait and see, what has come over me. Then you can see that it is our majesty, I'm sure you can agree that it's him that we need so take heed to my word. For it's truly God's word that we can depend on, this is only for a while don't be in denial. That all things that come to pass, they are free. Just look in the glass to get you where you need to be. In this I'm sure you can agree that this is for you and for me. That one day you will be free, and living in harmony. Psalms 116:5 The Lord is gracious and righteous; our God is full of compassion.

CHAPTER THIRTY-NINE

WHICH WAY IS THE RIGHT WAY?

Do you ever wonder if you are going the right way in life?" Do you ever wonder if you are at the right place and time where you are?" I sometimes wonder if I am supposed to be in a different state or country than I am now,or am I supposed to be somewhere else and if so where ?"and with who ?" I don't know why these questions always enter my mind. At times I feel like maybe I am misplaced. I think am I really doing what God wants me to?" Or am I at the right place that God wants me to be? Or am I Just doing what I want to do?" I mean, am I fullfilling everything that I was to do because I don't want to do a half job of my destiny. I hope I'm doing everything I'm supposed to do for the Lord, that I am pleasing him?" At times I wish that God could tell me what to do like a human person talks to us and I could hear him loud and clear like a human person. Yes I have goals in my life that I want to reach and there are dreams that I have that I want to see come true. And yes it is hard to wait for something to come now then wait for later.' Everyone is always in a hurry and maybe that's how we miss out on a blessing." I know that God wants me to be happy and fulfilled, and I know that he has only his best instored for us and that he wants us to be blessed by him. Here I go rambling on and on again.'`I guess mankind will always have questions that we may never find out the answers to. But for now I will take one day at a time. Then you won't be so overwhelmed. That's why maybe I should Just trust in God in him alone and not trust in man so much. Because man will try to take advantage of you or anyone else for that matter. As long as I am fast to forgive and slow to criticize one another I am sure that this displeases the Lord for our behavior and attitudes." And we keep looking to the king of kings, we know we will not disappoint him if we fail. We Just pick ourselves up and try again.`` God will be with us again and again. He will never fail us. He will be with us till the very end." With him there is no end." For that we can surely depend." I guess I will always have questions in the back of my mind, and maybe I will never find out the answers in this lifetime.. Maybe there is more to a mystery than meets the eye." I shall not cry as long as there is no stye in my eye. As long as I treasure each and every day. I will be glad and be on my way, because we are not guaranteed tomorrow. I will be glad and not drown myself in sorrow. Or feel sorry for myself because I made the wrong choice I still have a voice, and I thank God that I am here to share with you both far and near of what is important, and what is close and dear, do not fear for all things are possible to him that hear the word of God is so pure. In the end we shall see him face to face there is no one that can take his place. He has instilled his love and grace, this is very comforting to know that in the word of God we can find peace of mind, now remember to be kind. Because the way we live, has a lot to say that the Lord has blessed me and he is here to stay. Then I can be happy and on my way to my real home in time, I'll be able to sit and dine, there's no question in my mind, for the answers that I've been looking for are only a word that is not worth even a dime, so I won't have to worry about running out of time. Please do shine!" if you don't mind. Go ahead, take your time for this life is just for a time, we will have eternity with the great I am, I tell you time and time again there is no end. I'll say it over and over again!" there is no end. In whom I depend. John 14:6 Jesus answered," I am the way and the truth and the life. No one comes to the father except through me.

CHAPTER FORTY

KEEP A SENSE OF HUMOR

You will need to get a sense of humor, if you don't have one already." God has a sense of humor. You want to know how I know?" Just take a look around, he created me and you." I keep the Lord on his toes for he knows I am a challenge. I do keep him entertained.``He's never bored, he has made quite a creation, And there is no imitation. He knew beforehand every creeping crawling thing that creeps on earth and every teardrop of joy that a mother births, And if you keep laughing within your heart you gain Joy that spreads cheers and you prevent heart attacks and heart disease in part which is good medicine for the heart. So if you don't have a sense of humor you better get one soon before it's too late and there isn't any room. Now remember you want to make others laugh or get happy at the same time keep things in a perspective way. In other words. You want to make people laugh," or be happy but you don't want to be overwhelming, or obnoxious," or overbearing. Because people will think that you are a little coocoo" But you're really not." Now if you have the talent to keep yourself amused as well " Then You're a natural at being entertaining,to others and you even manage to keep yourself amused and entertained. You can keep yourself in pretty good spirits" 80-90 % of the time. That's great" For those that are mad at the world and those who are down right being mean or crabby to everyone and everything you need to rub some of your silliness off on those kinds of people. So, they can enjoy life while they are still living. Maybe that's the point they are not really living. They are just here and they are just existing and taking up space, in time they disappear without a trace. Nobody really misses them because they really weren't making a difference in this world. Because it's so cold, and in order for you to really live, you've got to give of yourself, and not act like you're just sitting on a shelf. They may need a little help to bring them to life, so they can start to live" and live life to the fullest. But not foolishly or stupidly!" Or dangerously." But to live life abundantly as God would want us to. Remember to put God first In everything we do or say, By the way even in our thoughts, life matters a lot. Since God created us in his own Image, so we could be a blessing to one another. But mostly to be a blessing to God for he created us for his pleasure." Now this I will treasure. God's love could never be measured because he first loved us." And we could never love as he loves us. Because he is perfect in every way, and he is in to stay. Sometimes people waiver to and fro, they turn their back on the Lord. Or they forget about him. When things are going good, then when in trouble they remember that there is a God, this is heartbreaking to my soul, I know the Lord sees it, and feels it as well, all I can do is pray for them because they are lost. They forgot who's the real boss. In time all that is lost can find the way back to have salvation and be on the right track. Please don't let it be only an act. But truly ask Jesus to come live in your heart and take away all your sins and fellowship with him and to read, learn, live as his word says. Let me tell you you'll be amazed and in a better place, he will bless you with his love and grace. Until we meet him face to face, I will rejoice and embrace his great kindness, love, and grace all over the place. For we will never have a love like him again. He is the beginning and the end, He is the great I Am."

What about those days when you are in a panic, and your nerves are jumping all around be quite don't make a sound because your mind is racing fast and you get up to do something. But you forgot what you got up for, then your mind starts to race all over the place. You know you've got to calm down a bit so you can concentrate and focus on one task at a time. You don't want to waste time. But you've got too much on your mind." Relax, take a deep breath, there hasn't been a death, so chill, take a chill pill but don't let all these things make a drill in your mind open your eyes, don't be so blind remember to be kind in the back of your mind. Just because you're having a tuff morning, doesn't mean the whole day will be that way. It can turn out to be the best day ever, remember to be clever in any kind of weather. You can laugh with somebody about your day then you've made it special anyway because you gave a smile to someone else,and you made them laugh in return, you've turned a frown into a smile, and a cry into laughter and you laughed about it the day after. This turned out to be a blessed day for another person besides yourself. And it's because you looked around and you heard God's voice in an audible voice and you really didn't have a choice for your desire to be used by God to do his will and not your own. This is what is shown that you are his own by the king of kings, And that you have been bought with a price that is paid in full . For this I am thankful and grateful for every little thing that God would choose me out of everything In which I will praise him every single day, as long as I live, breathe, and mind that he is forever so kind and devine. I am blessed that I have peace of mind. Because of our Lord being so kind, in him I can confide in most of my time." I'm willing to shine as I dine with him and enjoy every day as long as he is beside me and living in me to guide me, and show me the way to go. Because I'm not made of gold, as the story is told to the young and the old. This I have been foretold. Now stand up and be bold, for this lifetime span He will take your hand, so don't demand what you want or think that you need. For you can not see the future or know what's in store for the walk that he has for you. In time He will tell you what to do, don't be sad, don't be blue, for there is a lot to do. But be ready and alert!" before you know it, It will be time that we will be together forever to dine and yes we will shine because dining with him is so divine, I'm telling you it is time to let your light shine. For In a flick it will be time, can you handle all of this in your mind?" Now be steady, it's all in good time. Remember your sense of humor for this is very peculiar, then again who am I to say that you are different in each and every different way. But hey I'm here to stay until it's time to float away. For indeed we will be off to heaven so be on guard and be on alert that The true messiah will return In a blink of an eye. So take heart and don't cry. Just remember to take your sense of humor with you. I assure you that there will be no more crying there. Nor will there be killing or stealing, no lies, no sickness or pain. Never mind being ashamed. Our new life is fantastic!" And more than your dreams could ever dream. It's too hard to explain In time you can tell the story of God's glory, that this is not a fairytale. He's my God and That's all that I can tell. For the pages of this story, Is to give God all the glory." This Is not a story that is gorery refrain from playing games. This is the truth that he has chosen you. So don't deny his love and grace for his love is all over this place. Until we meet him face to face. I will accept his love and grace. In hopes you will do the same when all takes place. Can't wait to get there, In due time we will get there. We are Just waiting for more lost souls to find their way and be on the alert because you have heard. Wherever they go, because it's time to rise and shine for those who want peace of mind. Surely this is your time. To let your light shine, so you can wine and dine in due time keep this in mind, If you don't mind. Go ahead, take your time as long as you are on the right track this is no act. Be for real the enimey comes to steal, kill, destroy. God has come to give us life to the full and to have it abundantly. This we can surely see what is in store for me and for you, no matter what you are going through. He will show us what we need to do. So let our light shine and be a light that the king is here and he is here to stay, take it however, which way. And it is all up to him, what is the beginning and what is the end. And he is near, please don't be angry or have fear. Just be a dear and let him come near. So come on let's fight so we won't lose our ground that the Lord is here and he is profound and he is ready and able to take the stand so come on let's take his hand. This is not a demand, but if you prefer it to be then take it as you please that we are going home soon and it's hard to wait. All things are according to his will. That all things are possible which you desire, remember he gave you that desire, and he will fulfill what is due. He has not forgotten about you. Or give up on you. So hang on tight for the one who is right and know that everything is going to be alright. If you choose to live love, and be a light. Everything will be alright Just hang on tight and fight for what is right in the end we will all unite. So hang on tight!" You are in for a ride, don't get stuck on pride, let's take a ride to the other side. You will see just what I mean, that the king is coming, don't get left behind. Remember to be sweet and kind. If you don't mind, you are God's special kind. Just never mind what's going on, as long as you follow the one that can save the body, mind, soul and spirit. Fear not them that are able to kill the body but not the soul. Now this you have been told.There are mansions that are made of gold.You can not be sold please don't scold." Don't be afraid to come near it all in all. The Lord will take good care of you no matter what you do. Just stay true to the holy one, because he's the only one that can get things done. Let me tell you honey, It's not all going to be fun, and funny. But it will be on the money. So if you feel yourself being torn away, step up to the plate that he has garnished that will put you up to date you won't have to barrow. At the end of the day, God will have it his way and in hopes you stay true that you are his and he is yours. Please don't walk through any doors, but the door that's for you, then he will show you what you need to do, remain true to the Holy one, He is Christ the most Holy one. He is the only one I assure you his will, will be done here on earth as it is in heaven so straighten your shoulders, and take a deep breath, this may be a test, do not worry for he only gives us the best." He will give you a new birth, When you finally agree that he has paid the deed in full. Do you have the gull? I assure you it is finished that we have redemption, salvation, and of course a relationship, with the king of all kings. Who is the maker and creator of everything, hang on as he gives you wings, to fly home don't worry you won't be alone. The time is coming, the time is near, Pick yourself up and be a dear. For the time is coming the time is near. This will happen when he appears, please don't fear. Don't give up, the time and place is reserved for you and for me. That we will all live together in harmony. And unity we shall agree you shall see what's ahead for you and for me. Go ahead and tend to your deeds the Lord will provide for all of your needs according to his riches and glory. This is the end of this story. I will relax and take in his glory, for there is no better story that has ever been told, In which it never gets old. That the story that unfolded, protects, guides, blesses all of his children, that he is true to his word and will always remain true for both me and you. Now don't be bothered by what you should do, remember it's not up to you, don't get down on yourself and turn your face things will fall in place when he sends his grace you will be able to feel it all over this place. Now take your place you can see him all over your face that you will be able to be traced, upon his love and grace. We have been gathered together in this place. again and again. Proverbs 31:25 Strength and dignity are her clothing, and she laughs at the time to come.

CHAPTER FORTY-ONE
CAN'T DEPEND ON DEPENDS

So as I get older it sure seems like something goes wrong with me. Every year, It's like I am falling apart little by little. Well first of all I tend to almost fall down a lot.' I was walking my dog and the sidewalk was uneven, I knew that it was only a matter of time before I fell down. Well the time came I fell and busted my lip open. I had a fat lip and my mouth was bleeding." So, great, now I will have to use a walker. Then at times if I were laughing a lot I would pee a little in my pants." But one day it became more than a sprinkle. Once we were visiting my daughter as she was living in a facility. It was a bright sunny day and we all were laughing. I don't remember what about. But I could not stop laughing and I started to twinkle in my pants. Then it turned out to be more than just a sprinkle." Everyone was laughing harder and louder than before.``Well they could see my pee going down my pants." Boy did we ever laugh!" I had no control over this situation, We all had a great laugh!" I was humiliated." But I did manage to laugh along with everyone else." Years went on and little by little my health began to deteriorate. Now I walked with a walker inside of my building but when I went out to do errands I used a cane. Because a walker is a pain in the butt to have to lug around, It's more simple to Just take a cane. If I went shopping I would hang on to the shopping cart so I usually push the cart so that I have something to hang on to. I know they have a motorized scooter that I could sit on and drive, but to keep the public safe I better not use it. I tried it once, and that was enough to last a lifetime. Well I decided I should wear ``depends as a safety precaution. Let me tell you that you can't depend on depends." When I put one on as a precaution, by the time I know it the depends is almost down to my knees." Or so it felt like it. Plus they would make my pants fall down," I don't know why?" What's going on here?" How are these supposed to be of good support when they don't even stay up!" I told my worker and I showed her and she began to laugh about it. She said to me ``don't go around mooning everybody." I said to her, "Not for free." When I wore the depends I never had a problem but they did give me a blister on my butt." seems like it got bigger. It wasn't there before I started wearing depends. So now I stopped wearing them to go out. Okay so now I will never wear them again." Who knows what else they will give me!" I don't need whatever they want to give me. I've got enough issues all ready. I don't need anymore, okay. Enough about the depends that you can't even depend on." Yes, the things you take for granted when you are young can be taken away from you before the day is done. Like just opening a bag of chips, a bottle or a can. Can be a challenge for any older woman or man. I'll be damned, Just doing housework or cooking a meal leaves you all worn out. It is very frustrating that you can't do the things you used to do. In your mind you can do it. But your body says no you're not no spring chicken anymore I want you to know let somebody else take over. It's time to let go of what you can and cannot do anymore and go with the flow. It's time to realize this is a new day and that the Lord has something special coming your way. Don't be sad, don't be mad. Just accept God's plan that this is a new chapter for you and it's all of God's plan. Be happy and content. In due time you will learn to laugh again. Just remember when it all began where you were when God rescued you from death. Now don't get bent out of shape and out of breath. You can remember but you don't have to stay there. Because it's not good to dwell in the past, it will only bring misery and doubt and shame.and pain, what do you have to gain?" You don't have to play that game, you can step aside and reframe, what have you got to gain?' No you don't have to be a shame, what is your name? Please don't play that game, you must refrain from staying in the game. You know what I'm saying? I'll tell you over and over again. Play it cool don't be a fool, and please don't drool all over you, no matter what you do stay in school and learn and get the wisdom you need so you can succeed in today's world while it last, have yourself a blast but learn what you can then you can began to value the treasures of life, are not the things you can see with your eyes. To your surprise. You have become terrorized. And you have gained more than you thought. Because you can only see what is meant to be, I'm telling you for your own good, now this needs to be understood. That this is for your own good. Is that understood?" Focus on the here and now, then you can take a big bow, to the one who deserves your thanks and praise. This is king Jesus!' you will be truly amazed. You won't be in a daze, you will be totally amazed. You will never go back in a daze. This you will have to engage, you will want to stay on the same page if you were to be engaged this is not an outrage, to stay on the level that you feel comfortable you see. Take a deep breath and you will see what's in store for you and for me. Just you wait and see, what's in it for you, and for me Just be still and let it be real. This is between you and me. Truly I am telling you the truth indeed, in order to proceed what might and might not succeed if you truly want to be free and set free indeed. You will be able to succeed indeed, so let it be. This is for you and not me. Can we agree? Psalm 7:10 My shield and my defense depend on God, who saves the upright in heart.

CHAPTER FORTY-TWO

HITCHING A RIDE

For a walk each day I would walk to the store to get a few Items I needed to make a meal. Well I would seem to overdo the Items that I bought, I would forget that we were walking and had to carry the food back to our apartment. When I had a habit of going to the store everyday. Now as a grown-up I guess this was a walk for my kids and I, then I would buy too many things to carry home. So, cars would stop and ask if I needed a ride. I only lived a few blocks from the store But we had to cross the train tracks and that was hard carrying bags of food. Anyhow, guys would stop and ask if they could give me a lift." So I took the ride which was only a few feet away from home. I would take the ride because I was tired of carrying the bags of groceries.I know that this wasn't right to take rides from strangers, But I did anyhow."God kept my daughters and I safe from harm." So when we moved to my third husband's home with him and his mother. Here we go grocery shopping. That's a No no !" to go with your husband. So, my second husband and I go to the grocery store then we get into a debate of what we can and can't buy. This is totally embarrassing in public to argue and fight in public. Now I am used to shopping the way I shop and sense I do the cooking. I know what I need and my husband is overwhelmed by the cost and that we don't have enough money. Poor guy looks like he is a wreck from being stressed. I know being married and having a couple of babies and working two Jobs to make ends meet was draining him." But hey that's life. My mom's saying is, that's life in the big city. So, we finally got the shopping done. Then we decided to make a menu for the week. For the meals I will make Then we decide to buy a turkey. Because out of the turkey we could make lots of meals. This seems to work great." So, at first we had a turkey dinner with all the fixings, then we had turkey soup then turkey and gravy open faced sandwiches. Then turkey pot pie then turkey enchiladas When my first daughter was born she was so big and plump she was so strong and healthy You could swear she was 3-4 months old." I bet it was from all the turkey I ate." Well I had to stop getting too many things from the store if i didn't have a ride. Besides this was not a good thing to get rides from strangers in this day and age, you cannot trust anybody. This is the world that we live in. It's corrupt and dark. You can't take chances that can endanger your life all for a bag of groceries, It's not worth it. It's not worth the chance to come up with a different plan. Don't ever go in a car with a scam. Of course you don't know who is for real and who is a scam. Could be a murderer, a thief, you don't know what they have planed. That will leave you in grief, or maybe he could kill, steal, destroy you. Do not toy with the boy that you don't know,this may not be a show so let the guy go and be on his way. So that you can live another day. Stay that way, so you can be around to see who's stopping on your ground. Please don't make a sound so turn around, and stand your ground because your kids need you to be around. Besides, you need to be a role model to your children so they will grow up to be blessed and wise as they can be a light and succeessful in this lifetime. You won't have to worry how they are gonna turn out. You can be sure without a doubt that they have been blessed and there's no doubt, because you know what it is all about. Now give a shout!" For there is no doubt, what's it all about, go ahead and give a shout and tell what it is all about. Hebrews 13:5 Keep your life free from the love of money, and be content with what you have, for he has said, I will never leave you or forsake you."

CHAPTER FORTY-THREE

MAKING A SNOWMAN

As a grown up I decided to play in the snow with my kids. I don't ever remember making a snowman when I was a kid. I do remember licking big giant icicles that were hanging down off our roof. We didn't need to go in the house and get a drink of water we Just broke off a huge icicle that was hanging. Now I know that this was dangerous if you were to get hit on the head with one. It probably kill a person because they were so big and very thick." They were humongous!" Anyhow, enough about the icicles let me finish telling you about the snowman that I wanted to make with the kids." Well the snowman I made was crooked. He looked pretty funny like he was leaning to one side. It looked like he was about to fall over, that's how crooked he was." Listen to me, I am talking about the snowman like he is a person instead of a thing." I think I watched too many of the frosty snowman movies. I hope by talking like that, I don't make my kids think that he is going to come to life Naw!" he doesn't look like a normal snowman, he looks deformed." Well the next time I looked out the window to see how my snowman looked I didn't see him standing anymore." So, I thought I would go outside to see where my snowman went. But there was no snowman. He was gone so I thought some kids knocked my snowman down. But the truth was He probably fell over himself because he was already leaning over like he was about to fall over. Now that was my first and last time that I made a snowman. Now I will take the kids sliding but I won't even attempt or even think about making a snowman. Nope " not me not never again. Now to make a snowball perfect like some people do I can't even make a perfect snowball. Who cares if I make a perfect snowball?

Good thing winter and snow are only a few months I don't think I can handle anymore." Okay enough about the dum snowman I made. Here I am going on and on about a stupid snowman I made and I was a bit sad because I thought kids were being mean and knocking down my very first snowman that I made And the truth was He fell on his own." Who cares about a stupid snowman any how. Don't let snowman making get you down, or make you frown, it just takes practice, until you get it right it will be a delight!" Not a fright!" So you can delight, In repeating over and over again. You can even ask a friend to lend a hand. But do not demand or you'll be standing alone. Just you and the snow, you have to let things go. So that you can grow in wisdom, and knowledge" Then you're able to go to college. To learn some more, as you walk out the door. You remember your manners, no matter where you come from. Don't leave things undone. Even if you make a crooked snowman, it will melt away, then you can try another day. Just don't give up, there's room for improvement. So, don't be discouraged, There is no time frame so you can gain the most important truth. That it is the peace and love you endured from the ones who are so dear and near to you, they will be frank with you. Nomatter what you do they will always be here for you. This you can be sure, That the Almighty above, will be beside you and all heaven above will be waitting for you, you can be sure that it's in God's word. All that you want and need will be given to you yes indeed. As long as you trust him. Then you can truly be happy and fulfilled, to your heart's desires, that he wants to bring about, we can all shout and praise, To the one who truly deserves all the best can you take a guess, who that might be?" You know more than me, it's King Jesus, as you can plainly see that he has his best for you and for me. Psalms 51:7 Cleanse me with hyssop, and I will be clean; wash me, and I will be whiter than snow.

CHAPTER FORTY-FOUR

JOINING AN HEALTH CLUB

So the girls and I joined a health club like the YMCA. They had swimming, and other things going on there. We were blessed because we Just had to walk across the street to get there. It was fun but It was hard to be motavated to go at least three times a week. I know we had to get our money's worth, But this was exhausting yet it was fun. We mainly went there to swim. Once I walked around the track one day my daughter and I went out the back of the building to see what that looked like. It was dusk and the sun was going down soon it would be dark. But it began to storm my daughter and I got really scared because someone locked the doors so we could not get back in the building." We panicked, and began to yell for help. Some people who lived across the street were outside and heard us. They said that they would go in the building and tell them we were locked out in the back. Somebody unlocked the doors for us. We were so glad we told the Lady thank you for getting help for us. She was glad to have helped. Now as far as swimming goes the girls were like fish in the sea they loved the water and were excellent swimmers. They had no fear of the water." Myself I was afraid to go to the deep end and my girls would embarrass me they would say come on mom it's not too deep." When in fact it was the deep end I was still working on overcoming my fears. About swimming. Because when I went to california the first time I almost drowned I had never been to a real beach let alone swim in one. I had to be rescued." From that time on I had to work on my fears of swimming again." The apartment where we lived had a pool. So, in the summer when the girls had summer vacation we would pack a lunch and hang out at the pool all day." It took me seven years to overcome my fears of swimming in the deep end. But I did it.`` At times I still had a panic attack, while I was in the pool. So I tried to stay close to the wall incase I had a panic attack I could grab onto the wall, Once a kid Jumped in the water and he hit my head He got too close to me I began to panic and started drowning the kids father said do you need help I tried to say yes so, the man put his hand out for me to crab onto i pulled his arm and I used him as a step ladder." I was drowning the poor guy!" Well I bet this man would never offer a hand to me again."Then two other times I was drowning in our pool. Once a kid jumped on top of me He hit my head and my ear so hard the pain took a long time to go away. But I panicked" And began to drown again!This time a man asked me if I was okay. I said no but then I swam to the wall and grabbed a hold of the wall. The next time I almost drowned was when I was with my son. We were swimming on our backs and for some reason he pulled me down. I panicked and began drowning." My son was trying to help me but I was stepping on his head and using him like a ladder." My son yelled and said, ``Mom, you're drowning me." He said stop, I am trying to help you calm down. Well we finally got out of the pool safe and sound. The people who were out there sitting by the pool, in the patio area, were just watching us. I think they were confused if we were really drowning or not."Anyhow we entertained those people. There were a lot of Russians that lived in our apartment complex. They sure lived so free that they would change outside on the patio by the pool. Instead of going into the dressing room. At times it was hard to communicate with them because they didn't understand or talk English as well as they should have living here in Minnesota. One man was using the word shut-up to say something else. We thought he was being mean, but he wasn't. He just thought that was used for another word. We have all kinds of people living here. It has gotten so populated, that so many apartment buildings have been built and still more going up to acomadate as many people that we possibly can. In fact you have to go further to get to the country. Because we have really populated the Twin Cities. Saint Paul and Minneapolis are called the Twin Cities. This is home sweet home. This is where I was born and raised. 1 Corinthians 9:26-27 So I do not run aimlessly, I do not box as one beating the air. But I discipline my body and keep it under control, lest after preaching to others I myself should be disqualified." Disciplining our body like Paul is talking about here is an effort to keep our whole selves restrained from sin, for the prize of knowing Christ and him crucified.

CHAPTER FORTY-FIVE

TRYING TO JUMP THE HOOP

Back at our health club I took a peek In the gym, to see what was going on there were some women playing basketball so, I was watching them play through the glass window that was on the door. Then a woman came to me and asked me if I wanted to play So, I said sure I didn't expect for someone to ask me to play with them. I wasn't acting shy or anything like that. I said okay I'll play. I began to play with this group of women whom I didn't even know. But hey, I was having fun." dribbling the ball and just having a grand time" I hadn't played since I was a kid. I was playing like I was a pro. I have no idea where that came from, I was having fun. I was really having a good time." But I was going so fast I couldn't believe it!" I had the ball and I was out of control. I couldn't slow down, Wow I was on a roll." Hey I was having fun. I tried to slow down but I was going too fast. Everybody was trying to catch up with me, and the other team was trying to get the ball from me." I couldn't believe I was playing like that was my thing like I was an x- globe trotter." Then I Wiped out!" I fell face down. I did get hurt but I acted like I didn't get hurt. I am sure they saw the skin on my legs being scraped up." I couldn't fool them that I didn't get hurt. So, much for jumping the hoop!" The hoop jumped me instead!" I didn't ever see those women again, not to my knowledge. I was kind of embarrassed about wiping out!"And how the game ended for me."No more being an x globe Trotter." Then I played basketball with my husband and kids. We had a friend sitting on the bleachers cheering us on. We were not really playing, we just were running basket hoop to basket hoop and trying to make a basket. We were just having fun having family time. This was fun to do, sure glad I didn't wipe out!" Remember if you want to jump the hoop, don't act like you are a part of the troop Just to get in good with the higher-ups. If you don't get your way Just don't give up. You keep on trying until you get it right, go to the next level until you get it right. You better be hanging on tight, you can't just wait until you move from there. Sometimes you feel like you're floating in thin air. You are not in despair, let's clear the air. So you won't go home in despair because I really do care, and everything is up in the air, calm down, don't be in deep despair, I'll even give you a hug like a live bear, because you'll see that I really do care, now beware if you dare. 2 Timothy 2:5 An athlete is not crowned unless he completes according to the rules.

CHAPTER FORTY-SIX

HAVING PARENTS OVER FOR DINNER

Well I got an apartment for my son and I. It was a nice neighborhood where we lived upstairs of a duplex home. Everyday we walked to the park. My son was in head start preschool This was our first apartment since we moved out of the ministry home where we lived with our pastor and his family and some other Godly people that lived in the home. At the time there was a store across the street from us called Steves warehouse. My son did get to help the store a little; they let him stamp the price on some canned goods. We loved it there. I invited my parents over for dinner. I wanted to serve them something that they never had. So I decided to make taco pie. We had a nice dinner then they left to go home. Well I realized that I forgot to put in an ingredeant oh!" no I felt so stupid!" The truth was they didn't know and what they didn't know won't hurt them right!" wrong my poor dad had heartburn and indigestion and was burping all night!" Well I never did have them over for dinner ever again!" I never invited them again, and If I would have they might have said no thanks. Now I had invited a couple from church over for dinner when it was time for them to go home. The woman opened my closet and was going in there then she realized that it wasn't the right door she opened.' She was so embarrassed and humiliated. But we did have a good laugh." She did look funny going into the closet, sad thing she was wearing glasses apparently the glasses didn't help much." Maybe she was wearing somebody else's glasses and not her own.`` Now if you want to be a guest at my house, roll up your sleeves and button your blouse. I may or may not be the best cook in town but I assure you

you won't be bound. So take a taste please don't waste the food that I have prepared for you and for me, Just let it be, yummy for your tummy. And nice aroma to your nose, this will keep you on your toes. Remember to say please and thank you for this is a good manner to keep even if you think it's cheap. The next time we get together, It will be my pleasure to have you sit and relax. Now I couldn't have said it any better.What is your pleasure that you treasure?' Psalm 133:1 How good and pleasant it is when God's people live together in unity!"

CHAPTER FORTY-SEVEN

MOVING FROM PLACE TO PLACE

I had a luncheon at my place before I got married for the second time. My son says ``ewe there's a bug in the food!" One of my friends looked and said no. It's just spices. I was glad it wasn't a real bug because the place my son and I lived at, at the time, did have cockroaches and mice and rats. We did not know that there were bugs and rodents at the time we moved in. I was glad that neither of those ecky things came out while I had company.`` We had just moved there. We couldn't find another place that I could afford. Besides this was only for a couple of months until I got married. We had no Idea it was in a bad area, or a bad neighborhood. They had a night strangler going around killing women and they had the police and ambulance on our street all the time. Thank goodness It was for only a couple of months. Our duplex apartment we had previously lived in, the owners wanted to move in our apartment so my son and I had to move. We couldn't find a place that we could afford. And they didn't give us much notice. So we moved to a duplex home on the east side. The landlord stole our food stamps. At the time they used to mail them to you. The landlords and their friends would have parties. And you could smell the weed they were smoking coming through the cracks in the hall. The landlord was trying to rob us of some money but the Lord turned it around for the good for my son and I. We were glad to get out of that place. Well my son and I had our share of bad places to live and bad landlords. Brighter days were ahead of us. I knew that this was a temporary thing. Yes this was hard to be living in such horrible living conditions but there was a family that lived downstairs of us. They had four or five kids and the two parents must have been packed and wall to wall people. Now how could a family be comfortable in what little space they had without stepping on each other. They probably didn't have roaches or mice or rats because there was no room for them to go to their place so they came to my place instead. Ha-ha!" One day the fire alarm went off and my son panicked and he was so confused about what he should do. Poor kid" he kept running up and down the stairs he was frantic!" The people that lived downstairs of us came out to the hall to see what was going on. They looked at each other then they watched my son run up and down the stairs like a crazy man!" Then they went back into their apartment. They were just looking at my son acting like a fool." He looked hilarious!" He looked like a cartoon." But nobody laughed because we all knew this kid was in a panic!" Well this was the second time that we gave our notice that we were going to move and we could not find a place that we could afford in a decent neighborhood. But how do you know if it is safe or decent until you find out for yourself. I did have a friend of mine tell me that it was a bad neighborhood and to not move there. He also told me that I don't love my son if I move there. Well I had no choice but to move there. I was not going to let us be homeless." Besides, this was only a temporary thing. When we moved before We had trouble finding a place to live in a decent area for my son and I . We had a landlord that would have parties. One day My son was very sick. And the Doctor prescribed an antibiotic. I asked the Landlord if she would watch my son while I went to the drugstore to pick up my son's mediction. She said no, So I had to find someone else to come sit with my son while I ran to the store. I mean I practically and literally ran to the store." I didn't have a car and I did not drive. This was tough but we managed we had no choice.We had to make do with what we had. Maybe we didn't have much but we had what we needed when we needed it. That was God taking care of us. He was my husband and my son's father . We knew this was the hand of God. In the winter the pipes froze up so we had no running water in the kitchen. This was a big nuisance, a pain in the butt!" I had to wash the dishes in the bathtub. Then again we had to move. The landlord was having parties and the thing was that when they smoked pot, weed, dope, marijuana. Whatever you want to call it!" It would come into our apartment. Now this was strange because how could it come into my apartment through the cracks of our door?" I think they were smoking in the stairway that leads to my apartment. Because I could hear them. This was very ackward." I swear they were intentionally blowing it into my apartment. There was a crack on the toilet seat . I told the landlord about it but he didn't do anything about it." weeks later he told me that a plummer was coming to fix the toilet seat but how do you fix a toilet seat?" Put tape on the crack or you get a new toilet seat from the hardware store and put it on yourself you don't call a plumber. I had a feeling that this landlord was planning to scam me so I knew that he was up to no good, I didn't feel right about him calling a plummer. Well my assumptions were right. This guy had one of his friends pretend to be a plumber" They tried to scam me that I owed a lot of money because they had to replace the whole toilet. I knew better than that so I had a friend that was a lawyer and he came to do an expection on my apartment and he found a lot of things wrong. So he made a list as to what was wrong with my place. He gave the list to my landlord. My landlord dropped the charges against me concerning the toilet. I couldn't wait to get out of that place. I was thankful that I had a smart lawyer friend. I know this was the hand of God. God bless my friend that helped my son and I. This same friend came to my son's and my aid again. Our cat was sick and fell on her side. Apparently she ate some string and it caused damage to our cat's intestines. My son and I were crying. Our friend took us to the vet. Then the vet said that she could operate but chances are our cat won't live. So the best thing to do is put her down. My son and I cried even harder, plus we didn't have any money for the vet services. So our friend paid the bill for us, so our cat could be put to sleep so she wouldn't have to suffer anymore. My son and I cried and cried. This was so sad. But we did give her a good life while she was with us, we took care of her the best we could, now it's just memories that are all we have left. But it's good memories, and memories are the best. One thing for sure we will see her in the life that comes next. People always ask the question, Is there animals in heaven? I do think our pet's will be in heaven. Now I'm not the only person that thinks this is true. I guess there's nothing we can do but to wait until we get to heaven then we will see for ourselves, our long loved pets are not Just a memories any more, but they are waiting for us to come home so they can love us, and be with us again forever more, because we are the ingredient that's missing from near and far to be a blessing to each other and to live a life so special and perfect in every way you will be glad that you have stayed, to find out the answers to questions you've had for a very long time.Stop wasting your time being on line because everything that is on there is not true. You've had to learn this through and through. Now what are we to do?" But stay in school so you won't be a fool your whole life take it from me, so you won't live in strife. You better tell your wife so there will not be any strife. don't pick up that knife, because you will just add more strife to your life. If you know what I mean, don't scream, that's no way to get ice cream if you know what I mean go ahead and dream. But stay off that machine that is making you mean and makes you want to scream. So go ahead and dream because dreams do come true. If you know what I mean. So go ahead and dream, before I scream. Don't be mean. Remember to dream, dream, dream don't scream you know what I mean. Romans 8:28 And we know that for all those who love God all things work together for the good, for those who are called according to his purpose.

CHAPTER FORTY-EIGHT

MEETING A REAL LIVE BARBIE DOLL

Have you ever met a woman that was made up so much that It was hard to tell what is real about her and what is not!" It could be fake or plastic or what not" Well she has to be careful that her fake eyelashes won't fall down to her cheek, don't be bleak as you seek for a clue that will work for you so you won't have to lurk around because of some Jerk that's bound to make a sound, so stand your ground, and he is following you around. The sad thing is that she can't see anything, so she is making mistakes at work. She bumps into the wall a few times and almost knocks herself out!" Then staggers on her merry way. And the boss sees her stumbling to make her way back to her desk. And he Just shakes his head and tells her ``you better watch your step I am watching you" Now you know you are not supposed to drink or do drugs on the Job and she says but boss" I am not drinking or doing drugs!" Then she bends over and one of her breasts is lopsided." And she hopes nobody notices so she rushes to the bathroom to fix her breasts,so both are the same size and hopefully they are not lopsided." The hairdo she is wearing is only a fad. She is glad for what she's had." Because She can change her hair each day from the color, length and style. But it is for only a while that she'll be in style. Then she makes it to her desk and begins to type, her nails falling off one by one and they are all kinds of shapes big and small, long and short, chipped and all!" At the end of the day it is all done. And in the end she had a full day and it was fun.

In the end It is all done. But she's Just Living and she's not giving.`` She keeps to herself because she's a real live Barbie doll.``One day I was riding my bike and I saw a man riding his bike. I couldn't believe what I saw. This man looked like Ken the barbie doll!" Maybe he was on his way to meet up with Barbie. After all, they are a couple. Isaiah 64:8 Yet you Lord are our Father. We are the clay, you are the potter, we are all work of your hand.

CHAPTER FORTY-NINE

WATCHING FIREWORKS

Do you make it a habit to go watch the fireworks each year?" Either on TV or in person. Well let me tell you I will never try to go to see fireworks in person. I had one bad experience that will last a lifetime." You see I went with somebody to see the fireworks and it was quite the experience of a lifetime. This changed my whole perspective for going to watch them in person." Okay I never knew the reason for people trying to get out of where you are at a gathering to not be caught in a traffic Jam. Well I don't drive so I don't have to worry about a parking spot or a traffic jam. I have never been in a traffic Jam!" Well this particular time I did experience a traffic Jam." I refuse to ever go there again, I'm scarred for life. It got me in strife. I won't have to think about it twice, now I will be nice at a price. Shake them dice only twice if you want to be nice. Give me a surprise,don't minimize, you could be in a disguise otherwise pick your prize. Well we went to go see the fireworks and let me tell you it was horrible!" Not the fireworks but trying to get from point A to point B,This was very traumatizing for life."We were actually stuck. We couldn't move forwards, we couldn't move backwards, we couldn't move sideways or right side up or wrong side down, we couldn't go upside down or spin around.", we couldn't stand our ground. So all we could do is frown.." We couldn't do a darn thing!" natha!" zipo" And you know what?" We were not the only ones that could not move!" Everybody was stuck in a traffic Jam!" No more for me I will watch the fireworks on the Television or from my living room window." That's what I got to say about traffic Jams, I just thank God I didn't have to go to the bathroom. they might have made me take a bus because of all the fuss. Let me tell you never again until the end." Now one year one of my brothers decided to wear his firecracker. Somehow, someway he got the firecracker down the back of his shirt. Poor guy burned his back. It wasn't too bad. It also wasn't too good. Then one of my daughters wanted to hold a sparkler but she grabbed one that was already used up. And it was still hot ouch!" So she burned her hand. Wasn't too bad but then again it wasn't too good. Nowadays I just watch the firecrackers from my living room window. They do have enough fireworks all around the city. They start in June and last for months later. I thought it was supposed to be against the law to buy them and do them in our state so some people buy them from a state that is legal like wisconsin. Not all people follow the laws or rules. They even sell them at the store, Inside the store.with a display of the fireworks. And they sell them outside of the store. They will have a special spot and a tent set up with the fireworks. People will park blocks away then walk to the bridge to watch the fireworks display from the capital. There are more fireworks displays in different places, some people park as close as they can, then they sit on a hill, they bring a blanket to sit on or they bring some lawn chairs to be able to sit and relax. And watch the fireworks display. This is for everyone, not Just the gay, you better be on your way. Some like to wait for the grand finale display, this is the last for the night. They save the best for the last. If you don't want to be stuck in a traffic Jam you better not stay for the finale. This is a tradition that people do every year. Like I said I will watch from my living room window. I'm scarred for life. This was a bit tragic do you happen to have some cash, that you can spare do not throw it in the air, I can't hardly bear to see what is next I can only guess that you gave it your best and yet you won't have to guess why your a mess, unless you want to give it your best then you can rest. You know your best so don't pretend to second guess, please don't be a pest, take a wild guess and do your best so you can rest like you are a guest, you will receive the very best, in heaven's nest. For it's the best to be my guest." I know you will do your best. Now I can rest. Just remember to give it your best that you can rest at last. Have a blast while it lasts please don't pass gas." If you do, you will make the boy whose name is sue, very blue, then he will want to sue. Do you have a glue?' Take a look at my shoes. You need to know that they are new, what are you gonna do?' You know what to do, don't come uncluded. You need to keep it together, In every kind of weather from what I gather you can do it the day after and it won't matter. Just get it together. So then it won't matter the day before or after. Then you can have some laughter, and spread It around thereafter.

Matthew 5: 14-16 You are the light of the world. A city situated on a hill cannot be hidden. No one lights a lamp and puts it under a basket, but rather on a lampstand, and it gives light for all who are in the house. In the same way let your light shine before others, so they may see your good works and give glory to your father in heaven."

CHAPTER FIFTY

BEING AUTHENTIC

Okay so I like being creative and entertaining people when they come to my place for dinner. Right!" Well, I decided to make Chinese food even though I am not Chinese. I wanted to have people take off their shoes and eat with chopsticks and sit on the floor like real Chinese people do.Who am I kidding? That's only in the old fashioned movies. They really don't sit on the floor and take their shoes off do they?" Anyhow, if your feet have an order that can melt a candle stick to nothing then it's better to keep your shoes on." I made homemade chicken chow mein and it was delicious!" the special touch to make it tasty was putting cashews on the top." My guests loved it and I must admit I thought it was tasty as well. I even had chopsticks to eat with. Everyone was having a blast trying to eat with chopsticks.``I even had fortune cookies that we could eat and a message inside the cookie." Well, I started out right using the chopsticks. I felt good that I was doing a good job. I felt like I was a pro at doing these sticks. Everyone else gave up right away; it was too much of a challenge for them to try and try. So they all asked for a fork. So, I gave them all a fork. Then I began getting sloppy with the chopsticks. I decided to give up and get a fork. Anyhow it was fun as it lasted. Then all of us grown folks were sitting on the floor and began to play with a balloon. We were all trying to keep the balloon in the air. I guess this was funny how the evening turned out. I guess you could say we had a good turn out!" We all had a good time after all that's what it is all about. 2 Timothy 3:16 All scripture is given by inspiration of God, and is profitable for doctrine, for reproof, and for correction, for instruction in righteousness:

CHAPTER FIFTY-ONE

WHEN IS ENOUGH ENOUGH?"

Okay let's get real. Anything can be addicting. It can be your favorite food. It could be watching television It could be going shopping, it could be a million things, right!" Well I got addicted to collecting movies not so much as watching them, it was collecting them. Although I never got spooky movies or horror movies It was mainly comedy, suspense or love stories or fairy tales. Or should I say chick flicks. I admit I was addicted big time." At the time the vedios were in. I had so many movies that if you wanted to borrow a movie you had to ask a couple of weeks ahead of time, so that i had plenty of time to find it. Get this, I would be looking and looking for a movie so long that I forgot what I was looking for!" Now that's sad." Then my daughter decided to put the movies in order and number them and put them in the computer so that we could locate a certain movie we were looking for. Anyway, my daughter gave up." She didn't finish what she started. That's alright because times changed again. Now we use DVDs and in time that will change and we will be back to 45's then albums again because there is nothing new under the sun, we just give it another name right!" Take coronavirus, it's not new, back in 1918 January to December 1920 there was the flu pandemic, also called the Spanish flu. people were sick and dying. Now we call it a different variant name. Then while living in an apartment building, I somehow started to collect bikes. I don't even know where I got all these bikes." I had a garage, when I opened the garage door there were a lot of bikes. I had three kids, not 50. Okay next We live in a different apartment building. Then I began collecting cats. Not stuffed animal cats, but real cats." I took care of a giant African millipede. It was a huge black snake." I was scared at first, then I felt sorry for it. Because the owner was starving it in hopes it would die, because they didn't want it anymore. If you put your mind to not be afraid, then you won't be afraid but if you have a state of mind that you're afraid then you will be scared and not be able to touch or hold whatever is grossing you out." It's a mind thing. You can be amazed at how powerful your mind is that over takes the rest of your body. It's amazing. How powerful your mind is. So I took care of it, and after a while, I told the owner to take it back to where they bought it from, and so they did. At one time I had six cats, two ferrets, one bunny rabbit and a dog. Boy did my house stink like a barnyard. I did take care of other animals temporarily, at times some animals I ended up adopting as my own. Sometimes I found an animal that needed nursing back to good health, then I would find them a good loving safe home. Most of the time I took care of them, they ended up being mine for keeps. I took in animals that were being mistreated. Never got help to feed them or give them what they needed. Somehow God provided for all of us. The truth is I was always overdrafting in the bank every month 100.00 the exact same amount every month. Then when I lived by myself I started collecting plastic bags, of every kind and plastic that I could use to preserve something sentimental and meaningful to me. Or just something I wanted to keep for keeps shakes, my Junk drawer became a dump drawer packed with all these plastic things. Now I call myself the bag lady." All these strange habits I developed, as I am getting older. Is this the way I am gonna be, when I get even older?" Lord have mercy!" I hope I don't live to be 100. I wouldn't be able to stand myself." Now am I obsessed with collecting things, or is this hoarding?" Then there was a time I binged on sweets oh my!" I was so addicted to sugar that I would eat something that had sugar in it!" I ate a whole loaf of honey wheat bread that just came out of the oven. To me It was like eating my favorite oatmeal cookies that Just came out of the oven. I had to stop baking homemade bread and cookies. Everywhere you go they push the sugar. Think of it this way this is what I always say. I don't need any sugar because I am sweet enough!" Right!" You gotta keep that in mind. I am not being unkind. I am Just trying to make things a little easier, to look at things in the perspective that what you eat in the physical and in the spirit is who you become and it is scary when you don't have self control. Then again that's the fruit of the spirit And if you look to the one who saves you from all sin because let's face it almost everything we do is sin." we are not perfect only God is.`` And it's okay if each year I become more weird. That's okay I will even shout a little louder. As long as he is beside me I will continue my Journey.' And will try not to be in a hurry. Hopefully things won't look so blurry. I will try to keep things sturdy so that you can keep going on your Journey. In the midst of all this I will give you a kiss and a hug, to remind you you're not alone in this, because he promised that he will be with us, and never leave us or forsake us. He remains true to his word. Don't whisper like a bird. Instead scream as loud as you can, so that we will know where you have been. And in the end, you have spent your time well because he is within. The next day you get up, you do it all over again. For it will never end. Ecclesiastes 1:9 The thing that has been, it is that which shall be; and that which is done is that which shall be done: and there is no new thing under the sun.

CHAPTER FIFTY-TWO

WHEN IS A PET NOT A PET?

Okay so my grandson had a white rat and the rat had nasty tall and beady red eyes and a disgusting nasty looking tale that Just freaked me out!" I was scared to death of it.``Well in time my grandson helped me to get over my fears about this white rat. I had to keep this thought in my head and mind that ``It's not so bad." right!" Well I finally overcame my fear of the rats tail. In time I didn't believe it. I got a white rat with an ecky disgusting looking tail." I named him blanco And Blanco was a real clown he liked to make me laugh!"I never knew that animals could be comedians like people, only they don't talk. So if an animal can make you laugh!" And they know this. That means they are smarter than we think!" Well Blanco had a really cute personality." Yes he did like to make me laugh by the way he acted and he seemed to like it that he made me laugh. Then Blanco got a big bump on him. It was sad he died. But I was told that all the white rats get that growth of that same bump on them then they die. Anyhow, I guess they don't live long. Neither do hamsters. Speaking of hamsters We use to have a whole family of hamsters and they all had cute names. In Fact they had better names than some human people do" What a shame if your folks gave you a name that you detest!" Well you could change it But then that costs money so you figure I'll accept what name I got when I was born. Now my daughter has gotten a little mouse that was a tan color and she named him buttercup." I have to admit he was cute!" But for some strange reason the little mouse would bite her." Then she asked me if I wanted him because he didn't like her. So, I said sure knowing that I wouldn't say no because I have a heart for all animals." So I got the little bitty mouse and he sure was cute!" I couldn't wait to get home from church so that i could take him out of the cage. I would put my hand in his cage then he would use my arm like it was a ladder so he would climb up then I would let him crawl all over my shoulders he liked me to talk to him. I guess he liked the sound of my voice. Then one day he fell off my shoulder and hit the floor. I quickly picked him up. He seemed to be okay. But the next day he died." I was so sad I cried and cried." I felt so stupid a grown woman crying over a tiny tiny mouse I gave myself an headache from crying so much. I even called my mom on the phone and she said don't you have other pets? I think she was thinking of the hamster family." I told her yeah!" she said ``there you go!"I was so attached to that little bitty mouse I was devastated." I'm sure that God cares for all the creatures that he created. Genesis 1:25. God made the beast of the earth according to their kinds and the livestock according to their kinds, and everything that creeps on the ground according to their kinds. And God saw that it was good.

CHAPTER FIFTY-THREE

A REAL PARTY

Well okay my two daughters and I can get loud. I was helping my friend move, then I fell down and broke my ankle." All these years I've seen people wearing casts and using crutches. I never knew that it was so painful.`` Reminds me of a woman having labor pains!" All of a sudden you get very bad pain. Like hard core spasms!" This was intence." And you don't know when it's going to happen. There was a situation that came up where I Jumped up from my wheelchair quickly. It felt like I was standing on a stick. My ankle and foot felt very strange. I hadn't stood on my ankle or foot in so long. I would never wish a broken bone on someone because this is very painful. And if you happen to bruise your bone apparently it takes longer to heal. Okay so here I am with a broken angle. I couldn't even use crushes because of my dizzy spells I get and for not being stable with my balance at times. Well to get in my husband's van My girls were screaming with laughter!" Because I looked ridiculous trying to get on the seat in the car but I had to get in the car first I had no Idea what I was doing but I knew I needed help. But nobody knew how to help me." My girls were hysterical, laughing at me." I guess I was entertaining them.`Then I wanted to take a bath, But I didn't know how I was going to get myself in and out. Tammy was going to help me but she was shouting in my ear really loud, so again the girls and I were being really loud. This was quite the commotion." We all did a lot of laughing." Next I am trying to get dressed and my girls are laughing again," I said don't talk to me because you guys get me confused. Well I got confused all right from all the laughing, I'm surprised that I didn't fall down from laughing so hard. Sure enough, I did put on the wrong underwear, I put the ones that I took off before I took my shower. Then my daughter gives me old fashion underwear to try on. I did fall down on the floor, and laughed like crazy, silly." I wasn't alone. Everybody's laughing hysterically again!" This time we have my other daughter and her son. Now when we get together we have a ball!" So the young man next door to me says, ``Are you all having a party?" We say no this is the norm for us." Then he says you guys sure have a lot of parties." Then we laugh again because there are only three of us that live in our apartment." But it sounds like we are having a party. If he thinks that then I guess we have a party every night." According to him, Proverbs 24:1-2. Do not be envious against evil men, neither desire to be with them. For their heart studieth destruction, and their lips talk of mischief.

CHAPTER FIFTY-FOUR

WONDERING AROUND

Okay so I tend to get lost a lot even in my own home But if I am at the store trying to find something I tend to get confused. When the girls and I walked to the store I forgot which way we came from then my daughter had to lead the way." such a shame So if I am forgetting then I better put myself in a place where I wouldn't have to be alone. So there is this new apartment building that has just been built. And it says it is assisted living. And they have memory care there. So I decided to move there because I was falling a lot. I mean my arms and legs were all bruised up from falling all the time. And I was forgetting a lot.!" I decided to move there but the whole place wasn't memory care. Just a part of it was. I figure if I get worse then I can Just move to memory care. And this place is beautiful and humongous!" but it has been home for six years now." I can't believe it's been six years already." how time flies." I even forget how old I am at times but it's okay Because I can be any age I want to be and people believe me. Just so you don't believe it too," because what are you gonna do?"If you say you're twenty and you act silly and funny." Then people can believe that it is your age as long as you are not wrinkled up." They will believe it." One day I was somewhere doing paperwork and a person was listening to me. They started laughing because every time I was asked the dates of my kids birthday I guess I kept changing them. How do they expect people to remember your kid's birthday when at times you can't even remember your own?" Just teasing, I don't really forget when I was born. At least I am at the right place. I am glad I made this move because I am never really alone. That's important to me in case I have a need. I won't hesitate to ask for help!' All i have to do is yelp!"And when the day is done I am safe and my deed is done I will continue on. For the next chapter of my life is in God's hands and there's no strife. In the end God will win, he's my savior and he takes good care of me. His plan for me is more than I can agree that he has his best for you and me." Proverbs 26:2 Like a sparrow in its fitting, like a swallow in its flying, so a course without cause does not delight.

CHAPTER FIFTY-FIVE

TRYING TO BE NORMAL THAN NORMAL

Okay so when things that are taken away from you that are not in your control you got to work with what you got and remember you haven't forgotten. What it is like to be put on the spot." And it really seems that it is a lot!" But you try to do the best that you can. Don't forget who is within. The spirit of God will make you rich within, to be used for his glory and he will use you when you are not aware that time will tell because he really cares. If you can't do what you think you want to do," He's got something better in store for you. Even if you feel like such a fool it's all a part of learning and growing up, and you feel like you're in school don't give up and try to take control. You better wise up, don't be a fool. Sure it hurts when things don't go right." It's all in a good day of learning, relaxing and taking your shoes off. Don't be in such a rush and flick off the dust, But give God all of the glory!" Listen to the story, that can build you up, give you strength, wisdom if you ask him. He is able to make you stable, and upright this will surely make you bright and out of sight, That's right. It is the word of God, you don't have to sob, all you really need to do is to pour your heart out even if he knows what you're going to say, anyway.

Just give of yourself to the king of all kings,you will be amazed how much he cares, won't you dare? What is normal? You go to the Doctor, because you don't feel good and you try to get some answers as to why you feel like you do. Right away, They want to increase your depression medication. Then if they don't know what it is they call it a virus. Say you are a victim of a violent crime, You are quite out of the ordinary. If you survive, you have physical elements that are usually on an elderly person but who's to say that you have to be a certain age to have problems medically. I'm quite out of the ordinary. I have been diagnosed as having an organic brain -head syndrome!" What in the heck is that?" Did they just make up the name?" I'm telling you I really feel not normal with that dignose. How many people do you know that have a gunshot wound to their head and survived?" So you see, getting treatment from Doctors is unbelievable, In some circumstances. Sometimes they don't know what to do. They say ``Oh wow!" Once I went to the ER because my fake eye was stuck in side my eye socket, and they didn't know how to help me after waiting 4 hours before seeing a Dr. I felt like a freak."This happened a few times. Last eye Doctor gave me something to get it out if it got stuck inside again. Such as life. Romans 12:2 Do Not be conformed to this world, but be transformed by the renewing of your mind, that by testing you may discern what is the will of God, what is good and acceptable and perfect.

CHAPTER FIFTY-SIX

TRY TO KEEP YOUR PEACE

Try to keep your peace in the midst of a storm, If you let the devil steal your joy you're in big trouble Boy!" He will steal your sleep your health your mind your soul and your spirit and he will replace it with bad health, not to mention your appearance your eyes will have big bags under them and you will get a few wrinkles and more gray hair than you anticipated,Then you try to cover up the gray with dye, now who is the one telling a lie?" you better keep that spect out of your eye." I tell you no lie!"keep your mind free from clutter because you don't want to end up in the gutter. So be wise my friend and pay attention to who is withIn. Try to keep up and not fall behind, remember to be kind if you don't mind. You feel like you're not worth a dime. So you bide some time, you wish to dine so you can have peace of mind. In hopes you don't run out of time. So you try to catch up but you know not what to do. In hopes that God will rescue you. What are you gonna do?" It's up to you!" and your mind is two blocks behind and now you feel like you are going out of your mind plus you are running out of time that the boss gave you a deadline. But in time your health is in gear decline. There is no denying that you are slowly dying. By adding all these unpredictable sicknesses and Illnesses and worry and doubt, and infirmities.Don't let the enemy steal your joy, the only things that he will give you in exchange is a shorter life span than what the Lord had in his hand. All across the land people ask for God's Mercy that God would forgive us for our behavior, And ask God for his favor That we will work and do our labor so that we once again can win God's favor. So don't shorten your life over strife Don't lose your sleep at night, over worry It does no good for you to carry on as you are for the one is to help you overcome He's the one that can get things done. And he is the righteous one.`'So let your mind rest for a while please don't ignore me and be in denile. Now this will take awhile. But he who is in charge will always be with you; he will never let you down, for he is always near you whether you acknowledge it or not. He is the one that gave you that thought. And with his precious blood he has bought." Please keep that in thought.`'Remember to give him all that is within. and the whatnots. So if you are believeing then you should be receveing the promises of God for he will carry you through anything you might endure When the storm is over you will be a bit stronger Just hang on a little longer because he is coming soon and he will carry us home for now he is sitting on the throan Don't be afraid for you are not alone. In due time you will hear the trumpets horn. That long ago a special child was born. And when you follow that shining star no matter who You are . You are chosen from afar. And if you continue to keep your eyes focused on him you will be amazed of what's within.' We are all God's children and he lives today in every way, Just trust him and obey. He will be with us from the beginning to the end. In the end we will win. Numbers 6:26 The Lord lifts up his face to you and grant you peace.

CHAPTER FIFTY-SEVEN

ALL THE HUSTLE AND BUSTLE

When the holidays are approaching we all act all crazy and yes there might be more crime and killing but it's because we build ourselves up. In order to bring a smile to somebody's face We get all worked up if that is the case who's gonna take your place at the dining table. When it is fall we wait for the winter but not all. You see everyone is built a little different but we are basically the same inside yet we wrestle as we hustle to get things done for one day of event yet the season brings a spirit of love and yet why can't we love each other everyday not Just when holidays come our way For we know deep down this is how we should be Just to see the reactions to those that might be And Sally met Holly and they got together and sang in harmony. Let us be on bended knee that in our hearts we will agree that everyone that lets the holidays get to them Just remember who's withIn and it's only a matter of time when you wake up and smell the wine then you are ready to dine, No matter if you don't have much to share We really don't care what's on the outside. What matters is the inside where there is treasure that only God can see. In hopes that everyone can be Like true followers of Christ. This will make the Lord pleased that we are not far away In our thoughts and inner being because we belong to the king.This is the best place for human beings. In the end we will be seeing the Lord of Lords and the king above all kings, for all of us human beings.That this hustle and bustle is nothing but a fad. We must appreciate what we had and it's not so bad because of the risin Son that we are his children to whom we belong. He is my precious Jesus and he lives within. Now today it is hard to be content and stay content because things change too fast!" Now this is a gas to try to make it last If you like something and want to keep it in your heart you don't want to let it depart, Just wait a bit you'll change your mind when people are unkind don't Just wine, have yourself a good time because you won't have another opportunity to make this right because it will be out of site you won't see it again go ahead and tell your friend what you intend to end can I make an amends again and again." Shall I say it again?" James 1:4 But let patience have her perfect work, that you may be perfect and entire, wanting nothing.

CHAPTER FIFTY-EIGHT

BEING THANKFUL AND GRATEFUL

When I was a young christian everyday I went around the house and thanked God for everything I even pointed and touched what I was thanking him for. Good thing I didn't have much or I would Just spend time thanking him. When all I had to say was thank you Lord for everything. I was so thankful and grateful for even a little tea bag. I am still very thankful and grateful for everything. It's just that I am not so goofy about it now. Everyday when I wake up I say thank you Lord for letting me be here for another day and thank you for letting the sun shine.I Love you Lord thank you for taking good care of me and my cat. And for letting us live in such a nice place thank you for blessing us and taking good care of us. And for being our Lord and king of everything. Today is Thanksgiving day. Be happy everyday!" Because every day I wake up I thank God. That I can breathe, walk, talk and do God's will. Whatever he has given me that is around me that I have. For I know the one who has blessed me and that he takes care of me. When I look around and see people hurting maybe it could be physically it may be mentally it may be spiritually. I know I am blessed to be able to pray for them. I know that God hears me and he will answer my prayers but it is in his time and in his way. When we are thankful and grateful to the Lord we will see God move, you will see answered prayers and you will see miracles like you've never seen before. You will see God open doors, Then you need to walk through the door that God opens up.When you take the first step it will be easy to keep on for the future that the Lord has for you there's a brighter tomorrow for those of you that have sorrow,

And to those that have given up" you need to learn to trust not on you or somebody else But to the one that can get things done one on one!" It's the one who you can depend on, no matter what you have done. You don't have to be ashamed for the Lord took away that in his name. So that we may gain everything he promised in his name. The most beautiful name you've heard about his presence that you understood. That it's his best that we should depend on. For he is good to keep his word and his promises are endured. He will never let you down because he is always around. You might not like what he is doing in your life now. But he is purifying you and molding you into what he wants you to be. You may grumble and complain, ``That's just the opposite of praise" Now the Lord doesn't like this kind of behavior. He is good and he is our savior!" He is perfect and just, You should be glad and adjust, that we should be grateful and we need to trust.. God is good, he provides all that we need, tender hearted, his patience, his love overwhelms me as he waits to bless me. His goodness protects me, day or night I continue to look to him because in him everything is right and he is the only one that can make things bright. Let me tell you that's alright and out of sight!" 1 Peter 1: 6-7 Wherein you greatly rejoice, now for a season, if need to be in heaviness through manifold temptations;That the trial of your faith, being much more precious than gold that perish, though it be tried with fire, might be found unto praise and honor and glory at the appearing of Jesus Christ:

CHAPTER FIFTY-NINE

TWO SAINT BERNARD DOGS

There are two Saint Bernard dogs that happen to be prejudiced against black people. They didn't mind any other kind brown, yellow or red or white. It didn't seem like it didn't matter to them but the strangest thing that I can't understand about these two dogs is that the neighborhood that they lived in had a lot of black people in their surrounding. I don't know why they are hounding.``Now I think that they might have been hurt or traumatized from the color that they dislike, and maybe they want to get a big bite so they can show who's the boss of their territory. If they could talk they surely have a story. I've never heard of animals being prejudiced against the human race. I guess they have their own taste. But they have to be careful where they put their waste. I am sure you wouldn't want to taste,now I am not trying to gross you out!" Just give a little shout and I will tell you what it's all about. Maybe one day these dogs can overcome this thing that's in their mind and possibly be kind to all mankind. In hopes they can have peace of mind. I guess they are just living in time. They could be giving some peace of mind to some mankind that can give their time to just being a friend to the ones who need it in the end. Do not bend your feelings aside, so you won't hurt somebody's feelings. If you keep it to yourself and not tell anyone else. You will die slowly, the inside of you will be hurt, you don't want to get burnt. For the fire is hot, so this will hit the spot. Now I'm ready to trot, step aside and let me trot. Maybe it's Just a thought. What have you brought to the table?" Are you able to stay stable? Do not be disabled. Where there is a way this day that you can say, I can breathe in, and not have a double chin. I will win because the Lord is within, so let us begin to lift your chin and win, till the end. Let us begin to hold up our chin. Because in the end we will win. Take a spin, hang on tight and fight for what is right now that's out of sight!' Those things will be bright, If you don't fight. Everything is going to be alright. Philippians 3:2 Look out for the dogs, look out for the evil doers, those who mutilate the flesh.

CHAPTER SIXTY

THE FRIEND OF ALL FRIENDS

If you don't have that one special friend Then you need to ask the friend of all friends who happens to be the best in the world. This friend that I am talking about is Christ Jesus the Lord, now be quiet and don't say a word." Just for a moment be still and listen because we do all the talking but if we don't be still. How are we supposed to know what God's will is?" If we don't stop and be still for a while we run here and there and everywhere But are we really moving a bit? Or are you standing still Just to get hit? When what you need is a very big pinch for you to wake up and see what's around you. If you don't ask how will you know in which way you should go, shall you go this way or that way,or the other way any way at all or do you wait until you fall?" I'm telling you the best friend at hand Is the Lord Jesus the best in the land he will never leave you or forsake you He will be holding your hand and at times it will feel like he has you in his arms and you feel like you are flying and there's nobody else."He will always hear you from near and far and no matter where you are, he knows your thoughts and knows what's in your heart and when you ask him for something he already knows what your going to ask you can't fool him and you can't hide a thing and he knows what's best for us even if you think you can't discuss without a fuss, because he is our father and he knows all things don't be afraid to give 100 percent for he is the risen one God has sent. He is our Lord our God our savior our everything he is the master of everything And I am honored to say he is my king." I say Amen." Till the end. Please do not bend out of shape. I won't be late for this special date, I won't make you wait for the time is right and the future is at hand, I won't demand that you take my hand and we will stand in victory. We will shine, that your eyes will be blind from the healing touch of Jesus, Yes he wants to please us. We must want the same for him so that we can please him, Because he is so dear and so near, my dear do not fear. Because the doors will open up, we will need to shut all that doesn't belong to us, all the negativity can be pushed afar, no matter how old you are, the battle has been won. Yet there's things undone. There is a timing for everything. Be glad it's going to be spring, Then you can see what is meant to be, what's in it for you and me. You can surely agree, that what is meant for you is meant for me, can't you see we were made to be, God's creation, that he is pleased that he belongs to us, and we belong to him. You can plainly see what's in it for you and me. Can you agree on what's in it for me, that i just got to be me. Then I can be set free indeed. We don't have to speed, Time is only a vapor in the air, at times it can bring you down in despair, then it will disappear in thin air don't get all up tight because you've got to fight and hang on tight for what is right, Because time does not stand still hurry up get up that hill, when you reach the top, don't look back Just stay in the act. And that's a fact.

I Just want to say Amen again and again!" That's all right to do it over and over again. No harm done in giving praise as long as you're not in a daze, let me rephrase the importance of giving praise. This is important for your daily walk, that you walk the walk, and talk the talk of love to each other then you won't bother no other. Only try to keep peace and harmony, for this is God's way that you can live in peace, and all the wonderful gifts he has for you. He will tell you what to do. All in good time, so let your light shine, no one can take it away, because it's here to stay, hang on tight anyway if you want to be welcomed to the kingdom of God. You must be like the one in whom we trust. That all things are possible, to them that believe, that you can achieve, what the father has for you and for me. I'm sure you can agree that he laid down his life for you and for me. That the time is coming that we will be together for eternity. I believe this for you and for me. This is heavenly, for all who come to bow down to the throne of God, in which we have sought, all over this place, this is not the case to bring your sad face all over this place, In that case you can chase your dreams and visions, all you want. Or bend your knee to the Majesty, now this I know you can agree, that this is a wonderful passion to have, to be thankful for what you have, and to want to see it come to pass, and not looking through a glass, you surely will have a blast, when this comes to pass. You don't have to ask what the benefits are, you will surely get your kicks, when you see your visions, and dreams come to pass. You will have the last laugh. In this you will be glad and that's not all bad. So don't be sad. Be glad. Because as quickly as you get it, It can be taken away, you will want it to stay, so hang on for the ride, you won't have any stride. For he will be with you at your side. You will not be alone, He's got everything in tack, so you won't have to be the class act. You can be real, here's the deal: hang on tight when the time is right, put up a fight, then you will reunite with others, your sister's and your brothers. Just remember there are others waiting to be reunited with the Father. Remember there is no other that can take his place for he has blessed us with his grace and in the heavenly place. I say Amen and Amen again and again. This is not the end.

John : 15:13 Greater love has no man than this, that a man lay down his life for his friends.

CHAPTER SIXTY-ONE

FINDING MR. RIGHT

I see a few people that ask for prayer to help them find a spouse or a help mate, Mr. or Miss right. Now this shall be a delight. Nowadays the internet has online dating but you can't trust anyone because they turned it around for what they were supposed to do. You can be whoever you want to be and you can talk to as many people as you feel the need to be. But you can't fool people all the time, So they move on to the next. I had a fella that sent me a picture that was supposed to be him but I know that was a Joke because it looked so obvious that it was a clipping from a magazine. Yet I kept talking with him because it was fun to text each other everyday. I guess I developed feelings for him but I don't think he developed feelings for me. If he did he never said anything to me about it. He did say he had a daughter named Isabell. That his wife died then somebody else tried texting me while I was talking to him. This man got scared and sighed off in a hurry and I never heard from him again. There was another man that claimed to be a Doctor but he was nothing but a liar. He said he had a daughter then he wanted to talk to her but he could not get in touch with her. Then he asked me if I could go to the store to buy some cards so he could get in touch with his daughter. I said, "What's that?" Then I told him no because I don't drive plus I don't have any money. That was the last time I talked to him. Then there was another guy that claimed to be a general and that he had a daughter that was a teenager. Anyhow he was at camp so he said that he wanted me to send him 200$ I said what?" He says Just 200$ that's all, then he said when he gets back in the city he will pay me back. I said I don't have any money well that was the last time I talked to him. Then I talked to another man for a while. He has a son but he says his wife died in a car crash on her way home from work. Apparently she was a nurse. This man is in the Navy and ready to get out. He was going to retire. His son is apparently in a boarding school in New York city. Because he had no one to care for his son. He says he has a sister but they haven't talked in years since their mother died. The time is getting closer for him to come home and to retire. One day he is stressed out and I ask what's wrong. He says the place where he gets his mail from is closing down and that he needs to get his mail and his values sent somewhere. Can I receive his mail at my place? I said yes that was fine. Well we start the process then they are telling me I have to pay for the air freight and that was going to be over 3000.00 $ I said what!" I wouldn't even pay that for my own mail. I don't have any money then the guy says you don't love me if you don't give me the money. Then I said to him I really don't have any money. If you don't believe me then I don't want to be with you. Then there was another man before this guy that was in the Navy and he had a son." He says the nanny takes care of him and his house. Because his wife died. He was to retire in a few months and we planned to get married. As soon as he got out. Then he got transferred to a different country where they needed his help. It was really bad where they sent him; it was bad with the coronavirus. Tuberculosis, Pneumonia. We only talked a few times then I never heard from him again. I guess I will never know what happened to him. My heart was sad that I lost what I thought was my true love, my knight and shining armor. I did talk to many other men, But nothing ever developed or materialized from our friendships. Then I Just stopped talking to guys online. Because you're only asking for trouble I guess I will stay single so I am not going to mingle. It's safer that way but a little lonesome but I'd rather be lonesome than to have lots of troubles. At least I will have peace and my whole life I desired peace and now I found it. It's with the Lord. In him I find comfort that no human can give. If you find it in your heart to forgive this is how you should live. Now that's living. Now it is Ironic that every man happens to have a child and that their spouse has passed away. Well no more talking to guys on the internet for me. This is heartbreaking If you happen to fall in Love. I never knew that this could happen, that you could fall in love with a person whom you've never met in person or ever hearing his voice or seeing him in person.`` But the men take advantage of a lonely widow and especially if they know you are a Godly Christian They will take all that they can. Not all are like that but it's hard to keep up." of who is scamming you and trying the best that he can. Then you find out he's not a real man. He is only a scam and he will take you for all that he can. But that's living please don't keep on giving. You've got to keep up to know the do's and the whatnots. You have to be ahead of the game so you won't be let down and ashamed. For this world is getting darker and you need to know who is smarter. Yes times have changed but it starts out for the good then it turns into something that was miss understood. Then you're stuck with your head in a hood. But life keeps moving on and you want to know what you have done. To have all the mishaps that you have endured you think to yourself Is this a punishment or discipline for all I've done wrong. When in morality, This is you learning how mankind really is and that one day you will wake up and all this is nothing but a bliss. But in realality this is a test for you to keep moving on and that in the end you will be strong. That this is Just living Remember the key is don't keep giving. You need to also receive sure it will be hard at first then get better for only a time can you stand and not wither. Just try to keep it all together. James 1:17 Every good gift and every perfect gift is from above, coming down from the father of lights, with whom there is no variation or shadow due to change.

CHAPTER SIXTY-TWO

KEEPING UP WITH THE JONESES

Today's society it's like people are in some kind of race or competition with one another to see who has the better Job better house better spouse, better kids, better salary in pay and whose kids are really gay, this is sad that even in the church people stop going because they say they are tired of the competition of who dresses better than the other and if you had to you would sell your own mother people are envious of one another and they don't care they Just want the best that they can get no matter what it is And technology is outrageous you be lucky to use a phone or to know which way was home and then you began to get a little feel of what are the best deals. Now Christmas time is only about getting all that you can without giving it a thought of who is buying and who is giving or what you have bought the stores are all in for competition with one another even ask your brother. And the black Friday is even blacker than black it's Just a clutch to get you in to be their customer and their customer for life long. But you know deep down you don't belong. Then your neighbor says to you hey what's wrong because they are glad that you are wearing a frown then they can rub it in your face that they have no stress, they are happy, and stress free, but you can't agree because you know that just can't be. And their world is perfect and they brag about their child is doing so well so they boast and glolt that their child is a great success and how beautiful they are, on how they dress, don't forget the comparison of how much you spent to get what you are wearing and this is the intent. Now if you don't hang out with people like that you're in the clear but just remember you better stay clear. Then you won't have to fear. You must be dear. And this is what you call Just living, who are we kidding?" Are you being forgiving, or do you give to get back what you lack, don't let it be an act. In fact don't give to out give someone else. Just give with a cheerful heart, don't regret of drifting apart. In the end you win some, lose some, all in all you can recall that you are a doll. You keep it to yourself as I recall.``That's not all, Actions speak louder than you all." When we got our first house It was a nice quiet neighborhood. But my son was not treated well, because he was the only black person on the team. My son is half African American and half Mexican. So he did not get treated well. All the other kids were white. They were mean to my son and they would not let him play football. They beat him up for no reason, I guess their reason was for the color skin my son had. My son did get to be in boy scouts, then he got some badges to put on his shirt, I sewed them on crooked. I did not know that they were supposed to be Ironed on. No wonder my son got beat up!"

Galatians 6:4 pay careful attention to your own work, for then you will get the satisfaction of a job well done, and you won't need to compare yourself to anyone else.

CHAPTER SIXTY-THREE

YES MEANS YES AND NO MEANS NO

Have you had trouble keeping your word? Well it's hard to stick to your word watch and listen to what you have heard growing up. My mother would say one thing then she would turn around and say the Opposite, she said she feels sorry for who she is disciplining and then she gives in. This was confusing as I grew up to not know what is due and what is not. Of course I was not home too much because I became an workaholic in my teens I guess this was my way of escape of all the bad vibes that lingered in the house When i was at work I was happy go lucky because at home it felt yucky I never knew what it was Now I know our home was not a real home it was Just a place that we had a roof over our head. Now that I am grown I wished I had a real family and a place to call home. Where there was real love from God above. Because he is the maker and master of everything I am so glad that God," Taught me about love. He is my heavenly father from above. Yes there's time to live life like we were intended to. We can learn to give of ourselves whether it be time, money or talent, or your gifts. Be sure you give it your all, to get the best results that you have to give for we may never be given this chance again so walk through the door that has been opened to you. You'll be glad of what you've had because that's a part of living. Just because you were taught a certain way doesn't mean it's there to stay because there is another way there's always room for improvement especially if you know how to rule it. It's a matter of opinion of where you draw the line. Please don't step out of line; you have plenty of time to make your world shine. Please stop pretending you are blind you are always on my mind and always remember to be kind, you still have time. Please don't waste my time. Now this is reality of the real world, stop pretending that you haven't heard that this is the real world, it's all recorded in God's word. If you don't believe me, look for yourself, all that is expected from us according to God's word don't tell me you haven't heard of what's recorded in God's word. I challenge you this day to do it God's way If you feel this is too much remember what God's son has done for us. There could never be enough money to repay what sacrifices that God has paid with his own blood. He paid a high price for us so we could have freedom and an abundant life filled with all the good things that he has for us. Just remember you are a child of God so don't make a fuss or this would be truly unJust. If you can give him your trust. Another one bites the dust, don't be disgusted." Give him your all in whom you have trusted. Matthew 5:33 Simply let your yes be yes and your no's be no's.

CHAPTER SIXTY-FOUR

THE GRASS IS ALWAYS GREENER ON THE OTHER SIDE

I bet you wish you had this and that but only it's a fad, That lasts for just awhile. Then it goes out of style please don't be in denile rest your head awhile, don't worry if you are in style Just relax a while after you run a mile take a deep breath and hold it in for a bit then let it go as you go with the flow let us take a stroll Be carefull not to fall I'll be a doll and help you up Just stay cool and don't get worked up for the grass is always greener on the other side you must go on no matter how wide or how tall or how small. Just like dreaming that you be screaming about how fast the tide is coming take your time to jump right in then you will have time to begin, that life flies by and it doesn't matter what your age you want what everyone else wants and it is never enough because the more you get the more you want Now I'm telling the truth I'm being upfront. This will sound a bit blunt, this is not a front. For I tell it like it is now pay attention so you won't be missed. Now the grass is always greener on the other side it's because you want what you don't have then if you get what you want you'll look for something better than what you have it's instilled in you maybe you can't be still and wait for the bill because you have a long ways up the hill and it gives you the chill going up that big hill so take a chill pill and try to relax Don't go running to get your ax we don't want any trouble so hurry up on the double were not here to stir up trouble, now hurry up on the double. The grass is always greener on the other side. Please open your eyes wide. Because you have to have the best make sure you have a bird's nest to fall upon Incase you stumble and happen to get in trouble you have a back up plan to fall on it's all in a day's work and all is done. Then truly your life has just begun. Then another day has arived, don't stress or strive, let the other person go first and remember what God's word says. The first will be last and the last will be first Matthew 20:16 So the last shall be first, And the first last: for many be called, but few chosen. Luke 14:24 For I say unto you, that none of those men which were bidden shall taste of my super. Now this is the truth that is spoken to us if you don't believe me go look it up. For God's word is true to the tale of all these particles that are foretold. That God is alive and so is his word Please tell people about the good news Jesus brings to us. That he is our redeemer and if it weren't for him. You or I wouldn't be here. This is the truth I couldn't tell you any clearer. Now be a dear don't interfere with what God has planned so stay near. Jeremiah 29:11 For I know the plans I have for you declares the Lord. Plans to prosper you and not to harm you. Plans to give you hope and a future."

CHAPTER SIXTY-FIVE

CONFUSION

Are you in confusion?" You are not the only one there are lots of people that are in the conclusion that they are in a delusion of their confusion and so they get uptight and wondering if they are doing right or did they lose sight of the things that are really right and so this is my conclusion what I think is a solution of this resolution but if you are in delusion than that could lead to confusion. Therefore we don't want you to be confused. Please don't feel like you're being used. Because this is not a resolution to the conclusion of your confuseion This is not a resolution of delusion to your confusion to your solution don't be in confusion as we try to make a resolution to the thought that this could be a resolution to a great reunion. So if you're tired of being confused let me tell you some news that he and he alone has all the answers of the unknown Just try to focus on him that he will be with you through thick and thin if only you will let him In. And if you do so I promise you this will be the best decision you have ever made. Now you are on the right track. You let him take the lead and remember to have time to read the word of God for it brings life to those who seek his face. He will give us mercy and grace. Just keep seeking him and he will be there to meet you face to face. One day we can be with him then we can say grace in the most wonderful place. 1 Corinthians 14:33 God is not an author of confusion, but of peace of all churches of the saints.``

CHAPTER SIXTY-SIX

TRY ODELE IT'S SWELL

Now I'm not Just talking about a new product that came out let me tell you what it is all about then you can shout and rave what it's done for you.You can hold your breath until you turn blue." I'm telling you what to do to stay on cue!" This new stuff that you've been hearing about really does wonders for your hair. There is nothing that can compare. This will make your hair shine , it will feel devine I'm not giving you a line, I wouldn't waste my time. I have seen results when people have used it, they used it and didn't abuse it. The first time I used it I felt like I was on cloud nine but it was just for a short time. I could not believe the results this shampoo has done. It's amazing I have to shout and tell what's it all about. A friend of mine tried it out and the results that i have seen makes me want to shout and scream. My friend had curly frizzy hair after using Odele. We just have to tell it's swell. My friend showed me her hair. It looked silky and smooth and soft. It was so beautiful!" I couldn't believe what my eyes had seen. How amazing Odele is You don't have to be a wiz, to find out what it is. Now my friend will never be lost now that she's tried odele she says No more Freaky Frizzy now it's silky and soft. You don't have to take my word, try it for yourself. I guarantee you will never go back to your old shampoo. This I promise from my heart once you try it you will never depart. Because this is my secret for beautiful hair in which I am convinced that none can compare there's none like this none not one. Odele is swell I speak the truth about my secert I promise you will be blessed. I dare you to give it a try I am not telling you no lie. When you use it there will be a twinkle in someone's eye when they see your hair. Don't be surprised if you get complements about your hair you'll be glad for the switch that you have done. It's because of Odele let me tell you it's swell. You'll be glad you switched. This is not a hitch now if you are in confusion let me give you a conclusion that you don't have to be confused because Odele is swell you can tell let the results speak for itself let me tell you it won't be left on the shelf. It might cost a pretty penny but I can tell you this is not funny. This is worth the money you spend, how can I say it any other way, that you're in for a special day" It's best to be neat then you will be complete. So this is my secret that I liked to share with you.``That you don't have to be rich or famous to get great results, it's contagious. Just remember to try Odele, it's swell. Now how can I make this any more clearer? This is what you need to have as your gear. Just try it and you will be convinced that this is right and you are happy with the results. I can not express it any more than I already have. That this is the deal that you would want to steal. I am telling you this is for real. Is it a deal?" That I speak the truth you will find it in you once you try it you won't depart. Because this is like art in which you experince and take a chance to make something from nothing in the end you're anxious to see the results of what creation you have done with your hands, when you see the outcome is swell when you leave it to Odele. You can really tell that it's swell, who are you gonna tell?' That a gal, I can tell that you're quite the gal and that is swell that you're gonna tell others about Odele. Your quite the person to pay attention to what is important, that it makes a big difference once you try it, you will more than like it you will beam like a star no matter who you are this will be better by far, then you can play your guitar, people will know who you are if you want to be discrete lay low down to your feet be cautious and be neat can we agree? To a tee, that just has to be me. Then I can be truly free.Yes indeed, can you see?" The moment you are set free, everything will fall into place now I rest my case.

Romans 3:10-12 As it is written: There is no one rightous, not even one; there is no one who understands; there is no one who seeks God. All have turned away, they have together become worthless; there is no one who does good, not even one... for all have sinned and fall short of the glory of God.``

CHAPTER SIXTY-SEVEN

DON'T GO SHOPPING ON AN EMPTY STOMACH

I am warning you to never go shopping on an empty stomach. I don't care if it's a grocery store or a bath and beauty store. You put anything and everything that you think looks good to eat if it smells good you want to eat it." And even if it is not edible. Then when you get to the check out cashier you think that maybe you took somebody's cart by mistake because you don't recognize some of these Items that are in the cart. Everybody is in a hurry to get their things paid quickly and to rush out quickly. But that's not going to happen because you are holding up the line. The next time you are in a rush to get in and out of the store as quickly as you can. You are wondering why these strange items are in the cart. You've got shampoo that smells like strawberries and conditioner that smells like bananas.' Just to name a few, you start taking things out of your cart that you didn't have on your shopping list because you're not sure if you will have enough money to pay for all this stuff that's in your cart. So it's better to deduct things from your cart now than when you are at the cashier. Where you will be humiliated and embarrassed, and you're holding up the line. And people are getting annoyed with you for holding up the line. Then you put the shampoo in the produced items and some meat products by the toilet paper, Okay you get what I am saying. Now the next time you go to the store and walk down the aisle you see odd things in places they don't belong and you think to yourself ``hum!" somebody just stuck this thing anywhere that looks disgusting." And what about the coupons: buy two get one free. Oh!" boy that's a good deal, Then you think to yourself am I even gonna use these items. So in reality you lost money not saved.`` Then you see a tower built up in the aisle that may be of a product that the store wants you to buy. So you pull one out but the whole tower that was built up high comes crashing down and as they fall one by one it hits you on the head making you feel like you've been through a beating of your life" but you feel a little light headed because you've been hit on the head with each bottle hitting you. Now your memory is kind of off track. You call your friend's name but that's not her name. Then you make your friend a little nervous and worried." Because you're talking like you are delusional!" So you alarm the people that work in the store even more than the owners. They follow you around the store and keep asking you if you are alright !" not because they care about you or are concerned for you but because they are worried that you will file a lawsuit against them. you're not thinking straight because of being knocked on the head a few hundred times." Now a man that is sitting in a mobilized wheelchair runs into a tower of wine bottles that are stacked up high. Great, all the bottles come crashing down and the glass is shattering all over the place, not to mention wine splashing me. Now with my light headedness it really makes me look and smell like a real live wineo not to mention I probably have a head concussion. At the end of the day, you wonder why you are so exhausted." Matthew 25:35 I was hungry and you gave me something to eat.

CHAPTER SIXTY-EIGHT

SPREAD A LITTLE CHRISTMAS CHEER!

Okay so it is Christmas time again" sure does come quickly!" I went to the store with my friend. Of course I have to go with somebody, because I don't drive. I am dangerous Just walking and I am so glad that I didn't get a motorized scooter. I probably will be running into the wall and people and things. Nope not me I don't trust myself. At least I am being honest here. I think the old saying is true, if you don't use it you lose it!" As far as using a wheelchair or scooter. I wouldn't want to lose my ability to walk."Besides I have enough issues." Outside while I was leaving the store. A lady was yelling ``hey wait !" Wait, here, she has a plastic bag in her hand and in the bag was the coffee in her hand,that I put back because I didn't have enough money to buy it. She was holding it up in the air like it was a prize I won. She said this is for you. I said no I didn't have enough money to pay for it." The woman said ``It's okay here Merry Christmas." the woman touched my heart. I wanted to cry. I said thank you so much Merry Christmas to you too God bless you. It's nice to know that there are some kind decent people in the world. Then I started ordering stuff from the catalog. Well I started to get addicted to ordering from them. My bill got very high not once not twice but at least four times. That my bill was hundreds of dollars. So one year I decided to give everything away to people for Christmas. Now this was fun to do.`` It was on my heart to give to a certain family. The next year I found myself ordering things online for this family again but this time I kept myself from hundreds of dollars shopping spree." I decided to order stuff online all year around for these families that were on my heart to give. This was a very meaningful thing for me to do.``

This felt pretty amazing to give" than it was to receive I thought I had known what it meant to give with a cheerful heart and I thought i knew what it meant when the Lord says it is better to give than to receive" It's pretty amazing when you can continue to learn what you know already but in a deeper level and deeper understanding than what you thought you knew. That's amazing. But that is God's way of blessing us and enlightening us to be the salt of the earth. And to be the light that shines so bright even in your darkest hours and needs. God will remain true to his word, That all you have to do is believe that he will use you in ways you never knew He will make all things anew. He says he will supply all of our needs. Maybe not all our wants", But all of our needs His word is true Indeed. John 13:1-17 Now before the feast of the Passover, when Jesus knew that his hour has come that he should depart out of this world unto the father, having loved his own which were in the world, he loved them unto the end. And super being ended, the devil now being put into the heart of Judas Is-cari-ot,Si-mon's son, to betray him; Jesus knowing that the father has giving him all things into his hands,and that he has come from God, and went to God; He rises from supper, and laid aside his garments; and took a towel and girded himself. After that he poured water into a basin, and began to wash the disciples feet, and to wipe the disciples feet, and to wipe them with the towel that he was girded. Then he came to Simon Peter: Peter said to him, Lord why you wash my feet? Jesus answered and said to him, what I do to you, you know not now; but you shall know there after. Peter said to him, you shall never wash my feet. Jesus answered him if I do not wash your feet you have no part of me. Simon Peter said unto him, Lord, not my feet only, but my hands and head. Jesus said to him, he that is washed does not need to save to wash his feet, but is clean everywhere; you are clean, but not all. For he knew who should betray him; Therefore he said you are not all clean, therefore he knew the one who will betray him. This is why he said not all are clean. So after they had washed their feet, and had taken his garments, and sat down again, he said to them ``do you know what I have done to you?"You call me Master and Lord: and you say well; for so I am. For I have given you an example, that you should do as I have done to you. I say to you, the servant is not greater than his Lord; neither he that is sent greater than he that sent him. If you know these things, happy if you do them."

CHAPTER SIXTY-NINE

WHEN YOUR PET IS YOUR BABY

Some people can't have human babies. They want kids but for some reason they cannot conceive so they adopt kids and some adopt an animal. Just depends on what they prefer and some people can only have one then they decide to grow their family, but nothing seems to work. Then there are others that want to help those to grow their family by being a sergeant's mother. So they trust a stranger to carry their baby the whole nine months. Then they give the baby to the ones who have been waiting patiently for their bundle of Joy. This is a very hard thing to do. But if there weren't any people willing to carry your baby for almost a year to have the baby to see it born, and have to give them up, never seeing them again is a very hard thing to do. But it takes all kinds of people to make this world go around. There are people that are very intelligent, there are special needs people, there are people from all over the world, there are people near and far, there are animals that become peoples babies whether they have human kids or not. Now for myself my pets are my babies, And I tell you I spoil all of my babies, I love them so dearly. My pet is my baby . Because my kids have grown up and they have moved on. So it's Just my pet and he is my companion. I talk to him like he is human and my next best friend after Jesus. Sometimes your pet talks to you in his own way but this I can say that you do understand each other in your own ways. Your pet will stay true to you and he will protect you in any way. He will always be loyal to you. He will love and adore you. But of course, you will feel the same as he does because he's your second best friend. One thing that is so true you can tell him all your secrets and you won't have to worry about him telling anyone else. Another thing for sure is that your pet is your baby and will always be that in him you found a true friend. You stay together through thick and thin, no matter the obstacles that get in your way your baby will love you, until the very end. When it's time to say goodbye to this world Just remember that one day you will be together again. For now you can enjoy each other's company. My cat Rocky was given to me by my grandson, because the cat I used to have for 20 yrs. Had to be put to sleep because he got stomach cancer.This was so hard to say goodbye. I cried and cried, The vet let me hold his paw while they put him to sleep. So my grandson did not want me to cry anymore, so he said I could have his cat to take care of. Besides, they were not hardly home because my daughter works and my grandson went to school, and had sports and things to attend to. They had 2 chihuahua dogs, which the cat and dogs didn't get along too well." Besides Rocky and I needed each other. God is so good all the time and all the time God is good. To care for our every need don't you agree?' There is a woman who works where I live, and she tells people about Rocky that he watches TV, and when somebody comes to my door Rocky greets them. He's very smart, he's almost human, people say about him. He greets everyone and anyone, so they can say hello to him and pet him. And sometimes he's so loving he will touch somebody's heart so they will bring him a treat. Now tell me that isn't smart to put on his charm. The woman that works where I live tells people about Rocky, They don't believe it.But it is true. Now one day I had a friend come over and play cards with me. Rocky nibbled at her toe. She said to Rocky ``did you just bite my toe?" Rocky replied by nodding his head up and down saying yes." We busted out laughing." This was hilarious!" We couldn't believe it!" What we just saw. You know what I mean chilly bean. This cat is clean if you know what I mean. Because you have found a true friend. Luke 12:6 Are not five sparrows sold for two pennies? And not one of them is forgotten before God.

CHAPTER SEVENTY

WATCH OUT FOR THE TRIALS IN YOUR LIFE THEY CAN MAKE YOU OR BREAK YOU

Some people don't seem to have any problems in their life they seem happy all the time, deep down between you and me that's Just a mask that they wear because that's not real life everyone has hard times from time to time, that's Just normal to have some difficulties, Yes there are trials and complications, that come your way this is a time when you are being tested to see which way you will go. And a time when you toss and turn and you waiver to and fro, And you wonder which way to go. You keep your eyes on Jesus, he will show you the way. He will guide you, he will make you strong, he will always love you no matter what you have done wrong. He can make something gigantic look small, he can make a short person be very tall and that's not all. He can take all the hurt away, he can change the color of the day. And when you feel sick and weak he can heal you and make you strong to be able to carry on. You will be able to take anything that's thrown at you as nothing, because you are meant to carry on. For the good shall come to you if FDA aproved. He will build you up so that you can be used for his kingdom and glory. He will reign forever, you know he is clever." He has a special plan for you, and your life, that he is preparing for you but you are not quite ready for what he has for you. You're not quite tough enough for the battle that's in store for you. He will make you anew. Don't be in such a hurry, you've got plenty of time in which to be ready. You need to be steady, so get ready and always be on guard.

Keep close to your heart, don't drift apart, you know that you are a piece of art. and have gone through the fiery fire. I know you will get tired, but it is not my desire to see you struggle. All I ask is that you see me through the day, then you won't be in dismay. He will be beside you all the way . Keep on going and do not stop. It's very important to keep moving forward. At the end of the day.You've had it God's way so there is no delay for decay, Oh by the way, It's a new day. You are stronger than you were the day before. You are blessed because you have walked through the open door and you don't have to be afraid any more. Each day is a challenge and each day you break away and each day you fight to stay strong and courageous, let this be contagious"maybe you waver to and fro but in reality you take authority in Jesus name for the enemy knows this is not a game. Then each and every day that you tackle it. It will get easier than the day before. Remember who's walking beside you. so Remember to watch out for those trials they will either break you or make you stronger Just hang on a little while longer than you can get stronger. Be the best at God's request, be what God ordained you to be. He is our Father and he will not let us be. He is good, don't you agree?" I say Amen!" again and again." With all this praise I have spent, nothing compares for what lies ahead, so I suggest that you take the bid in what you have done, to make things right. If you do, you can pursue seeing the brighter side. Even If this doesn't make sense, It will work out in your defense. In the end this will all make sense. Even the things that happen to us, that we cannot control, we have to have faith that we will get through it. Even if we don't know what's happening to us. It may take awhile to find out. We can rest assured, that God's will is better than ours. I was having very heavy menstruations ever since I was a teenager, I would bleed for 12 days. And would get very sick.when I had a day off of work, I would take the day off of school and lay in my bed with very painful cramps. I would have a hot water bottle pressed against my stomach. Don't know if they have those old fashioned rubber water bottles or bags. Nowadays. After I had children it kind of lightened up. Where I didn't have them so heavy or so long. Then when I was in my early 30's they began to become really heavy again, I would wear a tampax and feminine pad and still bleed right through. Once I was at church I bled so bad that it went through my panties and dress and all over the cushion of the church. How embarrassing and humiliating that was. I am sure they knew who was sitting there. I rushed to the restroom and told my youngest daughter to let me borrow her underwear." She did not want to give them up. She said, why don't you borrow Tammy's underwear, instead of mine. I said just give me your underwear now," I only had a feminine pad in my purse so you had to wear underwear to wear a feminine pad. I was desperate." Then while I was having a garage sale in my garage, I had my menstruation, and I was bleeding very heavily. I went right through a tampon and a feminine pad that I had on, not realizing that it went through my pants that I had on.It was so bad it looked like I had been shot." I went to see the specialist in ob gyn. They did give me some birth control to try to lighten my periods. It really didn't help me. Then they did an ultrasound and found there was a cyst in my ovary that was as big as a softball. So the next thing to do is I had to get a Hysterectomy. I was glad that my mom and oldest brother were there when I woke up and they wheeled me to the recovery room. And I was so blessed that the Dr. gave me some flowers in a vase on my nightstand. I was so glad not to have any more periods. As far as having kids, I was glad I got to have 3 children, and I was scared to have any more children. Yes this is sad to not be able to have any more children. But it is for the best. I felt blessed that I had a few. Some people can't have any. That's why I felt blessed.2 Corinthians 6:18 And all things are of God, who has reconciled us to himself by Jesus Christ, and has given to us the ministry of reconciliation;

CHAPTER SEVENTY-ONE

TRYING TO GET AN ACCOUNT:

Nowadays trying to get an account open with the IRS. Let me tell you you won't be blessed they will make you stress unless you get a divine appointment then you won't be in disapointment" So you keep on trying over and over to get this done, And you feel like you are on the run, trying to get things done. You are going around and around in circles, because you have to keep repeating what you've already done. In order to get somewhere don't you dare give up. You've come so far in this process to get some progress. In this process, Now they have you confused Yes they lit a fuse But don't give up trying because you feel like you're dying, But you keep on trying and even if you know you will ever speak to a real live human being you still keep on trying there is no denying that you want to get progress. In this process it might take awhile. There is no denial it will take awhile. Just when you've come a long way doesn't mean you're almost done. When you think that you've come a long way they push you another way. You have to start redoing what you've already done and it's not fun to have to start it all over again another day. Please get out of my way, your insides are shouting that you are through pouting for nothing. So you try another day in your own way. And this is what they say won't you call another day, they might as well say you are in the way. Hey, hey what can I say!" Because the system is shut down. Now you've got a big frown and you are let down. And you feel like a clown because you have been let down. And you don't want to go back to town. You keep on being persitsant. You cross your fingers that this is the day that everything goes your way. And you say okay this is my day that I will make progress in this process to make an account no matter how long it takes no matter if you have to keep repeating yourself over and over you'll be glad when it's done and over believe me this is not fun." You will be glad when this is done but you've got to make progress in this process. The closest you can get to talking to a real live person is video chat. Let me tell you this is where it's at.!" When you finally get this project done you will be back on a run for all the time you spent trying to get things done. All this was very unnecessary because when you finally got an account you didn't get to find what you were looking for. Then this was all a waste of time. In addition you got a few gray hairs and gained a wrinkle or two. Now what are you gonna do?" Hold your breath, don't you stress. Let me second guess. Now you don't know what to do. I guess you could keep this acount You worked so hard to get. But it does you no good. It's just another app that's on your phone to clutter up your memory, In which you worked too hard to get. Now don't get upset, you don't have to get rid of it Just yet." Now that's just living right!" This is not the end but only the beginning. I don't need to repeat myself. Just because some people do, I am not like you, so what should I do to make things less uncomplicated? Well there's really no easy way to go around it. I must say be prepared for some new exciting things. It will get easyier the more you do it but who wants to keep repeating themselves? This gets old the more you do it. The more they ask and this whole time you're thinking, let's get done with this task. When you get done you think to yourself this task better last for all the pictures you had to keep taking over and over and for the information you had to re- submit, This is a situation that caused you to need a vacation." There needs to be an evaluation on the situation, for the cause of vacation" If you have been through what I have. Then you will clearly need a mask for this task. Now I'm not talking trash. Shall I give you some laughing gas? Because it is obvious that you need a lift to pick up your spirits that have been degraded. I will try my best to do what I do at my best. Then everything works out to the benefit of doubt. That all things work out without a doubt let me shout what it is all about!" This is the day I will be glad and give a shout. Philippians 4:18 a sweet smelling sacrifice that is exceptable and pleasing to God.

CHAPTER SEVENTY-TWO

WHEN THE WORLD GOES AROUND AND AROUND.

When the world goes around and around it may seem that you are standing still in the reality you are not, you're in a different spot and boy !"you're getting hot on the spot if you don't trot but be still then the wind will gust in where you began to wonder what is all this clutter that muttered, in this outered weather that is brewing don't be frightened of the gusty wind, stand still and take it all in. Then you can begin to win the battles within. I tell you the truth, there is nothing to lose. So be on guard about what regards you to a tea please remember me won't you agree that to be inspired from top to botom it really happens all of a sudden, And when you think you've thought it all through another thing comes and smacks you on the head and your left for dead Instead you are overwhelmed that you've gotten a second chance, you just want to dance for this is your chance, then you are thankful and grateful for every little thing and you wished you would have done things differently. you can't change what has already been done. And you wish you could have saved your special dish, now you have to make a wish. And when you wish upon a star I wonder how you are from up close to a far, how I wish upon a star. In regards to who you are, And when you wonder what to do next just remember you can't count on your ex for now it's just you and the Lord. He has promised me you will never be bored." When you have to be strong for long, you know where you belong and in time you learn the ropes, you know how to cope. So you deal with pressure your whole life through, you learn what you can do without pressure, or you learn when to scream and when to shout." let me tell you what it's all about!" Let me give you a little gesture. I will not love you any less. You can't go back and undo what's been done. Just let it go and be done it does no use to be on the run when your caught up you won't be so distraut just remember don't look back but look ahead then you will have the benefit of a doubt. That you are worth it no doubt. As the world turns around and around. Just remember you're not standing still, Remember to flip the bill." Now that I drilled it into your mind please remember to be kind and never mind what people say they always have their mouth running just as long as you stay true to your belongings. You know you are doing right, don't let them get you uptight."If you have to look any farther than your own backyard to find that peace that you so seek. Let me tell you you're missing the peek and when it's time to be meek I will give you a peck, oh what the heck"you don't want to be a redneck. you want to have an Impact. Of only good stuff to digest, now let me tell you this is far better to diegest I might even let you be my next guest. Remember my request at your best. Now I am guessing you 've come a little farther to work harder than you've ever worked before, it's you I adore. And this is how the world works year after year." Be a dear and get my gear, without any fear, can you hear?" nothing can harm me if you are near now step on it and push it into gear you better take a look in the rear view mirror now let's cheer. Now this is how it's laid out, That you may shout about what's taking place in my space. This is not a race, please don't leave a trace that we may be found it's time to take off from the ground, don't make a sound or frown. Stand your ground. The ground tells the dogs to not hound because we don't want to be found, don't move, don't make a sound or there will be more than dogs around so hold your ground. Hush don't make a sound. I'll be around. Maybe I can keep you abound, so you won't be found hush don't make a sound while I'm around. I don't want you to be bound when I'm around. Can you hear that sound?"Adios!" I'll see you around. Don't be bound because you found your rebound. Remember what it's all about, you can scream and shout!" All you want.

you can't go far without direction, please can I have your attention for this question or a suggestion that will redirect your direction. Excuse me, may I have your attention?" Maybe you need to take a break and focus on your meditation or do you need medacation? Now you've got my attention, did I forget to mention?" That this is a revolution. This is a concluetion to this illusion, so you won't be in confusetion, about this conclusion we will pay restitution. In this evaluation, Job 26:7 He stretcheth out the north over the empty place, and hangeth the earth upon nothing.

CHAPTER SEVENTY-THREE

FLYING TOENAILS

Now some of you may think this is gross," and some of you may think this is funny. But no matter how you feel about this chapter I Am still gonna share it. So you can skip this chapter if you want it's your choice but if you don't read it just because the name of it is gross then move on. You sure gonna be missing some giggles or maybe you think you will be missing in getting your stomach turned upside down. Who are you trying to fool ?" Well I want to talk about toe nails, Because people put it off and it's not a subject that is sweet to talk about right!" Well, I remember a guy went on American Idol and he wasn't planning on singing, he just wanted to be seen on the television well. He brought his nasty toenails that he clipped off for a century. Looked like dinosaur nails. Now that was disgusting." They should have not let him in the studio but he probably fooled them into thinking that he was going to audition yeah he was a sneak alright okay enough of the dinosaur nails," Have you ever clipped your toenails and each time you did a toe the nail flew somewhere but you don't know where it flew and so you search and search to pick them all up so when the cleaning person comes to clean they won't see any toenails lying around. Now that's just gross but it's life. Right!" It is said that if you have pretty hands you should have pretty feet. I don't know if this is true for me as long as they don't have an odor" It's fine but don't be wasting my time. Can you lend me a dime?" If you don't mind now take your time I don't mind don't let your mind slip back in time you've got to let go of what has been done and think of it as If it were a design if you don't mind, move on up so you can shine remember me keep me in your mind. But don't be blind and waste my time because I've got you on my mind all the time. Now you know I am worth more than a dime so give me some of your time. I don't want to wait in line because you are mine and you shine. Now come on, let's go wine and dine, take a load off of your mind, take your time, you won't be wasting my time. I've got you on my mind. Let yourself shine, remember you are always on my mind. So keep on keeping on having yourself a fine chime in time you will shine. Talk about toe nails, what about fingernails. you should see these crazy nails that women wear. It's too much to bear. They don't care who they scare. I will share what I cannot bear. This is unfair, would you dare?' The nails that some women wear these days do not phase them a bit how dramatic they look, and scary at times, to a toddler the most I would not boost the most if you're hung up in confusion you better get cruise- in so you won't get a bruisin. I'm not telling you to scare you. I only want to warn you not to get into a fight, because this would be a delight for you to reframe, and not play that game it would be a shame, what do you have to gain?" What about the lady at the post office, her nails were as long as a human can be. Of course they were fake.They were neon bright green, I asked her if her nails glowed in the dark. She said nope but they should. I put fake nails on my friend but she does alot of typing and she types real fast. She types 200 words per minute" Are you kidding me? nope she's not kidding. She's been doing this for over 20 years and she was supposed to retire years ago but she's still working. Anyhow I did her nails, they started to fall off one by one. I guess her fingers like short nails to be able to type. They did look nice for the little bit that she wore them. Such as life in the big city. A saying my mom always says.1 Corinthians 12:18 But now hath God set the members every one of them in the body, as it hath pleased him"

CHAPTER SEVENTY-FOUR

UNWANTED HAIR

Okay this is going to be a weird chapter so take it or leave it!" The choice is yours. Well sometimes you just don't feel like shaving your armpits or legs, yea this is disgusting if you don't." I know there are times when guys don't feel like shaving so they grow a beard or mustache or goatee. Let's face it we all get too lazy to shave. But this happens to be more disgusting for women than men. I know a woman that has to shave her face like a man. Now that's disgusting if you ask me. In some countries women don't shave their legs. Ours is not one of them but, I did see a woman not shave her legs. I thought to myself how disgusting!" Us gals were sitting at the table and we began to compare how long everybody's armpits hair was and we laughed about it." at the same time we said ugh how gross. One of the girls name is patricia but when she didn't shave her legs, she calls herself Patrick I think that is cute." Not her legs being unshaved, but her guy name that she gives herself. So us women can be disgusting at times. In our conversations as well. We are only human. We have faults, we fall short, we try our best to be an achiever and have the victory In what we are called to do. Well should I say some of us. What about you getting a haircut, then your hair decides to do what it wants to do. Well I've got a strange haircut right now. On the back of my head I have a cowlick then on the other side on the back of my head I have a Mohawk going on." How strange is that?" I feel stupid, and weird but hey" today anything goes. We are all the same inside if you cut yourself you're going to bleed red blood not yellow or purple or green or white or black nope we all are the same but our skin color may be different. If you take our skin off. We all have a skeleton.

It's kind of creepy!" right !" well it is what it is. Wouldn't it be strange if a black person got cut but his blood was black?" Or if an Indian got cut and his blood was brown. Or a Caucasian got cut and their blood was white?" I am only giving a peace of my heart and a peace of my mind. Please don't be unkind, tell me what's on your mind. If it is good it's okay If it's not, stay away. Because that's not the game we play. Let this be an ordinary day If you may Miss Sallie Mae, what can I say I must be on my way. But try to be giving and start chilling even if you're grilling because it's all about giving. If I'm not mistaken a part of your giving it may be time, or maybe even a dime. Just don't waste your time, keep this in mind, let your light shine then you will have peace of mind. All in good time. 1 Corinthians 11:14 Does not nature itself teach you that if a man wears long hair it is a disgrace to him.

CHAPTER SEVENTY-FIVE

REACH FOR THE STARS

Well have you had it said or heard someone say for you to reach for the stars. I think it means to dream big and to try to reach your goals, because you can try your best to reach and dream big because you can reach your goals and maybe you don't want to share some of your dreams or some of your goals to everyone. Because they would think that you are weird. But deep down you know you aren't and that Just because you dream big and expect for God to help you reach for the stars. I believe that God put those dreams in your mind and heart because he wants to bless you with these things that you had no Idea where these desires or dreams came from. Now until you take a step of faith, let me rest my case at this stage, let faith move in action you can reach the goals with action. It doesn't have to be perfect by a certain time Just as long as you keep on to reach as far and as high as you want. You know that this is not a stunt let me be blunt with you as long as you don't give up you must keep on to get to the front and everyday that you try is a step forward to get to go where you want to be this is not an Illusion to make you in confusion, that at the proper time this becomes reality now can we agree?" Even if you fail or fall down, get back up and try and try again.Sometimes you just need practice and sometimes you have been taught a lesson. Who am I to question?" May I give a suggestion?" Don't give up on yourself first believe in God and his word this reality this is real don't give up of what's important inside don't run and hide" look to the Lord in all things, for he will be beside you all the way and remember he will be your guide Don't worry of what's inside don't have stress or stride come along with me I'll take you for a ride so don't run and hide. Go ahead and reach for the stars dream big and wide don't put those desires and dreams aside swallow your pride and step aside nothing is impossible when you believe deep down inside Please don't hide you can wish upon a star or wonder about your life over and over but the real secret is deep within, You can't give up without even trying you can't keep wondering or you will feel like you're dying, now I'm not lying I'm trying to keep you from crying I'm not denying it's hard to get up and not give up but you have a purpose here on earth and you need to complete what you have started remember who's the one that had you parted for the things that you believe that started. Finish in what you began, try to hang on Just a little bit farther when you reach your goal you will feel alot better that you have a purpose and that you won't give up until you get through what you're gonna do. I've got enough faith for both me and you. Most people think that the more educated you are the more successful you will be. That you need to have a master's degree, in order to be successful in life. And to have it all. But the truth is, you don't need a master's degree to succeed. All you need to know is the master to succeed now this is reality indeed. For the things here on earth are only here for a while. Please do not be in denial, even the fashion will go out of style and this is for only a while. So be my guest and do your best 2nd Corinthians 4:18. While we look not at the things which are seen, but the things which are not seen; for the things which are seen, are temporal; but the things that are not seen are eternal.

CHAPTER SEVENTY-SIX

IS THIS A SAFE ELEVATOR?

Okay, how many of you have had a bad experience about an elevator either the ride or the wait or being stuck in an elevator?" I am quite sure there are plenty of you." My first bad experience was a bit scary. We had a family gathering event that was happening downtown. Most of the family lived out of state so we all decided to rent rooms in the downtown area of hotels. This was going to be fun." Winter was not quite over yet we still had some snow and Ice,some cold chilly weather. Since they had an indoor pool we took advantage of it. Then one day as we were done hanging at the pool we were on our way to get out of our bathing suits but something was wrong with the elevator. We stopped because the elevator was stuck. We wondered how long we were going to be stuck in the elevator stuck between floors. If you weren't claustrophobic before you got stuck in the elevator you were certain that you became claustrophobic while you were waiting to get help. You wondered if you would run out of oxygen and if so would you suffocate and die slowly." We really didn't want to find out," we were scared we had to not show it because then we would have a bunch of crying kids in the elevator and that would only make you nervous and then you would start to panic then that would lead to being anxious and that would make you breathe harder and faster. Then make you very nervous that you will run out of oxygen, you want to be able to breathe. Then you hope you don't have to go to the bathroom and if you do, how long can you hold it." So help does finally come and they finally get the elevator to open up but now you are too scared to trust the elevator again so what do you do?" Take the stairs even if it kills you to walk a few flights of stairs and you feel like you're going to pass out. Because you are out of shape." In time you have enough guts to ride the elevator again but you're afraid that if you have a panic attack or anxiety attack that you don't want to freak out while there are a bunch of strangers on the elevator with you. So you try your darndest to stay calm and cool for the sake of the kids on the elevator. Because if you lose it, the kids will start screaming!" and that will blow everything out of proportion. All hell breaks loose." Nobody knows what they are doing. And the kids won't be the only ones crying.``What about the man that is in the motorized wheelchair?" He tries his hardest to be kind and patient; he backs up to give people room to be able to get around him. Even though he does take up alot of room. He lets everyone get inside the elevator. By the time it's clear for the man to get back on the elevator the elevator shuts and leaves without him. Now how upseting is that?" The man has to start all over again." Somebody give this guy a break!" Isaiah 1:5 Why will you still be struck down? Why will you continue to rebel? The whole head is sick, and the whole heart is faint.

CHAPTER SEVENTY-SEVEN

TRYING TO KEEP UP

Now for some of you that don't have a disability you might not understand. The trials and hardships that people do have, it's not all peaches and cream. And maybe the person that has the disability doesn't want people to know that they are struggling. In your mind you can do it but your body can't,''Now Just to be in a crowded place and you are trying to keep up with the people you are supposed to be with and not follow the wrong person Just because you lost track of which way they went. Now you are frustrated and you feel like crying because people are pushing you every which way but the right way. You can't see much because everybody is taller than you. You can't see where you are going and you're trying so hard to follow the people you're supposed to follow and they walk faster than you. They don't know how hard of a time you are having Just to keep up." This is a nightmare!" No wonder I don't want to go out, I just want to stay home." It's a big ordeal for me. It's Just safer and I am sure the people I'm supposed to be following get frustrated because I am slowing them down because they have to stop and look for me. Besides, I really don't like to go where there are crowds of people. Especially now with the corona virus and the variants that they come up with every few weeks. It's probably the same virus but they give it a new name. I wouldn't doubt it." Plus you can't see too well. First of all your right eye is fake so there's no way you can see out of it." Then your other eye is partially blind they call it blind in the left field, something like that. Another word for it is peripheral vision loss. You can't see out of the left side of your eye. Then you have depture where you can't tell how close or how far you are from people, places, things, or objects. When you try to read something you only see half so you are seeing a different word than what it actually does say. When you lose your sentence that you were on, you try your best to find where you stopped reading. You are getting very frustrated and you want to scream." Then you think you found the sentence where you left off so you began reading and it's not the right spot you left off when you lost your spot. Now you keep reading the same sentence over and over until you realize that you already read that. Now you are frustrated you are at the point that you don't want to read any more. Or how about when you volunteer to read to your children's class and you don't know how to pronounce a word or not know the word and a child in the class says to you what the word is and a few teacher's are listening to you read to the kids. Well I Just mumbled the words I didn't know, then a kid screamed at me the correct way to say it." I was so embarrassed. I wanted to crawl in a hole and hide. In fact it was the Lion king I was reading to the kids and I was stuck on Maccudda Matada's name. Everytime It came time to say the lion's name I mumbled so nobody could understand what I was saying." Then that Mr. Smarty pants boy would yell Macuda Matada's name in my ear Macuda Matada." This was getting old. So I took work home for me to do to help the teacher. You know I actually forgot how old I was. I could tell the kids I was any age and they would believe me. Too bad We couldn't tell the grown ups we were any age and they would believe like a child believes. Only in our dreams. What about yor eye Doctor giving you eye drops to put in your eye that has little vision, and he doesn't tell you why you are given these eye drops. Then the nurse partisaner comes to give you a check up because your insurance company requires this yearly. You need to show her all your meds that you are taking and she tells you that the drops you are taking are for cataracts. Then you freak out because you think that if something goes wrong with your good eye you will be totally blind You can worry yourself sick, about something that has not happened yet, or maybe will never happen. Or Just take one day at a time. And Just go with the flow because remember God doesn't give you more than you can handle. Keep this in mind. 2 Chronicles 15:7 But as for you, be strong and do not give up, for your work will be rewarded.``

CHAPTER SEVENTY-EIGHT

TRYING TO FIND YOURSELF

I always say you never know what you're going to be when you grow up." Because I'm 64 and I Just found out what I'm going to be in my forties. I'm a writer and an auther. I never knew that's what I'd be doing. It's hard work but I enjoy this. Any how trying to find yourself in an unGodly world now this is hard because if you are in a Job and you have big demands and you want to excel in your career you've got to choose to please men or please God and if you work with Christians and are in a Christian environment you are blessed," not everyone has that kind of blessing. Sometimes you lose, sometimes you win. But that's life right!" We do the best we can with what we have." And if you are doing your Job like you were doing it unto the Lord you will be blessed but sometimes that's not the case and things don't work out in your favor you take it one task at a time. Trying to find yourself may be hard because a lot of the time we are searching yet we don't know what for and if we find what we are looking for we may not like it or be good at it. Sometimes it could be right in front of us the whole time. Yet we didn't acknowledge it." When you find what you are looking for, don't let it go because you may never find it again." That's just how life is. Ideas come and go, changes take place everyday, nothing really stays the same. Even time doesn't stand still, nothing stays the same, there's changes everywhere you go. Nowadays people change their careers at middle age. Because they want something different. It doesn't always turn out the way we have hoped. Then you need to cope. Today is here for a while, don't be in denial, stay for Just awhile, In time you will see Just what I mean that time doesn't stand still. In Fact there are days when the time goes so fast you wonder what happened the day Just flew by so fast you wonder how did it slip away?" then it's good that it doesn't drag on because you've got plans for later and so you want the time to last when you're having a blast so you wish the day will stay in your way. You can say that this is a kind of day that you would love to have more offten. When you realize this is what I've been searching for all along, that peace that fulfillment is what you've been after now you've found it the day after but yesterday is gone you will not see it again. So you try to hang on to memories you think that will do then you hope for something new. you try to be renewed in thoughts and memories that keep you alive because deep down you want to stay alive. you strive to stay alive. You try to keep things in perspective thinking this must have been a dream but inside you wanna scream. If you do you'll wake up and you don't want this dream to ever go away because you want it to stay. Then you realize that this is where you belong so don't fight because you are not in the wrong. This is where you belong now you have found yourself. Proverbs 3:5-6 Trust in the Lord with all thine heart and lean not unto thine own understanding. In all thy ways acknowledge him, and he shall direct thy paths.

CHAPTER SEVENTY-NINE

ALL IN GOOD TIME

How many of us try to rush through just about everything that has come our way? I know it is really hard to wait. And it seems we have to relearn over and over about being patient. Yes, especially when it's time to giving a gift to someone you can't wait so you give it then you have to get another gift because you gave the other one too soon. It's hard to wait for their special day because you want to see their face when they open their gift. One year I got help from a friend that is good at sewing. To make an apron for my grandma with her name on it. I had trouble sleeping because I was so excited to give it to her. Now I am not a sewer, in fact I should have been a fashion designer because what I was to make didn't look like the picture on the pattern. So a friend that is very good at sewing helped me to make it and a shirt for my son. I got a brand new sewing machine so naturally I was excited to use it. I do remember in grade school The teacher helped me to make an outfit. It was a pair of pants with a matching jacket. With the pattern of strawberries it was a cute outfit. It was white with a design . To tell the truth it was fashionable and so I wore it to a dance I went to. Since I made it I didn't have to worry about someone else wearing the same outfit. Like in the early 70's when the big platforms came out my cousin and I had a pair that were the same. This was funny because My cousin and I danced together if we were not dancing with a guy. I Imagined we looked funny with these big platforms, dancing our hearts away. But that was the style then. So I guess we didn't look funny." Although we were short, these platforms made you a few feet taller because they were so thick in height." Not too long after or maybe it was before that pants came out that were called elephant pants." Oh!" boy this was a trial hemming them up because I was short. I had to cut them alot and hem them up, this seemed to take a lot of time to do but this was the fashion they were way bigger than bell bottoms. What a chore!" Now the taller people didn't have to hem their pants." I did know of a few girls in school that didn't hem their pants up, they just let their pants drag on the ground so this looked bad, when their bell bottoms, or elephant pants dragged on the ground. Their pants had holes and were filthy from dragging on the ground. Nobody cared, it didn't bother anyone. such as life." They might have gotten some funny looks from people. But it was nobody's business. Patients are a good thing, keep expecting God is going to call our name, Just wait." How we wait is important to God. 1 Peter 5:8 Be sober-minded; be watchful. Your adversary the devil prowls around like a roaring lion, seeking someone to devour.

CHAPTER EIGHTY

THE FURTHER YOU GO THE HIGHER YOU WANT TO GO

Living life is as simple or hard as you make it. It seems the farther you go in life the higher standards you make for yourself. I think that might be a good thing if you don't beat yourself up when you don't reach your goal. Sometimes we set goals to reach that simply are not realistic. At least setting goals gets you moving and to get busy with life before life gets you busy then you turn out to be dizzy. In a jiffy. You don't need that " When you do go higher in your goals or in your dreams and you achieve what you wanted to do. You set more goals or dreams that you want to fulfill, be careful not to make yourself I'll. There are some people dying to kill because they don't want to flip the bill. Sometimes you come to a place where God will give you grace then you will need space to function in your time in your place. Now hold on and embrace the moment you are in this is a challenge a bit of change now you've got to rearange how you do things, because you didn't expect what just came upon you because you are blown away, That there is no delay anyway you press harder to make your dreams and goals come to pass but it's a hard task that you ask why is this happening to me Now I Just got to agree that the further you go the higher you want to go. For there are no limits as to how far or how high you want to go. Just don't be wavering to and fro keep your head up but not too high as if you want to reach the sky by and by. Keep in mind not to waste your time, don't get left behind, or be unkind you better unwind. Don't ever forget where you came from and get things done while you on the run try to get things done in order. If you can't keep it in order to complete your mission.

When you are done you add more to your addition. Try not to go into remission now look at who's grinning!" If you want to dream big and want to go farther or higher in life that's your preogative. you're Just living. Be kind and giving. Sure hope I'm not too intimidating!" Keep in mind there's no limit to time as long as you are on time . If you have a doubt in your mind, come let's have a drink of wine. You know it costs more than a dime. Don't waste my time, be diligent and be on time. You shine Just like a chime. Hebrews 12:1 Since we are sourouded by such a great cloud of witnesses, let us throw off everything that hinders and the sin that so easily entangles, and let us run with perserverence the race marked out for us.

CHAPTER EIGHTY-ONE

WHOSE CLOTHES ARE THESE ANYWAY!

Now if you live in assisted living or a nursing home you're going to end up with either someone's else's clothes or no clothes. Even if you do your own laundry, It's Just crazy how they do things, the different people that come and go each day In how much there is a turn over. In staff and in residence that's the way it is people come and go this is the way things flow and they gotta go. So in with the new and out with the old this is the way things go we must go with the flow or we gotta go but where do we go there's no place perfect no not one and there is no one perfect no not one there's only one that you can depend on. That's Just the way it is now my clothes are disappearing little by little and I get clothes that are not mine as it is I don't recognize my own clothes. So I am in trouble if I don't keep any clothes because I wouldn't have any clothes at all. My dad is in a nursing home and when my mom went to go see him she got upset because the shirt that she bought him did not exist and dad was wearing somebody else's shirt. My poor dad, he's getting older and more fragile and weak now that he is in his 80's. It is hard to see him like that but it is what it is that's life right well we're Just living. I don't like going to see my dad in the nursing home but I need to go see him because his days are numbered it won't be long then he will be gone and besides I will be in the same situation as my dad then I will feel lonesome and all alone with nobody to come visit me I already feel lonesome My family don't come visit me or call me this is sad that my ILS workers feel more like family than my own blood family. But it is what it is." If they all knew Jesus then they would have a change of heart then we wouldn't be so far apart I will keep on praying for their salvation and God will answer my prayers because one by one they will get saved for this is my prayer one day soon the day is coming both of my grandmas already got saved and mom and dad prayed for salvation I am pleased about that for there is hope for the lost to be found. lift your head up and stand your ground some of God's children have been found. It's not too late to pray the sinner's prayer and to make Jesus Lord of your life. For in him you will have eternal life and have it abundantly. In him you will have the things that money can't buy or the things that only heavenly things can give. It's things that the natural eye cannot see. It's what your heart and soul desires And only the Lord Jesus can give you what you desire and it's you that he admires. He longs to have us to be with him and the day is coming and coming sooner than you think so be on guard let me give you a wink. Don't you think I just need to know where to go. Be ready for the king is coming there's no denying he is stunning in the end we will win because Jesus is the beginning and the end and he remains faithful and true to his word this we can count on we don't have to be afraid soon we will walk through the pearly gates and home to be with the Lord where there is beauty in mid air we will see him face to face and he will give us the grace that we need to carry on what we have been called to do in him he will show us what to do. In him we can count on no matter what we have done he will forgive us and never give up on you no matter what if we fall he will pick us up." So don't give up because he will never give up, so take a stand and be in demand for the things of the kingdom. In the end you will have freedom. Now that's living, I've got that right, this is really out of sight!" With God all things are bright. Matthew 22:12 So he said to him, Friend, how did you get in here without wedding clothes?' The man was speechless.

CHAPTER EIGHTY-TWO

THINGS CONSTANTLY CHANGE

This place I moved to is brand new and people have gone and come so much that this can make your head spin." I've seen a lot of people that work here come and go all the time there is a turn over all the time. They are short of help all the time. The people who come to live here have come and gone. Some have died, some moved to nursing homes or other places that could suit them better. There is constant change even the menu changes, And at times the people serving the food get confused because what it says on the menu is not what they are serving. And so they change it." The thing I don't like is when they give an employee the keys to our apartment and maybe the person works only a few days then we don't see them again. Now how do we know if that person had gotten a key made. This is spooky when a strange man comes to your apartment and opens your apartment door and comes in. We have gotten rid of a few guys that people didn't want them coming into our apartment because they were scary looking. They are supposed to do a safety check. But now they have slacked off. They don't do safety checks everyday like they used to. This new company used to put apples and oranges and coffee in the lobby everyday. Now they stopped. In Fact they also would bake cookies and have them at the front desk. There are only a few employees that have stuck with the Job and have been here since it opened up. Not too many people have stood here from the begining, people come and go so quickly it's hard to keep up. Then we Just got to go with the flow. And make each day to be the best we can. Because we are not guaranteed tomorrow. So we should live each day as if it were our last. You want to treat people how you would want to be treated."

This is true. They do allow us to have pets for companionship. This is a good thing. Because some of us don't get visitors we also have activities going on every day when we have a lock down. Everything pretty much stops at a stand still motion. Slowly everything is getting back to normal, normal What's that? I highly doubt that things will ever go back to normal. Maybe this is the new normal of having to wear masks and have social disanting." and to be cautious at all times. And to continue to wash hands frequently and to be on guard at all times. Which means we don't have freedom. Which means we feel bound down to have all these rules and regulations. But this is the new normal because the variant keeps turning into another varient." Then they gave it a new name, and now the monkeypox has hit the states. I don't think this variant is going anywhere but in circles. And taking many lives each and everyday. Same as with cancer that it takes lives every day same with car crashes, takes lives everyday." Now what about the disasters of weather that's taking a lot of lives across our nation. We can't do anything about it. Except pray for the people that are being affected by these horrible disasters that have come upon them. Because only God controls the weather. Next thing you know human beings will try to control the weather. Like they change their sex. Mankind will always try to do things that are only for the Lord to do. Mankind will always put their nose where it doesn't belong. Now if you ask me If God wanted us to go to the moon we would have been born on the moon.`This is only my opinion. I think mankind tries to do things we are not meant to do. As the world continues man will always try to take control of everything. Things that are not in our nature to do. Now these pandemics are maybe our discipline for the way this world and people have turned. And we need to change and act and be like God intended for us to be. And when we got things shut down and things were taken away from us. It's because The Lord was disaplineing us. One thing for sure: God is Good all the time and all the time God is good. To us even when we don't deserve his forgiveness or goodness. I'm very thankful for the grace of God. This is God's love in action, grace is an undeserving favor from God.``Now people don't like change but change is normal and natural, change is good.

Romans 4:4 Now to him that worketh is the reward not reckoned of grace, but of debt.

CHAPTER EIGHTY-THREE

GIVING TO GIVE

Why do we give?" Is it to bless someone else or is it to get something back in return is the question? I love to see the expression on peoples faces when they open their gifts now I got a kick out of my daughter's two dogs I gave my grandson's one year a armor breastplate and the helmet to match they put them on and the dogs started barking at them they must of looked creepy to the dogs now that was a expression I did not expect I laughed because it was so cute." I don't know if the dogs were scared of the armor or breastplates or helmets. Or if it looked creepy to them or If they thought they would harm us or what !" I don't think that nobody paid attention to the dogs they were into opening gifts. I happen to like to watch people's expressions on their faces. Then if they don't say thank you that must mean they don't like the gift you gave them. Most of the time they don't say thank you so does that mean they don't like the gift?" or does it mean they are taking things for granted and they are expecting something so they don't have to say thank you. This Christmas stuff has really gotten out of control. I tried to get wrapping paper that maybe had something to do with Christ but to no avail. I found nothing concerning the reason why we celebrate Christmas nope, natha, zipo, not a thing concerning Christ. All I found was snowmen or Santa claus. How disappointing is that!" You see it's these little things of our behavior that we must grieve the Lord. Yes this may be why our world is in such a chaos right now. That this is a fallen world. So we keep getting plague after plague. Yet God is still good to us, when we don't deserve his kindness. Or goodness, or mercy. Yet the weather pattern changes all over the world. We are having disasters all over this world and we are having diseases and infirmities that are taking people's lives everyday. This is why we are having the world in chaos!" And our country is in shambles!" And we have the wrong people in authority and in office?' If it saddens me I am sure it saddens the Lord. Now when it comes to wrapping that's another story. I am so bad at wrapping the gift that it looks like it has been opened already and it's Just trying to cover the gift. And the person I'm giving it to didn't have to open the gift it opened up for them." I Invented a wrapping paper that opens itself up!" How do you like that!" Well I've gotten better at it. Still not the best." But now I don't make wrapping paper that opens up the gift itself. This is one of the Joys of Christmas Is wrapping gifts up. Let me tell you about a few of my husband's gifts, well one husband tried to give me some flowers, but by the time he got to me all that was left of the flowers were the stems. So no flowers for me. No wonder I never got flowers. Well husband number three gave me a sweater that had snowflakes on it. Now this is the month of May for Mother's day. We knew he caught a sale," then another time he gave me some beautiful flowers, But they were not real and not only that they were shaped in the form of a heart. And these flowers were for a grave." We all busted out laughing. We could not stop laughing." Was he planning to bury me soon?" I hoped not. He had no Idea why we were all laughing." historically!" He was speechless, and puzzled. He had no clue. He just looked at us all with a blank look on his face." Nobody could tell him why we were laughing, because none of us could stop laughing to be able to talk. Well eventually we finally stopped laughing to be able to talk. We asked my husband, "Do you know what this is?" He didn't respond. Then we told him these flowers are to be put on a grave at the cemetery by a tombstone." He said he didn't know that. So I didn't want him to feel bad, I wanted him to know that I appreciated the thought of him getting me something, even if he didn't know what he got me. Yet it was pretty. So I hung it up on the wall above the head of my bed. And the shadow of the flowers was an image of a devil with horns. Kinda creepy. But to keep peace between us, I said nothing about the shadow image of the devil to him. He was already laughed at. Besides, if I told him about the devil image he would get mad and throw it in the garbage. How I know this is because there is a vacuum cleaner that is called the dirt devil, he would have nothing to do with it because of the name devil. I had a hand vacuum and he refused to have anything to do with it. In fact I think he threw it away. He also didn't like Adam Sanders because of a movie he did where Adam Sanders peed on the wall. My husband got mad. I told him it's just a movie, it's not real. But he doesn't like Adam Sanders because of that movie Nobody can change my husband's mind. To each their own. I did feel bad for him when we were all laughing at him about the graveyard flowers. Besides I knew he meant well. Now I know why I never got flowers. That's living in the big city!" a saying my mom always said. 2 Corinthians 9:7 Each of you should give what you have decided in your heart to give, not reluctantly or under compulsion, for God loves a cheerful giver.``

CHAPTER EIGHTY-FOUR

GETTING OLD

Yes this is a topic that some people don't want to talk about or face. In Fact I've heard a person say they are afraid of getting old." Yes it's a little scary but it is a part of life. And it is something that we all go through. People age differently, some get unhealthy every year as they get older. It's almost as if our bodies are getting worn out and everything is falling apart little by little. You get hard of hearing your eyes are not 20/ 20 anymore so you have to wear glasses then they get worse so you have to get bifocals. At first you're having a hard time seeing out of them. It's a real headache trying to get used to these strange glasses. You're afraid to walk down or up the stairs because you are seeing double. You don't even want to move, these new glasses are freaking you out." But you need to trust the eye Doctor because apparently he knows what he is doing. At night your knees are in pain and you can't even sleep so you go to the Doctor then you find out you have mild arthritis, And you think to yourself if I only have mild arthritis, I hate to find out what severe arthritis feels like." you have pain everywhere out of the blue and all your bones hurt. It is hard to move because your whole body aches. And you think to yourself "Why do I hurt everywhere?" You realize you sound like an old person, you think to yourself "Yikes I sound old!" Just the simple things you used to do without a problem is now a hard task. Like trying to open a bag of chips used to be easy, now it's a hard task. You say I swear they make these bags different than they used to because now they are stronger and tougher than they used to be. But the truth is you just got older and weaker than you used to be. So the littlest simplest things you were able to do when you were younger is now a big task then you have to ask someone for their help. Now if you are the type of person that is independent, It's going to be hard for you to ask for help. You will insist on doing it yourself so you try and try but you can't get this task done. Someone will see you struggle for a long while then they will say ``can I help you with that?" You say I can do it but you're getting frustrated and getting tired." So you give In and say okay even if you didn't want their help you wanted to do it yourself you had to give in. In your mind you want to do things but your body is not the same as it was 20-30 years ago, so you have to except the way you are now even your eating habits have to change because you get heartburn, or bad acid reflux the first time I experienced this I was up in the wee hours I was so sick it felt like firecrackers going off in my system I felt like I was gonna die I didn't know what was happening to me. come to find out that the reason why I got bad acid reflux was from cranberry juice. The cares person that answered my call light brought me some cranberry juice to drink she thought this would help but we didn't know at the time is that the cranberry juice is what caused this acid reflux, so I couldn't eat spicy foods anymore I couldn't eat alot like I use to when I was younger because my metabolism had slowed way down so I couldn't eat like i used to or I could gain weight." Then when you smell an odor that smells old you have to confess and realize that yes you are getting old. But there's no shame or harm in it. One day I got up, and I went to the bathroom, I looked in the mirror. I got scared because my stomach had blown up, like I was pregnant. My boobs were touching my tummy. I had to look on the bright side. At least when I looked down I could see my feet. Because if I couldn't I would cry. I already felt like crying when I looked in the mirror. Because I looked like I was pregnant. I got scared. I thought maybe I had something wrong with me like I had a deadly disease, like cancer or maybe a tumor. I was scared to go to the Doctor and find out why my stomach blew up so big overnight. I told my sister about it. She said I better go to the Doctor because if it's something that I could get treated for right away I better take care of it. Before it gets worse, I went to go visit my mom, and she asked me if I was pregnant. I said nope I can't have anymore kids remember I had a hysterectomy, she said oh yeah that's right you and your younger sister had that done. I told my mom that one day I woke up and my stomach had blown up.

I got scared and yes I'm going to the Doctor to find out why this happened, I finally got an appointment to go see the Doctor. Then I thought about canceling, but kept my apointment. I went to see my Doctor. She said that i was just bloating, that i needed to take some over the counter stuff to help with the bloating. Also fat. I was scared she was going to make me get some tests I didn't want to go through. Besides bloating, I'm getting fat and old. Great!" I'm going to be an old lady with a big stomach that looks like I'm having a baby. This is life, live it right because you only have one. When I was younger I could eat anything and everything and not gain weight but once you get older everything changes. Well besides getting older every year and my health deteriorating little by little and getting more aches and pains I seem to be going to the urgent care a lot" because I can't get in to the Doctor's office I got bad pain in my shoulder and arm and back of my neck, I had to go see the orthopedic Dr. to find out why I'm having so much pain." I was blessed I got to get in right away. I needed relief from pain and I needed some answers. Well I got it. Now I've heard it said and I began to say it myself, "If it weren't for bad luck, I wouldn't have any luck at all." I got diagnosed all right. I couldn't even pronounce the word in fact I don't even remember what it is called. Some fancy name meaning having inflammation in my shoulder. So the Doctor suggested getting a cortisone shot. I said yes do it I was so desperate!" For some kind of relief, Oh my" I didn't even have to see the shot to know how big it was because I could feel it quite well. It felt very long and thick. I had to take deep breaths, to be able to stay cool and calm, and to be able to finish letting the Dr. do their Job.The botox shots were nothing compared to this one. I've heard it said that you can only get a few of these cortisone shots in a year, because this will make your bones thinner, and deteriorate. I didn't get any sleep all night!" I was in so much pain. Well it seems as though the shot made things worse, The Doctor did say that this will take a few days to get the effects of the shot. A few days pass then I do get some kind of relief, I still have pain but it's not quite as bad. You know why it's because I've developed other aches and pains that are more severe. I fell on my back while helping my son move a couch. So now I'm back at the urgency room again." The Dr. asks me if I had this before I said no. When I got home I did remember years ago I had this happen to my back while I was in my kitchen heating something up in the microwave. I started having severe pain. I went to the emergency room. The Dr. wasn't quite sure what I had, because he didn't see anything show up on the x-ray. So the Doctor gave me some muscle relaxer pills, and said if it doesn't get better to come back. Well it Just got worse and worse, every day. I was having a hard time bearing the pain. I decided to go back to the ergentcy room. Well they turned me away because they were at their capacity of people. There was a hospital not too far from where we were at. I went there to their emergency room and they did a cat scan. This is what they found out on the test. My CT showed evidence of a compression fracture in my lumbar spine at L2. So I get in the next day to see the orthodontist, she says I've got to come back to get fitted for a brace for my back then I will have to wear it at all times except when i go to sleep at night for 4-8 weeks. Well I got fitted for the brace that I will have to wear for the holidays 4-8 weeks. This brace is heavy and very awkward to wear trying to get in and of a vehicle. I hope nobody was watching, If there were, they would have a good laugh!" I know my daughter did. Although I was in a lot of pain I managed to laugh too!" even if it hurts to laugh. I tell people I'm a football player. Because I feel like one with this big plastic brace on, you feel like you are carrying a ton of bricks, now to go to the bathroom there's no way you can wipe yourself in the front or the back or sideways, or upside down, or inside out or right side up you only go the wrong side in. There's no way it can be done so you have to take the brace off. Now this is a pain in the behind, It takes forever to get it back on and fasten tight. How troubling this is. My housekeeper saw that I was having a hard time fastening this huge brace. She said here let me help you, then she helped me to fasten the brace. She then fluffed up the pillows on the couch and said to me, Here lay down and rest. But there was no way I could lay down with this big heavy brace to relax. Now I look in the mirror to be able to see what I'm doing. Yay!" progress" Try to brush your teeth or wash your face. You are farther than you think you are with this big piece of plastic you have on, I don't need to ramble on. And to bend over to pick something up or to put food down for my cat. Is very painful having the plastic brace Jab you hard on your skin, this is treacherous, simply torturous to bare. And to walk from one room to the other, don't even bother you feel like you ran a mile Just dragging yourself with this hideous thing that you have hanging on you weighing you down. It's easy to frown. At least God cares, he knows my pain and won't put me to shame. Great, now I will look like a freak for the holidays." I figure I'll just stay home with my cat for the holidays, since it's hard to move around with my turtle shell. I guess my nickname for now is Turtle turtle. Come to find out the reason this brace was killing me was because I had it on upside down and backwards!" Now how did I do this trick?" I amaze myself sometimes!" Then I always have a good laugh, and anybody who is with me at the time." I sure know how to cheer someone's day up, even my day too. That's the truth. My daughter came over thank God she did. She says mom something isn't right with your brace, let's take a look. She figured it out for me. But it still is in need of adJusting, because I can't wipe myself if I need to use the bathroom. I don't want to drip dry. Or what if I have to go number 2 how am I supposed to wipe myself?" The brace is too big for me to reach." I'll Just stay home for the holidays with my cat. Besides, my cat doesn't like me to leave the house. But if I have appointments he will have to deal with it. He acts like he's my husband. Yes I swear he's part human. That's life!" In the big city!" as my mom would say. I say, `` That's Just living!" 2 Corinthians 4:16 Therefore we do not lose heart. Though outwardly we are wasting away, yet inwardly we are being renewed day by day.·

CHAPTER EIGHTY-FIVE

OUT WITH THE OLD IN WITH THE NEW

Okay so I weaned myself off this terrible turtle shell. Then I decided to be done with it. The Doctor told me I only have to be in the back brace for 8 weeks. But it has been more like 12 weeks, I think it was longer because we thought we had an appointment to see her but we didn't. So I had to wait longer for things to proccess. Anyhow I cut my thumb on a can. It was bleeding and I thought it wouldn't stop. Eventually it did, I put antibiotic ointment on it so it wouldn't get infected. A day later I cut my thumb again, but not the same spot. This time with a sharp piece of plastic. I didn't put ointment on it this time because it did not bleed. Well in time my thumb began to pain me, It started to bug me. The pain began to get worse, in fact the pain began to spread on the palm of my hand. Then one night it did get a little swollen, my son came over and I showed him he said it looked infected. So I made an appointment to see the Dr. But the pain was getting worse and it was hard to bend my finger. I thought I should go to urgent care because my Dr. appointment was not for a while. And I needed to be seen now. The emergency would have taken too long and they probably wouldn't help much anyhow. At first they told me that I had to make an appointment for my kind of problem, I thought to myself "when did they start having to make an appointment for urgent care." I thought this was strange. So they said the next available time was in a few hours. I said I'll take it. I figured since I was already there I might as well stay and wait. Well I didn't have to wait as long as they said. The Doctor that was on duty was a very smart older man. He knew exactly what was wrong with my finger. He said you've got a trigger finger, I said "what is that?" He said you have a cyst in the joint of your finger, there are a few options we can go, we can give you a cortisone shot, if that doesn't help there's surgery. But you need to see a hand specialist, an orthopedic. I said I already see one for my shoulder, I get a cortisone shot from, then I see one for my back. He said you can just see the one for my back to look at my hand. He was wrong about that because each orthopedic specialist specializes in a different part of your body. So they put a splinter on my thumb risk, psalm. So out with the old,which is my back brace. In with the new, which is my splinter for my thumb and risk. There's not a dull moment with me. I'll say it again, If it weren't for bad luck, I wouldn't have any luck at all. Since I'm going to the Doctor's so much, I thought I better make that appointment for the podirest Dr. that I"ve put off for years. When I had a bunion removed and a pin put in, my toe got infected. The Doctor said if it did not clear up they would have to abitate my toe. Boy did that scare me!" Since I had the gift of healing, I decided to pray over my toe, then The Lord did heal it." I never went back to the podiatrist again. But my toe was never the same, and I've had trouble all these years. It's time to get it checked out."And what a time to go, when we are having a snow storm all this week. Like I said out with the old in with the new. We'll see what tomorrow brings. Well I did manage to get an appointment the very next day. It had been five years since I saw the Doctor for my toe.They took x rays, then he felt my toe and apparently a bone grew on top of the other one so that's why my toe is painful and turns red. So the Doctor prescribed some cream to put on my toe four times a day. Now if that doesn't work they will give me a shot, If that doesn't work surgery is the last resort, they will shave the bone down. Now we wait to see what's the next step.

CHAPTER EIGHTY-SIX

YOU LEARN AS YOU LIVE

Time and time again it is said the older you get the wiser you become. Is this a meth or a fact?" Well I believe this is the truth. When you're young you don't know much and so you think that old people don't know much because they haven't been out in the world to experience life on the streets but the truth is the elderly do know what they are talking about. When I was talking to a man on the internet my mom said he probably was after my house. The man thought I owned my house. And I believe she was right. I thought to myself how she knew. Maybe she didn't experience it herself but she knew what this man was after. This made me realize that this saying is true about you getting older means you are getting wiser. So you can say this is not just a meth , it is a fact. It is true. Maybe not everyone agrees but I believe this is true. Now with the internet and the computer kids nowadays are so smart. Technology has made it for kids to be pretty smart. You can ask a smartphone to get you information on Just about anything. And it will give you information on whatever you ask. You can get the correct spelling of any word and the meaning in a split second. How amazing is this?" So if you haven't had a smartphone you better get one because you don't want to be caught with a dumb phone. Right!" When you are a teenager going into adulthood you think you may know something better than a grown up and think again that this is a possibility they know what they are talking about." Because you're the one that doesn't know what you are talking about. Because even as times have changed and the world is so crazy, and everything is moving so fast, hold on tight because it won't last. Don't be afraid to take a step forward and see what you can gain for knowledge that will be with you your whole life. Try to remember the good and not all the bad because there is good in Just about anything and everything that you can think of. Try not to focus on the negative but the positive in each circumstance for where there is a will there is also a way. This I believe to be true. You can believe it to be true. Believe in your heart that this is the truth, go after what inspires you and the Lord will give you the strength to do what you were born to do. And when you find out, give a shout and do it with all of your heart. Make sure you don't depart what you've taken to heart for you will never depart and this is from the heart. This is Just living, trying to remember to be kind and giving. The next time I get advice from an elderly person I am going to take heed to what they are telling me. I'm not going to have a deaf ear, or refuse counsel, as if they don't know what they are talking about. Because God could have sent them to me to give me a message from God." When I was younger I did that but I was being foolish. Now I better listen to what is being said. Not all things Just some. Maybe the one that is pertaining to my situation in my life, and maybe it should be a Godly person, one that knows God would be a plus for me. You just don't know who God might send to you to be a friend or a mentor for guidance and direction you just never know. Sometimes you will get a divine appointment: Now this is a time that the Lord had planned for you that will be very important and very much needed and benafical." This time is so special for you it will feel like God sent this person specifically for you." This will be a blessing in disguise not only to you but to the person that is blessing you." And you needed to hear what they have to say, that It was meant for you and they were blessed with meeting you and having fellowship with you. So you both were super blessed. You both benefited from this divine appointment. at the right time, at the right moment.This is called a divine appointment. But you pray you make the right choice and that it feels right and comfortable but most of all that you have peace within yourself within your heart. PHILIPPIANS 4:6 -9 Be careful for nothing;but in everything by prayer and supplication with thanksgiving let your requests be made known unto God. And the peace of God, which passeth all understanding, shall keep your hearts and minds through Christ Jesus. Finally, brethren, whatsoever things are true, whatsoever things are honest, whatsoever things are just, whatsoever things are pure, what are lovely, soever things are of good report; If there be any virtue, and if there be any praise, think on these things. Those things in which you have both learned, and received, and heard,and seen in me do: and the God of peace shall be with you.

CHAPTER EIGHTY-SEVEN

THE OLD GET OLDER AND THE YOUNG TRY TO STAY YOUNG

This is how the world turns, the old get older and the young try to stay young. But in reality it can't be done, well the ladie's can have face lifts and guy's also if they want then put anti age cream on everyday and every night, but it won't do the trick, because the old will get older and it is hard to see your own parents go down hill as they say." They become hard of hearing and hard to see and all their teeth fall out and they fall down alot."But if they lose their glasses and can't see a thing then you wonder why they just want to sleep all the time." You need to keep up on what they need no matter how hard it is to go see them like that, you better or you will regret in time that you didn't take the time to go see them and have to get them some new glasses so they can see. And get them new dentures so they can eat regular food." And not have to eat like a baby sitting in the high chair. Yes it is hard to see the old get older but this has to be done for this is a cycle of life some live longer than others but you come into this world as a baby and you leave as a baby. Then there are people who don't want to admit that they are getting old so they sell their silver and gold. They dress younger than their age, so they can keep thinking in their head that they are still young. But It's going to take a lot of convincing on your part and others, that you are not getting older you're just getting better." Then you dye your hair so there's no gray hair. But the dye is making your hair fall out!" So, now you are freaking really bad. Now you have to wear a wig. Now you are In a panic. That your hair is falling out!" you're balling and screaming that you wanna sue the company that made this hair dye, but all you can do is cry and cry." Then you realize that you're acting like a baby, and you think to yourself that grown folks don't act like that. I guess I really am getting older. I better not try to hide it or prevent it from happening too fast. Because you're just here for a while so you might as well be in style. Try to keep a smile. Getting old is a mindset, and aging is a fact of life.

Psalm 92:14 They shall bring forth fruit in old age; they shall be fat and flourishing;

CHAPTER EIGHTY-EIGHT

SING YOUR HEART OUT!

Okay so suppose you don't have a great voice to sing solo but you sound good when singing with others, So I sang in a choir at church and most of the people in the choir are elderly right!" Well we wore robes and I had to ask someone to zip me up. Instead of me helping the elderly they were helping me." At times I would lose my place in the song we are singing so what do I do?" well I just lipped it and pretended that I was singing the right words that everybody else is singing. It's a good thing the Lord looks at our heart and does not listen to the singing. He probabably plunges his ears or laughs at me. At least I keep him happy. I do lose my voice a lot. I don't know why I lose my voice a lot.``I think it's from acid reflux. Okay so the activity director asked me if I have any musical talents or gifts. I said nope all I ever did was sing in the choir then she asked me if I could sing a few songs by myself well, I've never sang by myself I guess I could try. What she had in mind was a Christmas program for the people that lived in my building. I had a bad headache and thought that this would be my chance to back out of this." But I felt like maybe I should at least give it a try, maybe it would be fun. So I went and when it came time to sing by myself I started to sing ``oh holy night then my voice started to snap" crackle and pop!" and the laryngitis started to kick in, then I stopped singing and said I'm not a singer!" nobody said a thing.'They probably were thinking in their heads you got that right, this was a bit embraressing." Then I said I can sing in a choir because I am more confident when I sing with others plus they can drown my voice out. To blend in with the others. I used to be a soprano, now I sing snap crackle and pop!" I told them before I started to sing that they might want to put ear plugs on. It's a good thing I sing with my heart Amen!``You know My headache went away, so this was worth going to join in the fun because we did have some good laughs!" Now the next day we will put this program to action and I am sure that some people's hearts will be blessed just for our efforts to want to bless them. You know I'm sure we will bless the Lord's heart and To me I believe that's all that matters. Psalm 105:2 Sing to him, sing praise to him; tell of all his wonderful acts."

CHAPTER EIGHTY-NINE

THE CLOSER YOU ARE THE BETTER

Okay so I am talking about the Lord the closer you are with him the better all the way around. You will be spiritually, emotionally, mentally, physically, protected. No harm can come to you only if you are right with God. yes harm can try to attack you over and over again but the Lord only allows so much harm that can be done to you and he will use your strengths and guide you to where he wants you to be and there is nothing you can do to change his will." Besides, he knows what's best for us.`` He sees the future and already has a plan for your life span. So take his hand and take a ride lay low, and do not try to take things in your own hands and try to do things in your own way or in your time, because you will fail time and time again so don't rebel for I have a story to tell when you do things in God's way it won't take up the whole day, Just for you to think things through there is nothing else to do. But to sit back and take a view, now I'm telling you what to do. Pay attention to what I'm saying don't take matters into your own hands be still and see the Lord move in ways you've never thought possible for in him through him all things are possible now if you believe you shall receive so faith has a lot to do with the answered prayers, it also has a lot to do with how close you are to God and his word. You know who can be against you if God be for you. John 10 : 10 The thief comes to steal, kill, and destroy ; But Jesus came so we could have life abundantly and to the fullest." Jesus is the good shepherd; He gives his life for the sheep. Being his sheep he'll have to keep me close to him, there's no other that I will let in shall I begin? Over and over again until i get it right, for there's no other sight that is worth my while do not be in denial Just except the truth it will be worth your while. I guarantee you'll leave with a big smile, and all the while people will wonder what's wrong with you. You'll Just have to tell them you're brand new. Then they will wonder what you are talking about. You'll Just have to give a big shout, and tell them what it's all about. Then you pray for them that they will receive eternal life; please don't get in any strife, you have begun a new life.

James 4:8- 10 Come near to God, and God will come near to you. Wash your hands, you sinners, purify your hearts, you double -minded. Grive, mourn and wail. Change your laughter into mourning and your joy into gloom. Humble yourselves before the Lord and he will lift you up.

CHAPTER NINETY

REARRANGE OR CHANGE:

With my second husband I could not rearrange things. If I did he would change it back the way it was originally. So we fought like this. I rearranged, then he would change it back. This went on for days. I don't even know who won their way or who Just gave up. I know this was exhausting to keep moving furniture around everyday. I know when I did this when I lived alone if I rearranged the furniture a lot the furniture would start to fall apart. I had to learn to not rearrange too much. In life We want God to change things for us, without changing us, Because we are afraid of change. We don't like surprises, stay surprisable" Do something that you never thought you could do. God wants to surprise you, you are stronger than you think; We should have a surprising spirit. We ought to be a little more surprising, and less intact. My daughter gave me a large glass table that was shaped in the letter L. This was very heavy there was no way that this heavy table was going to break no matter how many times I moved it. One day I carried this heavy awkward shaped piece of furniture up the basement stairs. Now this was a miracle that I did it myself, and it was a miracle that I didn't fall down the stairs. This was the hand of God I knew the Lord was helping me to carry this big heavy piece of furniture. God is good all the time and all the time God is good. Although I should not do this type of thing again by myself, I was only blessed that God gave me the grace to do this myself. This was not a wise decision that I made. I shouldn't take risks like this anymore.

It was nothing but a miracle that I didn't fall down the stairs. I do believe that God and the angels were helping me to carry that big awkward heavy table up the stairs, and out to the back yard. There's no way I could have done it myself. I sure have my guardian angels working hard. 2 Corinthians 5: 17 Therefore, if anyone in Christ, the new creation has come: The old has gone, the new is here!

CHAPTER NINETY

HAVING A GREEN THUMB:

I never was much of a gardener, but I was fascinated in how some people kept their land scapes and took real good loving care of their yards. I knew of a woman who worked in her yard eight hours a day. She had a beautiful yard. She was really tanned from being outside all day in the sun. She would rearrange her landscape all the time. She put in all her hard work, with her whole heart." I think she was obsessed with rearranging her yard and landscape. That is what she put her whole heart into. She did have a beautiful yard. I had a nurse assistant to help me with my girls, because they were a few years apart this was like having twins. I had a dead plant in my house and I decided to pray for this plant because it was dead and there was no life to it. I didn't want to throw away this plant because a friend gave me a piece of it to start my own plant. Well, it did grow big and tall on its own. It grew big and then it seemed to have gotten old and died." well I prayed over the plant, and long and behold this plant came back to life!" My nurse's aide couldn't believe what she saw so she began to laugh and said she never saw such a thing."In all of her life" She was amazed!" I was too, I had no Idea what would happen to this plant after I prayed over it. In time I went to my daughters house to see the trees and plants that she planted. There was an apple tree, a lemon tree, some raspberries and rubarbs, peppers, cucumbers and tomatoes. She wanted me to come pray over them because they didn't look too good. So I did, and then I asked her how they were doing, she said good. People might think that it's strange to pray over things, and not Just people. But you can say a prayer for anything you want. God doesn't think it is silly, or strange. When God gives you a gift he expects you to share it." Jeremiah 17:7-8 God's green thumb. Blessed is the man who trusts in the Lord, and whose confidence is in the Lord. For he will be as a tree planted by the waters, who spreads out its roots by the river, and will not fear when heat comes, but its leaf will be green, and will not be concerned in the year of drought. It won't cease from yielding fruit.

CHAPTER NINETY-ONE

THE WINDS BLOWS WHERE IT WILLS:

I never used to be afraid of the wind but when my son and I got caught in a storm that left me scared of the wind forever and a day. Well my son and I were on our way to visit my grandparents at their new house. It began to strom. The winds were so strong, I thought I was going to fly up to mars, or the moon, I must have looked like a goon. So I grabbed onto the telephone post, I must've looked like I saw a ghost. My heart was pounding fast, I felt like crying. But I had to be strong for my son. Because if I cried then my son would cry. I couldn't let that happen.So now I am wounded forever, not true i can be clever, and pray the fear away, and that's okay. Well, we tried to get into the store but the electricity went out so the doors did not open, so the people that were in the store were stuck in the store, until the electricity came back on. In time the storms got even worse than before, there were trees and telephone poles, and street signs and other things that were up rooted and flew in the air. lying all over the sidewalks. That you couldn't even walk on the sidewalk. One storm tore up all the bike trails at Fort Snelling. It looked like we had an earthquake. The trails were all cracked and split apart. We could not use the bike trails until everything was restored. This was bad. It was good to know that I am not the only one that is afraid of the wind or of storms. It seems that nowadays the wind is a lot stronger than it used to be. And the storms are intense and stronger and more deadly than they used to be. I see all the damage that storms do now more than ever before. And so much destruction and many deaths, and countries have been destroyed. Now more than ever before.Time and time again, God says in his word do not be afraid Over and over again. So we must not be afraid of the gusty winds, the winds blow here and there, but what do I care do you have time to spare, do you dare.You must be a brave one, for all the things he has done in the end it will all come undone, was it fun? Make it worth your while, I'm sure you won't see a crocodile, especially when you smile for a while, take your time, you've only have a mile then you can decide if it's worth your while, don't forget to give me a dial, and remember to smile that's the style; can you stay awhile? Luke 21:11 And great earthquakes shall be in diverse places, and famines, and pestilences; and fearful sights and great signs shall there be from heaven.

CHAPTER NINETY-TWO

WHEN YOU FIND JOY IN THE SMALLEST THINGS:

I find Joy and laughter in the smallest things that most people don't even pay attention to now this is so true. I could name a bunch but I don't want to bore you. So I won't go there, anyhow one day I was trying to find my file cabinet because I kept my laundry money in there, apparently I kind of rearranged my living room I had this gigantic fake plant, so here I am fighting and wrestling with this fake plant now you would think that I was in the jungle fighting for my life against some deadly creature by the way I was carrying on. My housekeeper came into the dinning room, and she saw me fighting for my life!" She said, ``What are you doing?" I said I'm trying to get to the filing cabinet!" she said it's over here remember you moved it!" I said oh!" really" she said yeah really she began to laugh and laugh so hard." Then I began to laugh and laugh!" we both are laughing hysterically!" and we were loud!" My daughter came out to the dinning room to see what all the commotion was about. She thought that I was crying" when she found out that I was laughing and not crying she laughed and rubbed my back. We could not stop laughing, my housekeeper and I. We had a great time laughing." Now if I'm in a hurry I grab the wrong jacket which happens to be one of my daughters. I would leave them jacketless, now if it is winter that's not good but they can always wear one of my jackets so it's not that bad. We just have to adjust and compromise a little bit because with me you don't know what to exspect!" but that's part of the joy that only I can apreciate." I say Amen!" Being thankful and grateful for every little thing puts a smile on peoples face for they think that you are weird because you have the joy of the Lord. And to them you are making them bored. That's quite all right because you know you are out of site in the site of the Lord. Because you know this pleases the Lord to be thankful and grateful for every little thing, When others take things for granted and they seem to think that God owes them some blessings or that they deserve all good things to happen to them. This is not a fairy tale for he is the great I am, I say it over and over again!" Yes Just going to the drug store and waiting for a prescription, and the store is busy with lots of people. But there is two seats waiting for you and your ride to be able to sit and wait." that's a blessing in disguise it's these little things that i just thank and praise God for, Just to get in and out of the shower without falling down or getting dizzy or losing my balance is an answer to prayer. The Lord does not demand but he gives us a free will to do what is right. Just to get in and out of the shower in one piece is an answer to prayer. Just looking up tends to make me have a dizzy spell. We are God's precious ones and he is ours. When he brings us home we will feel like we flew into mars, take a look at his scars, and the blood that he shed was red. And the scars that he had from the strike of a whip, that ripped the skin on his back. He did this so we can live the life that he intended for us to have for he loves us and this had to be done. That he is Jesus God's only begotten son that his will shall be done in whom we have become one. 1 Thessalonians 5:16-23. Rejoice evermore.Pray without ceasing. In everything give thanks: for this is the will of God in Christ Jesus concerning you. Quench not the spirit . Despise not Prophesyings. Prove all things; hold fast to which is good. Abstain from all appearance of evil. And the very God of peace sanctify you wholly; and I pray God your whole spirit and soul and body be preserved blameless unto the coming of our Lord Jesus Christ.

CHAPTER NINETY-THREE

DON'T LOOK BACK:

It's okay to look from where you have come from and see how far you've come, but to not dwell on it or let it get you down which can lead to depression, which will lead to everything negative against you which can lead to sickness, diseases, which can lead to even fatal things such as death. Set some goals, and try to reach your goals. It is good to have goals and dreams and if you don't reach your goals it's okay. Because at least you tried I'm certain this gave you a purpose and a plan for your life, and not Just existing. But that your life matters, you do make a difference in this world. Because you belong to the one and only most holy God!" And if you make mistakes, that's okay, there is room for improvement and besides we learn from our mistakes. Have you heard this saying ``You have to learn the hard way!" Well I guess this is true but when we were born we weren't given a manual on how to raise your child. Actually we have been given a manual. It is the word of God. The bible tells us how we should live if we want to be Godly people, pleasing to God. But we take chances, we take advice from people, as life goes on for you to learn as you grow older. Then you become wiser with time and with aging. Some people are blessed that they don't have to go through many hard times, or conflicts, or trials, or storms as much as other people. Think of it this way that the hard times will make you stronger inside out and in every area in your life." You will be used in time to help and bless somebody that needed the words you spoke to them. It's like your life is a puzzle that God is putting the pieces together little by little. You have no Idea why you have to go through things and stuff, nobody else does. That is because you are specially made and very unique from the next person. We are all the same but yet different in our own way. Just remember who is in control and who has your back before you were even born. How awesome is that?" For God is good all the time and all the time God is good. Don't look back because you may have a heart attack, now that's a fact it's not an act so kick back and relax and reminisce on the good times, and not the bad. Remember all the good times you have had, stay focused on what's in store for you surely you know what to do. Don't waver to and fro stand strong even if you don't have long to search for the best of what's in store for you. Now you know what you should do. remember all the good times and in what you have had that things aren't quite so bad try to remember who's your real dad. In this you can be very glad. PSALMS: 139:14 I will praise thee; for I am fearfully and wonderfully made; marvelous are thy works; and that my soul knoweth right well.

CHAPTER NINETY-FOUR

CHANGES OF SEASON"S

Depending on where you live you may or may not experience the four different seasons. Now if you live in Minnesota you have four seasons: summer, spring , fall and winter. Nowadays the weather pattern has changed so much it's hard to know what the season is let alone what the month is. The fall can feel like winter or the winter can feel like fall or the summer could feel like fall. It is very confusing all over the world right now. Florida had more snow than Minnesota Texas had a bad snow and ice storm which they never had before, they've never experienced cold or snow before, hopefully it will be the last. so this was a big surprise. Or should I say a shocker." First time in history, they got sidekicked and got out of breath!" Thought that this was death. All they ever used was air conditioning. They have never used a heater to get warm because in that state all they ever tried to do was try to keep cool. Storms have become deadly to mankind. Now I know a few people who work where I live. They lived in Minnesota but went to visit friends who lived in Texas. Funny thing is, the cold and snow seemed to follow them. They decided to move there, then Texas had a big snow storm. I bet these people wished they were back in Minnesota. Because at the time Texas was having an ice and snow storm, we were having nice weather. Now how confusing is that!" Sure seemed like they took the cold ice and snow with them to Texas. Now they moved there to be in nice warm weather. This is not what they expected, I wonder if they moved some place else or stayed there and stuck it out because they were used to the winters in Minnesota. I'll never know. Everybody is confused. I think even the weather itself is confusing, all the seasons are mixed up a bit!" We don't know how to dress ourselves and the storms have gotten out of control . We really need to get a grip on life before the grip gets a hold of us, and how do we do that? How do we stay a step ahead of these treacherous disaster storms that hit us out of the blue? We can't predict when or if a storm is coming no matter what !" We really don't know and all we can do is predict." I've heard it said that there's only one Job that can lie and get away with it, and that is a weather person. Well I know today I thought it was going to be up to 50 degrees, and next week in the 60's I was going to go out and do errons but when I found out it was 11 below zero I decided not to go out!" I guess I must have been reading some other states' weather reports. Or maybe it was Wishful thinking!" Here in Minnesota, we have a saying, that we only have two seasons, winter and construction.

Acts 1:7. He said to them it is not for you to know the times or epochs which the father has fixed by His own authority

CHAPTER NINETY-FIVE

WHY DO THEY CALL CHICAGO THE WINDY CITY?

Well, my husband and I went to Chicago city for our nephew's wedding. This was my first time going to Chicago. I couldn't believe in how busy downtown was. A man approached us showing all this Jewelry asking us if we wanted to buy some we said no." Then the freight train was even more crazy!" It was my first time going on a freight train. I was scared and apparently I was confused. The train started to leave without me. My husband was already on the train. He was yelling at me to get on but I was scared and confused because another person was shouting something to me. I don't know what he was yelling, and trying to tell me. The more they both yelled the more nervous and confused I was getting." I put my foot on the train then took it back out. This went on for a few minutes, I finally had enough guts to step up on the train before it left me. At the wedding reception they were serving the best of everything. My husband and I danced a few times, then a man asked me to dance. I said no sorry I only danced with family for I knew this man was looking for more than a dance. It was better I didn't dance with strangers, or strangers who are strange. Throughout this whole trip I kept asking my husband why they call this the windy city?" But he never answered my question. Well my husband and I took a tour bus. This was my first time going on a tour bus. All of a sudden my dress flew up in the air, and I quickly pulled my dress back down. I showed the people on the bus what I had on underneath my dress. I was so embarrassed and humiliated!" This was the answer to my question that I had been asking about this whole trip." Because the winds blow a lot and hard. But this is not the only city that has strong winds, back home in Minnesota the winds can get strong and there are days that it is windy all day in fact I was walking to church one Sunday and I had put on some knee high nylons because I didn't have pantyhose to wear with my dress. And sence my dress was below my knee no one could see my knee high nylons right!" well I was wrong, my daughter and her family were looking out the window, the winds gusting through hard and strong." My dress went up a bit so when my daughter and her family saw my knee high nylons, they had a grand old time laughing at me. When she told me, I felt like a real old lady, not a fake one. Because my grandma used to wear knee high nylons with her house dresses that she wore around the house. I don't know who else was laughing and looking at me. The church was only across the street from where I lived. I sure hoped I didn't give a funny show to anybody else. Then again I probably cheered somebody's day up. Palm 78:26 He caused the east winds to blow in the heavens And by his power he directed the south wind.

CHAPTER NINETY-SIX

EMBRACE LIFE:

You hear people say lifes shorter than you think this is true. You are not guaranteed tomorrow, so embrace each day and live it as if it is your last day here on earth. This is hard for some people to even think about whether you may or may not get hit by a car or you could be dying slowly from some type of disease. I know that this book started out to be funny, then did some strange writing kinda like poetry. And now I am being serious. I'm Just being led by the spirit and going with the flow." I sure hope everyone is getting ready for the coming of our dear Lord and Saviour's second coming." This is a topic that many people don't want to talk about but this is reality, this is for real, this cannot be avoided for too long so be strong and courageous. Get ready to go to your real home with our Savior!" our King, our all be careful not to fall and if you do he is there to pick you up he will shake the dirt and dust off, he will never remember your sins anymore, because this would be a bore, and it would be a real chore, your the one that he adores he will not make a mistake or hold a grudge he might give you a shove to go the right direction. Did I forget to mention, he wants us to forgive others as well as ourselves and try not to remember your mistakes because the one who loves you will give you a break. He will not hold us accountable for unknowing mistakes but learn from them and seek his face. He is a God of Mercy and Grace so continue to seek his face. In the end we belong to him and to us he is the only one that you can truly trust." Only him that you can have peace, and harmony, True Love, these are the things that matter and it's things that money can't buy things that will forever stay with you forever they will not fade away they will always be Just like heaven and true harmony. So try to remember that this world is only temporary and to get ready to live eternally for that is the future our true home and in this I will treasure and not moan and groan. This is what is recorded in God's word: you cannot change or rearrange his word to be true and it will come to pass that the righteous will have the last laugh. Ecclesiastes 3:1-8 To everything there is a season, and a time to every purpose under the heaven: a time to be born, and a time to die;a time to plant, and a time to pluck up that which is planted; A time to kill, and a time to heal;a time to break down, and a time to build up; A time to weep, and a time to laugh; a time to mourn, and a time to dance; A time to cast away stones together; a time to embrace, and a time to refrain from embracing;A time to get, and a time to lose; a time to keep, and a time to cast away; A time to rend, and a time to sew; a time to keep silence, and a time to speak; A time to love, and a time to hate; a time of war, and a time of peace;

CHAPTER NINETY-SEVEN

THE LOST, AND THE HOMELESS

It's sad to see the people that are lost and just existing in this world. They are here in body but their minds and hearts aren't. So pray for them that they may find Christ !" Though we do tend to find it hard to keep on praying for the loss because things seem to be getting worse, the more we pray the worse things become but don't give up praying because things are getting shooken up. That just means that Our God is working on that person that you are praying for. It may take years before you get an answer of prayers. It will happen in God's timing in God's way. What about the homeless animals they can't even talk to tell us what is wrong. Now this is sad but we can't rescue every animal that we see on the street!" There's not a house big enough for all of them, so all we can do is pray for them." And hope that they get a home and family that love them and treat them right for this is God's creation that he gave to us that we may take care of them and love them as God does for us for he gave us all that we need and to enjoy and respect what he has given us. So stand tall and shake off the dust, because the Lord is not done with you yet, he gave us a lot to enjoy and take care of, he wanted only the best for us he entrusted us to do his will, now we must do what has been placed within our hearts and try to do the best on our part keep him near and dear in your heart then things won't fall apart. And if things get all out of place remember he will fill you with his mercy and grace do not let anything, or any one take his place. Now for the homeless I guess some like that lifestyle and some don't have a choice, but they should yell loud so we can hear their voice. Some like not having responsibility and then there's some that don't mind sleeping under a tree. Then there are those that can turn their life around, because they're tired of sleeping under a bridge. They never have a good night's sleep or rest. they have to be on alert so they can stay alive to see another day. let me guess their stomachs keep growling of hunger, and that's another reason they can't sleep. Then they grow weary, and weaker by the day then the Lord takes them away. What can I say?" I Just sigh so no one does them wrong. They fear for their life every single day that someone may come and take them away. Or perhaps take their life before it is supposed to be gone, then you wonder what went wrong. So you keep praying for people that you don't know and maybe ever get to meet but that's okay because your prayers make a difference. So don't give up hope, that things will get done. You may never see the answered prayers, but you know who's the one that really cares. And to you that's all that really matters because this is who you want to please even if people make fun of you and think you're a tease. It's fine and dandy they can have their fun, even the little ones are shooting guns. This is sad and out of hand that the world is out of control. Be still and let God stretch out his hand." Don't try to hide, don't try to run for the one who loves you will take a stand, for his people he is in demand. He has his best interest at heart, remember he is here for you even when you are apart, for He remains the same today, yesterday, and forever he will be the same. This is not a game, be patient" be kind. Be wise" Be still and let God's will take place because in the end he will have his way anyway he's the king of kings. He's the Lord of Lords, he's the great counselor, the great I am, let me say it again and again. He is the prince of peace, he is everything and much more that you can desire, he is more than your heart can desire, he is the one that you should admire for your heart's desire. You must come to desire you will be inspired once you see what he wants you to be, then you can be set free Indeed. You cannot see Just yet of what it is that he wants you to become, you can not see all the beauty that is with In, for he has Just begun a new work in you, In all that you should do that you may be the best, that you can be, that's why he's Interested in me. So you can be the best of me and become all that he desires for you to become. He will not leave things undone remember he is the same yesterday today and forever more remember what he has endure for you and for me he is the great I am he will never leave or forsake you he will always be faithful forever more this you can be asured he will rescue you when you are in danger or wipe away tears, and your fears for he knows what you're gonna ask for before you even thought about it to ask. He will help you through any task all you have to do is ask. Now this is not a hoax, nor is it an superstishion, nor is it an rumor, or some kind of tradition. I'm talking about the Lord our God who made this creation. Now you can take my word for what it's worth or take heed to the truth of this universe. But I tell you the truth that there is not much time to repent, to change your mind, and your ways to turn to Jesus in these last days. So I will keep praying until I'm all prayed out!" then I will give all the praise and glory to God and I will give a great shout!"To our Lord and savior. For he deserves all the praise, and all of the glory, honor belonging to him give God all that is within. Proverbs 29:7 The righteous care about justice for the poor, but the wicked have no such concern."

CHAPTER NINETY-EIGHT

BEING CONTENT:

Nowadays it's hard to be content the way things keep changing. Yes I wish I could go back to the 60's and 70's when things were more simple. But the truth is changes keep happening and it's hard to keep up with the new technology. you can fool some of the people some of the time, But you can't fool God any time." with the technology that keeps changing every few months it is almost impossible to stay content and satisfied. Unless you live in a community that has nothing to do with the things of this world. Take like the ammish people they do a good job at being more Godly than Christians today that claim they are Christians now will the real Christian stand up!" I gotta admit that the Ammish people do live a clean and peaceful life, they don't need to think about it twice and they do beautiful work with everything they make. They are very talented. And hard working people that keep to themselves I tend to think that they are living like the way Godly people should live to be at peace with everyone, and keep to themselves Not being busy bodies with their mouths instead with their hands. Seems to me this is how the Lord would want us to live. But of course I only see what has been on the television about the Ammish people so maybe in real life they really don't live like that all the time. I don't know but from the shows I've seen on the television they look like peaceful people. But then again they are only people. So they are not perfect, there is no one perfect, only God alone." They stay in their own group of people, which is probably a good thing because then they won't have any bad or negative influences for their people. These people are very interesting people, but then again we all are interesting because God made us for his pleasure. I'm sure he is pleased with his creation yet I'm sure he is disappointed in us, in how his people turned cold wax in some areas of our lives. If we keep asking for forgiveness, and truly repent of our evil wicked ways. He is just to forgive us of our sins. He is a wonderful God that forgives and does not hold it against us.God is good all the time and all the time God is good. Hebrews 13:5 Keep yourself free from the love of money, and be content with what you have, for he has said I will never leave you or forsake you.

CHAPTER NINETY-NINE

WHICH CHURCH SHOULD I GO TO?

Since my husband died I really haven't gone to one church steadily. Well I don't drive and I really can't take the bus because my balance has gotten worse since I fell down and have to use a walker, when I was getting physical threapy the therapist said that I move like an eighty year old. Now that was not a good thing to hear but the truth hurts. And people don't want to go out of their way to pick you up." Mind you these are supposed to be Christians" Like I said will the real Christian stand up here!" I think people are trying to be cautious!" And they are being too cautious!" Besides, it's probably safer to stay home with all these variants of coronavirus going around. I do watch all the preachers that come on everyday. I wish I had money to give all of them and their ministries. But I don't maybe someday I can at least give some to the TBN channel. I love all the preacher's that come on everyday. They are wonderful men of God. And Joyce Meyer I love her too, I like listening to her everyday. Her grown kids are blessed to have a Godly mother and woman of God. She is a blessing. The Lord has blessed us with good teaching from good Godly men and women of God.``Then again we have to be careful that these other things that we do, does not take time away from God If it does then we need to prioritize our time wisely. Because the Lord and his word should be first and number one in our to do list.Then things will fall into place and It would make your day go smoother. When you have your priorities right and in order.Try it you will see how good it is to be right with God. You will be amazed at how your time can be used wisely, and you will accomplish much. You never stop learning and growing in your walk with God. Maybe the horrible illnesses that are going around will disappear one day and we won't have to be on guard when we do go to a public place. Because now we don't have peace when we leave the house. We don't feel freedom anymore and what about the Christians that are being persecuted for their faith. How long do they have to suffer before the coming of the Lord Jesus?" Nobody knows these answers to our questions, only God the Father knows the answers to these questions. Now In the Catholic churches, some people say they stopped going to church because it was Just a competition In who dresses better. Now how ridiculous is that?" Now we wait with antipatation for the Lord to come and take us home where we will be safe and happy for ever more. We hear people say that this is the end of the world and that the lord is returning soon. But what is soon?" Nobody knows what soon is." We only wish and hope and pray that it won't be long, as we desire to get out of this horrific world. We are tired of seeing people suffer. We are tired of seeing people die everyday from coronavirus from cancer, car crashes, or killed by crazy people that have weapons they should not have. We are tired of seeing the rich get richer, and the poor getting poorer and the innocent babies being murdered everyday because of abortions and unwanted pregnantcies. We are tired of seeing people committing suicide. We are tired of seeing people dying in vain. We long for the lost to be found. We are tired of how they took God out of everything. When he should be about everything.This world is not what the Lord intended it to be when he created us. And that is a shame, and sad to see we should be weeping for forgiveness and a transformation in our hearts and lives. Because people's hearts have gotten stoney now I am talking about all people including the so-called Christians."It's no wonder people don't want to get saved because you can't even trust so-called Christians. And people are desperate for the Lord to come. But are we really ready for his coming?"I don't think so, maybe it is a good thing that the Lord hasn't come back yet because he knows what's best for us. I see this just about everyday on the prayer list that somebody doesn't want to live anymore because people are being mean to them. And that they don't want to be here on earth anymore. That they just want to go home and be with Jesus. But you know that's the easy way out. Is to commit suicide. Even though God said he wouldn't give us more than we can handle, It sure doesn't feel that way at times. This is when we are being tested for our faith if we are to give in to temptations and do self harm or to just end our life because the trials we are going through is to much for us to bare, but who really cares people are caught up in their own world, and that this world is so bad it's only getting worse so you don't want to be here anymore. and that this world would be better off without you here. Now you know that this is not from God. This is satan himself yes he's trying to get you to do something stupid. Yet some people give in and end up taking their lives; this is truly sad. Because the devil is attacking more people everyday because he knows his time is short. The world must have been overpopulated, because people are dying everyday. When God said to multiply the earth we had no problem doing that." Yet people only listen to what they want to listen to. This is man's will. We are strong willed people if only we use it for God's glory!" Now if we believed in God's word and lived by his word we could reduce so much of physical bad health. Because stress, and worry really do cause lots of troubles this can cause many sicknesses and infirmities such as strokes, heart attacks, heart diease, diabetes, cancer. Oh!" let us not forget about the wrinkles, and gray hair and looking so old !" just to name a few If we really took God's word serious" we could avoid a lot of discomfort , pain, shame, humility embarestment headaches lack of sleep mind fogg, and so much other ailments from worry or stress. Our bodies are amazing to put up with a lot But our bodies are not meant to go through a roller coaster of bad emotions. This really takes a toll on your body. We were meant to be happy, healthy, successful and to have life abundantly. Don't be hasty, or in a hurry you have to think straight and don't be late for important decisions that have to be made, don't put off things that need to be done. Just because you want to have fun, while you're on the run. Or maybe just put it off, because you don't want to do it. In reality you have to do it, so you won't lose it. In the end it's up to you in what you do, but don't put the blame on anyone else. Take full responsibility, in your actions, and in your words. You can't fool anybody, not even yourself, get it done but do it gracefully, and with good motives in your heart. Then things won't fall apart, take it to heart what I'm saying I'm not trying to fool you, but only to school you. Matthew 18:20 For where two or three gather in my name there I am with them.

CHAPTER ONE HUNDRED

REMEMBER GOD'S BLESSINGS:

When we get to complaining we need to remember that we don't have it so bad after all, because Just take a look around and see all the chaos going on around the world. God doesn't like us to complain, besides it is sin to complain. It seems like it is hard not to sin. Because most everything we do is sin. If you don't have your favorite foods but you have food you are blessed." If you have clothes on your back you are blessed. Who cares if you don't have the newest trend. If you have a roof over your head you are blessed. There are lots of homeless people, and animals. If you have some spare change in your pocket, you are blessed that you have a pocket to put change in, and even more blessed you have change. Maybe that's all you have. you are blessed, there are alot of people in this world who go to bed hungry, wake up hungry and do not know when they will be able to eat again. If you have a bed and pillow to rest your head you are blessed. You are truly rich. My friend, If you are in good health you are blessed, some people can't afford to go to the Doctor. And so they have to hope that they don't get sick, because they can't afford to miss work and they cannot afford to go see a Doctor. If you can go to any church and be able to pray or read your bible in peace, and not be persecuted, you are blessed if you can live one day without pain. You are blessed, because there are a lot of people that live with pain 24/7. If you have family and not totally alone you are blessed. If you can look forward to another day you are blessed If you can sleep at night in peace you are blessed. If you can look forward to tomorrow you are blessed. Now if you think you've got it bad, Just take a look around you, you will see that somebody else has it worse than you in any area of their life you will see that you are truly blessed. Then you will agree and see that you have nothing to complain about. So count your blessings, Instead of complaining. You will see a great change in your heart and attitude. And you will be more grateful and thankful. For this is the way that will be good for you and your soul, and be a blessing and pleaseing to God. I am so amazed of the blessings of God.`` I believe the more thankful and grateful you are I believe the more God blesses you. I can have 40.00 in my checking account the next few times after I've checked my account there is 75.00 I don't know how that happened I know it is the hand of my Lord. Okay it was laundry day and I needed my clothes done so that I could have clean underwear to wear, so I have to wear a pair that is four sizes too big for me that someone gave to me, that someone gave to them they bought the wrong size. I have to be on guard because the underwear falls down to my knees. Then the next week I have more than enough underwear that I need for a week and some extra days so I don't need to be in a rush to get my laundry done. zNow I'm very puzzled about this, these are mine but why weren't they there last week when I needed clean underwear?" I'm very puzzled about this. Is God playing tricks on me or what?" 1 Philippians 4:19 And my God will supply every need of yours according to his riches in glory in Christ Jesus.

CHAPTER ONE HUNDRED AND ONE

PLEASE DON'T COPY WHAT YOU SEE ON TELEVISION OR HEAR ON THE RADIO AND THE NEWS:

Okay so the kids watch a cartoon on the television then they decide to do the same thing they saw. They hit and kicked their little sister and left her out in the cold, not knowing where the parents were. The little girl ended up dying. How sad. The parents asked the boys why they did this to their sister?" and the boy's said that they were just playing. They saw the cartoon do it, so they wanted to copy the cartoon. It's no wonder why we have so much violence it's everywhere, even Tom and Jerry cartoons are violent!" That's why I never let my girls watch Tom and Jerry. At first it looks cute!" but then it gets violent, my oldest daughter always did something to my youngest daughter. It's a miracle that my youngest daughter is alive!" My poor baby had black and blue marks, scratches. Once my oldest daughter was going to hit my baby with a large glass object. Thank God I caught her on time, another time she was giving my baby a cleaning supply to drink. I caught this on time." This was getting dangerous!" Even the three stooges were violent!" They were supposed to be funny, but I didn't see anything funny about Moe smacking the other two guys all the time. And then he would pull curly by the hair, and pull Larry by the ear. That's what my dad did to us kids and he would kick us in the butt. I wonder if my dad did that to us kids, because he saw the three stooges do it!" Now Laurel and Hardy was another one that was supposed to be funny. But I only saw the big guy picking on the little guy." Same thing happens when one school or child does something, another school or child has to copy what they heard or saw." One school has a shoot out so another school will copy. They are having shootings at concerts now. People are just copying other people and this is sickly crazy." Now there have been movies or shows on the television where a person faked their death. Well some guy fled the U.S. Now he has been found in Scotland and is infected with Coronavirus." This guy is getting double portions of justice for the crimes he has committed. The Bible says Be sure your sins will find you out!" Then again they are just living," Get real do not steal that's not how you get sex appeal This is the real deal, so take a stand and do not let things be fasely unreeled, for the truth to be revealed now can we make a deal on this appeal to be revealed so don't try to steal what is for real and try to make it yours when you steal it from someone that is being real. Let's make a deal for real because this is the real deal. Now don't try to steal what has been revealed now pay attention, because this is real. Can we make a deal and make this real then you won't have to steal you won't have to worry about you making an appeal. Because this is the real deal. So you won't have to steal, can we make this simple and make a deal because I can truly feel that this is the place and time for you to re design everything that you had in mind, do take your time, don't whine I'd prefer that you take your time so that you can shine, as we dine and wine. Go right ahead and shine because you are mine. I'll talk to you later if you don't mind. Don't be in such a hurry, take your sweet time. I don't mind. Romans 12:2 Don't copy the behavior and customs of this world, but let God transform you into a new person by changing the way you think. Then you will learn to know God's will for you, which is good and pleasing and perfect.

CHAPTER ONE HUNDRED AND TWO

WATCH OUT FOR WOLVES IN SHEEP'S CLOTHING

Nowadays, It's hard to trust anyone even if they say they are a christian, because they pretend to be holy and righteous. But they can't fool all the people all of the time or some of the people some of the time,because the true christian will know the Lord will give discernment and wisdom of who is for real and who is not. I seem to be taken advantage of money lately. A woman pocketed 200.00 dollars cash that I gave her. and didn't record it and I forgot to get a receipt. My mistake. I won't make that mistake again. Then the first publishing company got all the royalties and I didn't get my share of the royalties. Then I got a different publisher and they lied to me as well then the third publisher lied to me as well. I guess this business is not good to be in. So I'm thinking that I won't get my 6th book done and published but it's really up to God in what he wants me to do.Then I switched Insurance companies. I was supposed to get 400$ back and they only gave me 300$ and when I moved to a new apartment building I had to pay for the hook up for cable, and I felt cheated. Later I did read in our handbook from where I live that if we wish to get cable we can do so it sounds like we have to pay for the hook ups. Because this building is brand new. So I am the first person to live in this new apartment. Then somebody else told me that I shouldn't have had to pay for it. But what is done is done.I Felt cheated out of a lot of things lately. I trusted the person that I gave the money to. Which I shouldn't have. My fault. It's just hard to see them working here and getting promotions, when in reality they should be fired. I dread seeing them. when I see them. I know I have to forgive, but it is hard to see them almost everyday. And they get away from doing wrong. When you truly forgive within your heart you can actually smile at them with a true smile, and better yet you can even say some words to them that are kind. When you can do this, you know you have truly forgiven like God wants us to forgive. They have scammers all over, The cons are pawling all over everywhere. Now they pretend to be the social security administration, so beware of these kinds of calls. Because the social security administration office says that they will never call and ask for our social security number. Also some scams will call and demand payment for something you ordered months ago. And they will talk just right to get you all nervous and confused. They will make you believe that you do owe them money. Then there are the landlord's scams. If you are trying to move they try to find something wrong that they want you to pay for and they will make it bigger than it really is. Trying to get you to pay lots of money. Then there are the mechanics that rip people off of thousands of dollars. When there was nothing wrong with your car in the first place. Then in the second place they make things up and since they are charging by the hour they will take their ever sweet time. And usually they tend to pick on women more than men. Because they figure that men should know about cars. Then there's the plummer, now he gets paid by the hour so he will sit in his car for an half hour before he decides to come to your door. And since most people don't know much about plumbing they will make up stuff to charge you more money than you had planned. So they will tell you that you need a part and he has to order it. So it will cost more. And he will come back again and he will take his ever sweet time, to just figure out what is wrong. In the meantime you have to go to the bathroom, So you try to hold it for as long as you can. But the plummer wants to take his sweet time. Come to find out you didn't need to call a plummer after all because you could have just used the plunger yourself until you feel like you have rubbed the skin off of your palms.and your palms are throbbing red and in pain. But that's okay, it's better than paying a plummer right!" I went to a woman's house because she had a scooter that she wanted to give away. I had a hard time finding someone to help me to go get it." A friend took me to get it. And we had a hard time finding the women's location. The woman acted like she was a christian, but it was just an act. I asked the woman if she could charge it for me before we got there. She said no because the cord didn't reach the outlet. I should have known that something was up. While we were there the woman put her arms in the air. And said thank you Jesus!" She was happy to get the scooter out of her house. My friend took awhile to get it in his vehicle without scratching his car. This scooter was very heavy." Well he got it home to my place then I let it charge overnight. Come the next day, the scooter was not charged. This woman used me and my friend to get rid of the scooter because it was no good. She used us to get rid of her trash. Apparently it costs money to get rid of it." I was upset that this woman conned us into taking her trash. I wanted my friend to take it back to her place and leave it at her front door. But my friend said no that wouldn't be right!" I said well it wasn't right of what she did to us." I was glad I got rid of it for free, the maintenance man where I live took care of it for me. And come to think this woman pretended to be a christian. As far as life goes you can't trust anybody!" Now in God's word it says that we are to take care of the widows. I have been a widow for a long time. But people do not seem to be doing what God's word says. Maybe it is my fault that people are not helpful. Because I do keep myself isolated. I do remember when I was going to church, people seemed to not be helpfull. I would think to myself what happened to brotherly love? What happened to the church?" Even the women's bible study that we had all day once a month wasn't the same. Seems like there was no time for prayer, or the important things that we should have been concerned about." Boy do we need a spiritual revival!" Seems to me all the churches need this. Because ever since the pandemic happened, something happened to people's hearts. But then again who am I?" I cannot judge anyone. I am responsible for myself. When judgment day comes, I am gonna be held accountable for myself. People say they want Jesus to come now but are we really ready?" Be on alert!" But to be ready. In other words, be ready for the coming of the Lord Jesus' return, We must not be asleep,don't be caught off guard. But to be prepared, and ready for the coming of the Lord Jesus. that we need to be observant, what if Jesus came right now? Are we really prepared? How many of our family members and friends have not accepted the Lord as their savior? Now this is sad, because it is our duty to share the gospel to everyone.

So that none should perish, but have everlasting life. What do we do if they don't want to listen? We don't give up praying for them. Things may seem like they are getting worse and they probably are, but we must not give up praying, because God is going to answer our prayers. In his time we must keep on believing that the Lord hears your prayers. He will always answer, maybe it may seem like God isn't listening to you. But he is, and maybe it feels like God is so far from you. Maybe at the time you don't feel the Lord's presence or wonder can he hear you. The truth is if you don't have a relationship with him, he will put a damper on hearing from you and that you may not have God's favor on you and your life until you surrender your all to him. you may feel like he is so far away from you, so what do you do? For one thing you have to acknowledge the Lord every day every hour every moment that you are awake. Not just when you need a favor or a miracle." and press into his word, This will guide you into what is the right thing to do when you come to a place of uncertainty. You are not alone, it's sad to say there are alot of people that mistreat the Lord. They use his name to cuss and swear and not even care they go on with their day as if they did no wrong or harm. This hurts the Lord, I'm sure because his people reject him and his word. Yes things will get ugly before they get better. It is all in his time and in his way. We can not give up praying for the lost souls that are blinded by the ways of the world. Keep on praying. Because the Lord doesn't give up on us. Aren't you glad that God is a good God? I sure am. He doesn't give us what we deserve, he gives us what we need. Matthew 7: 15 Beware of false prophets who come to you in sheep's clothing but inwardly are savage wolves.

CHAPTER ONE HUNDRED AND THREE

HOLD YOUR PEACE:

Okay somebody hurt you or miss treated you, don't try to get revenge because God will take care of it for you. It may take a long time or it may be taken care of right away. But it will happen in his time and in his way. For God knows what's best for us. We see what we want, and we think we know what is best for us. Not seeing ahead, That's why we have the holy spirit to guide us, protect us, give us insight!" of what the natural eye can see. Now I know some people would not agree with me. But if we take it in our own hands there will be consequences to your actions. When you think that you have it bad that the trials and troubles that come upon you are more than you can bare. Remember God said he would never leave us or forsake us. And he also said that he would not give us more than we can handle. Yes, at times we are tired, and it seems as though life is too hard to go on suffering as you or someone you know are going through. And we have a lot of questions, and we want some answers but we don't get them, you will always get an answer, but sometimes we have to wait a very long time before you get the answer. And it may be the answer you've been waiting for. You will always get an answer. Take these diseases that have become deadly to us humans. This is a consequence for our sins." Maybe you feel that the wrong people are being punished at this time on earth. There are some people that have been suffering for most of their life with sickness, or we ask ``why do innocent people have to suffer and die?" because they were a good person, or innocent babies, being killed everyday. They did no wrong, they didn't even have a chance to be fully developed in their mother's womb. They got their right to be born taken away. They didn't get to taste life." That was taken from them. What about the man that transforms from being a man into a woman, because he feels he was supposed to be a woman. God does not make any mistake. If you were born a man then that's the way you should live as. We can't go around taking lives, or changing lives acting as we are God." God is the only one that has that right!" But of course us humans try to control everything and anything. That's what the fallen angel did, Satan himself. As far as the infirmities go, this was foretold in the bible. So if the bible says this will take place. So then it shall come to pass. Exodus 14:14. The Lord shall fight for you, and you shall hold your peace."

CHAPTER ONE HUNDRED AND FOUR

BE INTUNED TO HEAR FROM THE LORD:

Keep your eyes on the Lord and read his word. Know that God has planned everyday for you. Now maybe God placed it in your heart to do something, and you think that it is silly, then you think that it wasn't from God that you heard from, but in reality it was really God speaking to you. Then you need to act on what he has placed in your heart to do. At the time you think that you can't do it, but you better, even if it seems hard for you to do. Because there has to be a good explanation for you to do this but you should not question God. Because he knows all things and it's not our place to question God, maybe I'm wrong, maybe it's okay to question God." Because he is my best friend. Well some things are hard to understand but it is good for us to fall through of what God wants us to do. Because you don't want to miss out on a blessing for the person that God wants you to bless and also a blessing for you as well. Sometimes, things don't make sense to us, of what God wants us to do. In the end it will come together, as the Lord wants us to be in submission to him and his will. Besides, we want to be on good terms with God, and not rebel." right, I used to rebel against my parents when I was a teen, I don't know why? Now that I'm older and know God, I was so stupid to not listen to what my parents told me not to do. I did it anyway against their wishes, almost like to despite them, that was a foolish thing. I believe I paid for my rebellion, I lost the sight of my right eye. I guess I had to learn the hard way to learn to not be rebellious. Once the Lord laid it on my heart to buy a bouquet of flowers for a woman that lived in my apartment building. She happened to have back trouble and was in alot of pain, she had to have back surgery. I tried to reason with God. I told the Lord that I couldn't because the woman would think that I was a lesbian and think that I was trying to make a move on her. Because this woman was kind of strange one day she would be nice and then the next she would be stuck up and just strange. So I kept my distance from her. But I knew that I had to do what the Lord wanted me to do. So I did as soon as I left I heard her cry. She was so moved at getting flowers she was speechless. I had no Idea that she was in so much pain, or having trouble with her back, and needed surgery. But God knew. What a wonderful God we serve!" God wanted to let her know that she is loved, and that she is not alone. Isaiah 30:21. And your ears shall hear a word behind you, saying this is the way, walk in it,"When you turn to the right or when you turn to the left.

CHAPTER ONE HUNDRED AND FIVE

SOME LIKE IT HOT SOME LIKE IT COLD

Well there are a few kinds of people in this world, some are heartless and cold. Some are kind hearted and sweet, and easy- going. Some are very vulnerable and fragile But the kind and sweet, warm hearted people get mistreated because people take being sweet and kind for being weak and naive." Now this is so sad but this is how the world and people have become. Then there are the people that are ruthless, they use people for anything and everything they can get. They don't care who they hurt, in fact they don't like themselves, so of course they don't like anybody. They seem to get a good partner, doesn't seem fair. Well who says life is fair? I don't think anybody can say life is fair, because it's not. I hear that saying all the time that it's not fair. Especially when something bad happens in our life like a tragic or horrific thing happening in our lives. I was sick with the second vaccine. But the booster shot really kicked my bootie. I was down for five days, my daughter had the virus but she was not sick at all, I guess I took her sickness for her. My father is in a nursing home and he got the corona virus twice," and had no symptoms. I guess I took his symptoms for him also. Crazy right!" If they come up with another shot I'm not going to get it. Because I was so sick, Then if I got the virus I would be a lot sicker. So they say even if I am vaccinated I still could get the virus. There have been people that were vaccinated and still got the virus and died. I have been around a lot of people that had the virius and I was protected. Nothing is going to protect you if it is your time to go, right!" This virus has been a headache, to many people it has been ruff to wear masks all the time and we don't feel at ease when we go out in public because we have to be cautious about what we touch, who is too close to us, and then you wonder people get the virus, they don't even know that they have it. There are no symptoms. I know people ask when is this pandemic going to end? We are sick and tired of it. It has been bad for so many and still taking a toll on our lives. No one knows but the Father so just take it one day at a time. The president said that the pandemic is over, but it really is not. People are still getting the virus, there are people still dying. Well I've also heard that the virant will be treated and diagnosed as the common cold. Many wonder and ask God when is this going to be over?" They keep coming up with new names for the next variant. I wish that one day I would wake up and this will be gone for good and never to return. That this is just a bad nightmare. I am sure I am not the only one. But time keeps going on and there still are people living, Time seems never to run out. It just keeps going on and on.So we have to keep pressing on. Maybe one day we'll wake up and all this chao's will be gone. And we can experience true peace. But I don't think this will happen in this lifetime. And so we can't wait until Jesus comes and takes us home. Our real home. For all this is temporary. This is here for a while then taken away as fast as a blink of an eye shall I tell you why? Tell that guy to take that sty out of his eye then he may see what's in your brother's eye. I tell you bye and bye, stay close to him that is within where shall I began, over and over again Let's win this battle for it is good to lay back and don't attack be on the right track as a matter of fact don't be a class act, stay low in profile then you won't have to make an excuse or be in denial stay for awhile now give me a great big smile that will last a while. 2 Peter 1:13-14. And it is only right that I should keep on reminding you as long as I live. For our Lord Jesus Christ has shown me that I must soon leave this earthly life,"so I will work hard to make sure you always remember these things after I am gone.

CHAPTER ONE HUNDRED AND SIX

WEARING SPIRITUAL MASKS

Okay so there are people that are truly Christans then there are people that are good people and truly want to serve the Lord and truly love the Lord. But only have a head knowledge but not have been truly born again and have surrender their all to the Lord. So they put on a spiritual mask on Sunday which would be their best for Sunday to go to church. But all week long they are carrying on the oppsite of what a real true Christian is supposed to be. They think that doing nice things for others will get them to heaven like getting brownie points then at the end they get rewarded and get to go to heaven because they are a good person. Nothing can be farther than the truth." God doesn't play games nor does he give you brownie points and at the end of the day you get rewarded in how good you have been then you get to go to heaven. At the right time we will be rewarded for our deeds that we have done on earth.Where your heart is there will your treasure be. Yes we will be held accountable for our deeds which we have done here on earth, but this is not a religion, this is about a relationship and that relationship is with Jesus Christ. Now this is the true way to get to heaven by your communion with the Lord. And the reading of his word and doing what his word says. Which is the Bible. The day is approaching his return and come Judgment day he will say that he never knew you. Because all the years being on earth you did not have fellowship with him and read his word and you did not seek his face or his word Please don't let that be you. God forbid that any should perish but to have everlasting life and to be with God forevermore. This is his desire, and I am sure yours too," time is running out. The time is short to be able to turn to the king of kings and the Lord of Lords" he is waiting with open arms. Won't you come to him and surrender your all to him?" Now if you have doubt just ask God for more faith, It's not that you don't have faith it's that you misplaced it. And have a lack of faith, maybe you lose your focus. Ask and you shall receive. Matthew 7:7 ask and it will be given unto you seek and you shall find. Knock and the door shall be opened to you. Now God says you have not because you ask not, so ask then you can receive.

CHAPTER ONE HUNDRED AND SEVEN

DETOXING FROM DIGITAL DEVICES AND TECHNOLOGY

I read something on the internet about detoxing from elecronic devices, yes this world is so much into electronic devices we spend way too much time on these devices. If it's not the internet it's video games if it's not video games it's texting on the phone. Or maybe talking on the cell phone, or maybe playing a game on the phone. Or maybe you are at work and you are on facebook or Instagram or Just checking your e-mails. Now if you're in a hurry, and you have to be somewhere and you're yelling at the kid to get going because they're running late and you're kid says wait until I make it to the next level, then you say it's now or you're going to be left behind. What about the kid that is in the bathroom playing on his phone and everybody is screaming for them to stop hogging up the bathroom. Other people need to use it too. The kid isn't even concentrating on going to the bathroom, he's just playing games on his phone. Or how about making sure that your phone is always with you wherever you go. You can't be without it. How about those crazy drivers that think it's okay to text and drive!" They already are crazy at driving, Don't give them a phone to text or talk. You know what I'm talking about!" No doubt. Don't forget about watching movies on your phone or labtop, Let's not forget about the television so we are on some kind of device all the time. It seems to me we are addicted, big time. And get this, some companies would rather you text each other than talk on the phone. So when you do talk with someone how do you know if it's a human or a robot. There have been times when I thought somebody was talking to me, but they had headphones or earbuds or whatever they are called, you get my drift right!" on and talking on their phone. I've done this a few times and I answer them back. This is embarrassing, most of the time the people don't even know that I'm talking to them good thing. Times are getting crazier and crazier, can't put the world in low gear or somehow slow it down. Then you've got to make a frown, and prove to them that you are not a clown. Keep on going because things are going down, I'm not fooling around, take off that frown and look around, can you hear that sound?" You've got to be found and hopefully you're standing strong on solid ground. Take a look around so that you may be found. Until you are not so attached to these technology devices you better stay low until the sun rises. Even if the sun doesn't shine, don't get left behind that way you can wine and dine make sure you shine, yes take your time then it will only cost you a dime. And your world will shine. Keep in mind that you will have peace of mind when you're set free from these bondages that hold us down. Remember don't make a frown. Instead turn it around so that it becomes a smile, then you can laugh a while and you will still be in style, keep away from the crocodile, remember to keep a smile. Mathew 24:14 In which he commanded us to proclaim in. Mathew 28:19-20. God's goal for mankind isn't to advance as far as we can or to know all that we can discover, but rather that all should come to repentance. 2 Peter 3:9 Keep looking to the Lord he will never fail us. And I say Amen again, and again. PROVERBS 19. There are many devices in a man's heart; But the counsel of Jehovah, that shall stand. Take his hand in time you will understand from the beginning to the end. This I recommend. And I say Amen!" again and again. May the Lord's blessings be upon you:

[: Slogan for book number five: Just Livin:]

Just Living you ought to be giving. Take a seat you're in for a real treat, swallow your pride so you won't have to hide. All you have to do is take a step aside and glide. Each day you live, take it as a gift, yeah you're Just living.

www.ingramcontent.com/pod-product-compliance
Lightning Source LLC
LaVergne TN
LVHW091533060526
838200LV00036B/589